SYLVIA MERCEDES

THE VENATRIX CHRONICLES BOOK 6

© 2020 by Sylvia Mercedes

Published by FireWyrm Books

www.SylviaMercedesBooks.com

Cover design by Deranged Doctor Design

This one is for Emily, my NaNoWriMo buddy,
With many thanks for all the encouragement.

THE VENATRIX

Drauval Borough

Skada Mountains

Aalis River

Castra Brecar

Wodechran

Sang River

Tehanor City

CHRONICLES

Aldreda Borough

The Great Barrier

Dulimurian

The Witchwood

Sang River

KINGDOM OF PERRINION

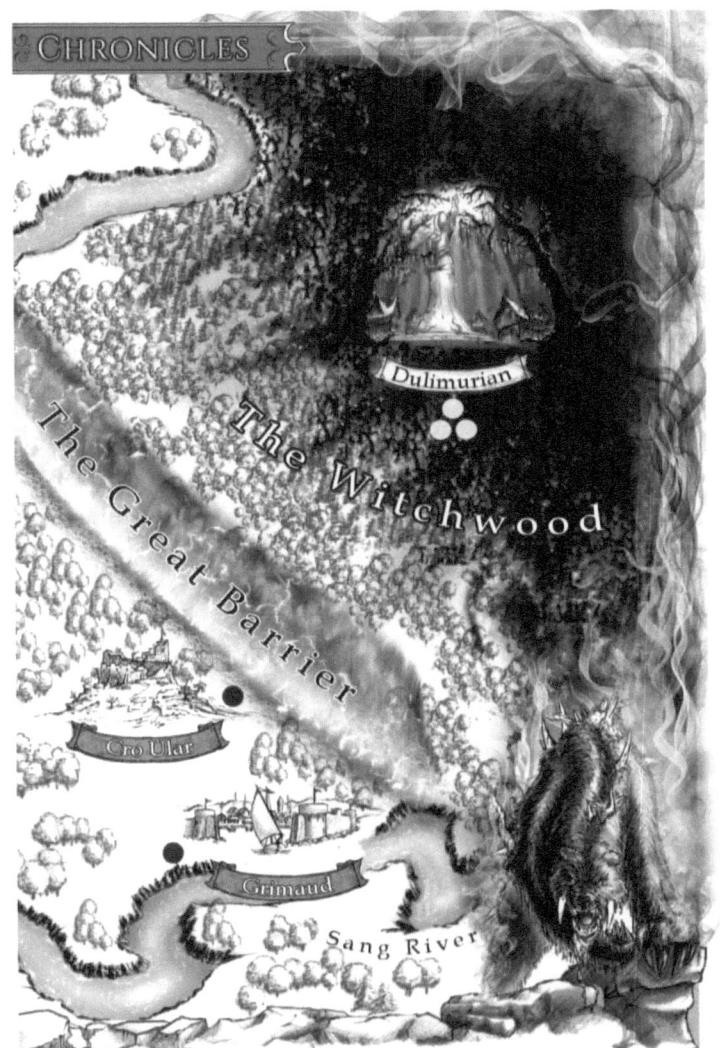

Dulimurian

The Witchwood

The Great Barrier

Cro Ular

Grimaud

Sang River

GLOSSARY OF SHADES

Shades: Disembodied spirit-beings who have escaped from their hellish dimension—the Haunts—and entered the mortal world. They cannot exist in a physical reality without mortal hosts, whom they possess and endow with unnatural powers. If left unchecked, they will gain ascendancy within a host-body and oust the original soul, taking full possession.

The following are the known varieties of shades as catalogued by the Order of Saint Evander:

ANATHEMAS
Abilities pertain to blood and curse-casting.

APPARITIONS
Abilities pertain to mind control and manipulation.

ARCANES
Mysterious entities with abilities not fully understood, but which seem to pertain to energies such as heat, motion, light, magnetism, and electricity.

ELEMENTALS
Abilities pertain to the natural elements of wind, fire, water, earth.

EVANESCERS
Abilities pertain to *evanescing*, or instantaneous distance-travel.

FERALS
Abilities pertain to heightened senses, augmented strength and agility.

LURES
Abilities pertain to enchanting voices and siren calls.

SEERS
Abilities pertain to visions, foretelling, and predictions. May also look into the past.

SHIFTERS
Abilities pertain to temporary transformation of host-bodies.

TRANSMUTERS
Abilities pertain to the transformation and manipulation of material substances.

PROLOGUE

IT IS ALL A LIE, YOU KNOW. NOTHING MORE THAN A *beautiful lie.*

Don't think you're the only one who has dreamed this dream, the only one who has felt this longing. None of it is real. Not in this life. Not anymore.

I was like you once. Long ago. Eager to devour all the lies they could feed me. Eager to ingest them and make them my own. But you will learn, as I did. You will learn, or you will break.

Olena.

My love. My pretty child.

The time has come for us to be acquainted with one another. The time has come for you to know who I am.

CHAPTER I

TERRYN HAD NO CHANCE TO CRY OUT BEFORE HE broke the lake's surface and water closed over his head. The cold was so sharp, so sudden, it shocked him to his core. For the space of several agonized heartbeats, he thought his body had frozen solid.

But he didn't have heartbeats to spare. The poison would paralyze him in under a minute. He had to move. Now.

His body jerked. His lungs spasmed with the need for

air. Then, as though responding to the overwhelming outer cold, heat roared inside him, surged through his limbs. A heat of spirit, stemming from his core where his shade reared its ascendant head.

The pain was so extreme, he could not stop the scream that tore through his throat. The last of his air escaped in a stream of white bubbles, but the pain was enough to shock his limbs into motion. He pulled hard, desperately hoping he was still pointed toward the lake's surface. His head broke through a paper-thin layer of ice into open air. He gasped hungrily, drawing breath into his lungs.

Something splashed in the water near his head. He swiveled, arms rotating wildly, and his eyes rounded. A dart, a venator's dart, floated past his nose, fletched in black. The Gentle Death.

A spatter of water hit his eye as a second dart flashed too close to his cheek. Terryn cast a desperate look overhead and spied the two hooded figures leaning over the parapets high above, their scorpioni raised, taking aim.

With a curse he dove under again, taking refuge in the

frigid darkness of Loch du Nóiv. How much time did he have left? Already his left arm was a dead weight hanging from his shoulder. His ascendant shade fought against the effects of the poison, but it would succumb sooner rather than later. The poison was formulated specifically to influence and subdue Arcane shades. It wouldn't be able to resist for long.

His heavy clothes and boots pulled him down, but he kicked against the drag and used his right arm to pull himself through the water. His eyes flared with shadow-light an instant before he struck the webbed spell song of the barrier. The barrier he himself, under Fendrel's orders, had set around Dunloch days ago. Even if he had the time, even if he had the strength to swim for shore, he couldn't break through that.

He surfaced again, and his right arm flailed in the air, desperately grasping at nothing. Light flared in his hand, in the center of his palm, mounting with power he could not understand, could not control.

Trust me, a voice whispered, a hissing heat in his head.

Fingers outspread, he struck at the song-spell barrier. Where his hand touched, light flashed in a blinding bolt.

The spell threads burned, broke, and the air shivered with discordant notes as the spell came undone. Not completely—just a seam, a narrow slit.

It was enough.

He burst through the snare-like threads and out into the open water beyond. Paralysis spread swiftly now. He couldn't keep his head above water anymore. With a last gulp of air he went under, and despair overcame him, as heavy and cold as the ice-laced waves. It didn't matter that he'd escaped the barrier. It didn't matter that he'd avoided the deadly darts of his pursuers. He would drown—and his soul would be damned to the Haunts forever, heretic that he was. The Goddess had surely forsaken him.

Trust me.

He shivered at the heat of that voice searing through his brain. But suddenly his eyes widened as light flared in the darkness underwater. His right hand, still only just under his control, burned brilliantly with the light of a fallen star. He felt the power building in his arm, building in his soul, power enough to shatter him into a million pieces if he did not let it out.

Trust me, mortal.

Terryn turned his hand, pointing it behind him. His fingers clenched into a tight fist, gathering all that pent-up force into a single point, a ball of pure magic energy.

Then he opened his hand and let it burst free. The force of the blast propelled his leaden body through the water faster than a leaping salmon. Magic channeled through his arm, so hot he was certain his bones would melt.

In a few seconds the poison overtook his shade, dousing its power so completely, the effect was like a solar eclipse. But it had lasted long enough to fling him to the shore, to leave him tangled in weeds at the shallow edge of the Holy Lake, where the water was no deeper than his knees.

With a final propulsion of pure will, Terryn flung out his right hand, caught hold of a stone, and pulled up his head. His mouth and nose broke the water's surface. It would do him no good in the end, he knew. He might not drown, but he would surely freeze to death long before the paralysis wore off.

Darkness closed in, darkness more absolute than the

lake depths. He couldn't fight it. Not even shade magic could drive these shadows away.

"Ayleth," he whispered, his numb lips scarcely moving. "Ayleth . . . Ay . . ."

The darkness claimed him.

THEY FOUND ME ON THE DAY OF MY WEDDING.

I will never forget how they came riding into my cousin's estate, their red hoods pulled over their heads so far that you could not see their faces. I will never forget the shock I felt when the foremost of their number threw back her hood and I saw that she was a woman, and that she was the leader of the other two. I had believed a woman's lot in life to be limited only to that which I now faced—marriage to some fat, hideous old man, to serve in his household, most likely to die bearing his brats.

The woman on horseback before me was a figure of power. She commanded the respect of all who looked upon her. One could not imagine her submitting to the indignity or the danger of childbearing.

I wore my linen wedding dress and clutched a handful of posies in my hands. They were marching me to the chapel, where I was to meet my bridegroom and say my vows before the Goddess. But that was never to be.

The woman pulled her horse to a halt but did not dismount. She looked down at my cousin, who groveled and scraped and wiped sweat from his eyes. "My lady Venatrix," he wheezed, "if there are shade doings in my household, I swear to you, I am unaware of it!"

He babbled in this manner for some while. She regarded him silently, waiting for his self-exonerations to wind down. It was a long wait, but she was a woman of infinite patience. When at last my cousin paused for breath, she said, "I am told the last of the House du Mauvalis dwells here with you."

"Yes, yes." My cousin all too eagerly snatched my arm and pulled me in front of him as a shield. A skinny, linen-clad shield. "This is she. My cousin. My second cousin once removed, actually. Hardly any blood shared between us, but I made a promise to my old mother, you know, and the girl is—"

"What is your name, child?"

My cousin's voice broke off at once. His hand, still clutching my arm, trembled. I wished he would let me go, wished I could distance myself from him.

I looked up at the Venatrix. Though she frightened me,

everything about her made me wish to be more courageous than I was. So I made certain my voice was clear and firm when I answered: "Odile di Mauvalis."

"And your mother's name?"

"Odessa di Mauvalis."

"And her mother?"

"Odiane di Mauvalis."

One of the other two Red Hoods leaned forward in his saddle, his voice rumbling deep as he said, "It is she. It must be."

The Venatrix nodded. Her gaze brushed over my wedding garments, my veil, and the flowers in my hand. "You are to be married today, Odile di Mauvalis?" she asked.

I hesitated. Then I nodded.

"Would you rather come away with me?"

"Oh." My breath left my body in a rush. "Yes!"

And that is how I joined the Order of Saint Evander.

CHAPTER 2

PAIN CAME AND WENT IN WAVES.

Just now it had her in its grip, and the more she fought against it, the more it pummeled her, dashing her against the rocks of her consciousness until her very spirit was bloodied and bruised. She could not escape it, could not fight it, could scarcely endure it.

But she knew it wouldn't last. Not like this. Not for long. If she could only hold out a little longer, just one more heartbeat, and then one more after that . . .

Ayleth let out a gasp. "Festering Haunts damn," she growled, squeezing the words through her teeth. But the worst of the wave had passed. Little by little, breath by breath, the pulsing agony decreased. And as it slipped away, her awareness slowly returned.

Not that the reality of the world around her was much better.

But at the very least, there was the solid feel of horseflesh beneath her. She could be grateful for that. It had been much too long since she'd last been on horseback, and the sensation of those solid muscles moving, the sound of those heavy hooves clumping on paving stones somehow made her feel more complete.

However, when she slowly cracked her eyes open, her heart sank. It wasn't Chestibor's brown neck she saw before her, nor his black mane fluttering in the breeze. This was some unknown gray beast.

And she was tied to the saddle. Probably to keep her from falling when the pain got too great.

She grimaced, looking down at her hands. They were encased in iron mitts, an Evanderian implement of restraint. Or torture, to put it more accurately. Less than an hour ago, she'd been brought to her knees and forced to submit her hands to these manacles. The inescapable proximity to iron was enough to nauseate her, but iron alone wouldn't cause such waves of pain.

No, the torment came and went because the inside of each mitt was studded with small spikes. Unless she took care to keep her hands tightly fisted, these spikes plunged through her skin, down to the bone. Whenever her horse took a jolting step and her hands involuntarily jerked, numerous punctures drove iron poison into her flesh. Into her soul.

For the moment, the road was smooth and she could avoid the spikes. But every muscle in her body tensed with dread of the next round of agony, which was inevitable.

"*Laranta?*" she whispered inside her head with no real hope of response. The iron poison had driven her shade deep into hiding, leaving Ayleth alone. Or not entirely alone.

Teeth gritted, she lifted her gaze from her iron-encased hands to the riders in front of her. They rode with their red hoods pulled up over their heads—three of them in front, two more on each side, and two behind. Escorting her as if she were some witch on her way to execution.

She studied the shape and slope of their shoulders, the set of their heads. Was Kephan among them? She'd last seen him in the halls of Dunloch with a paralysis dart in his throat. It would be hours yet before the drug wore off.

No, she couldn't hope to have a friend among these people. They were strangers. Enemies. She didn't know any of their faces . . . except one.

When she glanced to her right, her lips pulled back from her teeth in a snarl. Fendrel du Glaive rode close enough that, if her hands weren't trapped in iron, she could easily have reached out and caught him by the throat.

He knew she was looking at him; she could tell by the way the muscles in his cheek tightened ever so slightly. He rode with his black hood thrown back across his shoulders, his face exposed, and his gaze fixed on the horizon, on the sky brightening with dawn's vivid colors. But she could read nothing in his expression, no hint of whatever thoughts lurked behind that stone façade of a face.

Had he really done it?

The thought pricked in Ayleth's mind before she could stop it. She tried to pull back. If she let her thoughts go that way, she might lose herself in the grief and fear waiting to swallow her whole. But the question continued to pluck sharp, vibrating notes in the back of her mind.

Had Fendrel truly ordered Terryn's death?

She knew better than to doubt it.

The horse took a faulty step, jostling Ayleth. Her hands smashed against the iron spikes, and dozens of points of pain burst in her skin, sending shots of poison straight to her soul. The pain swelled, rising to dizzying heights before crashing down over her, and she could think of nothing again for some while. Only pain, pain, pain.

When at last she emerged from it, day had broken in good earnest. It seemed strange that the sun should rise so bright and the sky should be so clear, so blue, when everything good in the world had shattered into a million pieces.

She lifted her heavy head and looked around at the cold landscape through which they traveled. To her surprise, she realized they hadn't come all that far yet. They were only just leaving behind the formal gardens that surrounded Dunloch and making their way to the main road. What was Fendrel thinking, anyway? This didn't feel like a hell-bent pursuit of witches. It was more like a solemn processional for a feast day. Or a funeral.

Taking care of her hands, Ayleth carefully turned in her saddle to look back the way they had come. She could still barely discern the turrets of Dunloch Castle above the trees. Somewhere in there, Prince Gerard was locked in his suite of rooms, a prisoner in his own house. And Hollis . . .

Was she still alive? Fendrel had left two venators behind to hunt down and dispose of any shade-taken remaining in the castle. Would Hollis be among those eliminated? An ignoble death for a loyal venatrix.

But Hollis was no venatrix anymore. She was a traitor to the order. Ayleth was living proof of her perfidy.

Suddenly aware of Fendrel's gaze on the side of her face, Ayleth turned to him, teeth bared. He looked away at once and faced the road ahead, his expression hard. What was he thinking behind those locked-down eyes of his? Of his brother lying cold and stiff in Dunloch's chapel with a gaping hole in his chest where his heart should be? Of Terryn lying dead in some back room, his body hastily bundled to one side, out of the way, his soul and his shade's both banished from this world?

Of Gerard, the young man he'd raised to be king, whom he'd imprisoned?

"It won't work, you know."

The sound of her own voice half startled Ayleth. She hadn't fully intended to speak the words out loud.

But Fendrel wasn't startled. He didn't even blink.

Well, now that she'd begun, she might as well continue. "You can't make it right. Not anymore." She leaned in the saddle, taking care not to jostle her hands. "I know what you're thinking: 'If I can just get the witch girl to do what she needs to do and fix my mistake, no one will ever know.'"

She chuckled viciously, vapors puffing in the cool air before her face. "Even if we succeed, even if I manage to kill Dread Odile, even if you then kill me and murder each of these men and women, these comrades of yours, so that none are left alive who know the truth . . . Gerard knows."

Had that dart struck home? It was impossible to tell. Fendrel's stillness was so absolute, so unbreakable. How could he be that calm in the face of all that he'd done?

"Do you honestly think he will take his father's throne now?" she continued relentlessly. "Do you honestly think he'll submit to your will, become your puppet, your pawn? You know him better than that. You may have driven him into a corner this time, but he'll not be driven by you forever."

Still nothing. No reaction, no quick side glance.

Ayleth laughed, a cold sound in that cold air. "I hope for your sake, Venator Dominus, that you're a better liar than I think you are. I hope you're lying about what you did to Terryn. Because if you're not, if you truly had him killed, Gerard will never forgive you." She spat out the next words, foam flecking and freezing on her lips: "He'll see you dead. He'll see you damned."

At this, Fendrel turned. Slowly, calmly, without once breaking his horse's even stride. His face was blue with cold beneath the stubble on his chin, and wisps of pale hair dangled over his forehead and framed his cheeks. But his eyes were what struck Ayleth, making her draw back as though from a knife's point. They were the eyes of a dead man.

But in their centers, deep down, a furnace burned.

"Don't think your petty threats mean a thing to me, witch," he said. "I am damned already."

She moved too quickly, jolting her hands again, and cursed as the pain returned. She had to find a way to deal with it, to tamp it down. She couldn't know how long she'd be forced to wear these mitts, and she couldn't afford to be lost in this miasma of agony every few minutes. She couldn't—

Then the pain was too much, and all thought fled.

When she came to again, her hands throbbed and her throat felt raw and burned. She realized she'd been sick, but had no way to clean up the mess spilled down the front of her jerkin. The road stretched before them through the countryside of Wodechran Borough. Lifting her head and peering between the red-hooded figures on horseback in front of her, she spotted another horseman coming their way at a fast clip. Another red hood . . . a scout rider, she guessed.

A minute later he was close enough to recognize; it was Kephan. Ayleth's stomach sank. They must have revived him from the paralysis, used another poison to counteract its effects. An agonizing process, she knew from experience. But they needed every man for this hunt.

Kephan rode at a gallop down the road until he reached them, and the three Evanderians in the front of the line parted to let him through. He pulled up short in front of Fendrel, offering a swift salute.

"Dominus," he said, not once glancing Ayleth's way. "I found the anchor."

He must have been sent out from Dunloch on reconnaissance, to find the Phantomwitch's curse anchor that had allowed her and the other witches to escape Dunloch's vaults. These anchors always put off a powerful magic trace once activated, and Kephan's Feral abilities would have had little trouble in locating it.

"Is it near?" the Dominus demanded.

Kephan nodded. "It's broken and discarded, but I

picked up the witches' scent. I followed them from there, about five miles. All the way to Camon, a village just up this road." He paused. His face was very gray in the brilliant morning light.

"Well?" Fendrel said. "Speak up, man. Are they waiting for us in the village? Or did they *evanesce* again?"

Kephan shook his head. "I called my shade as far ascendant as I dared and searched for any sign of a living soul in the village. But there was only one—a witch's soul, bound with an Anathema. Otherwise . . . nothing. Neither human nor animal nor shade."

Silence fell as those listening considered the venator's words. Ayleth, her brain still half numb with pain, didn't at first understand. Then it slowly dawned on her.

"The Corpsewitch." Fendrel spoke Ayleth's own thought out loud. Another moment of silence hung in the air. Then he added, "Haunts damn."

The Evanderians shifted in their saddles, casting each other wary looks under their hoods. They knew that Gillotin du Visgarus was among the Crimson Devils who had broken into Dunloch last night. The Order had renamed him the Corpsewitch due to his unique curse-casting proclivities. Du Visgarus could plant curses that allowed him to take over the actions of others, controlling their bodies like puppets. But he found living bodies difficult to manage, so he preferred to channel his powers into the dead.

A whole village, though? Could it be possible that Gillotin du Visgarus had killed and cursed the entire village? Men, women, children, animals . . . all of them?

Despite herself, she looked to Fendrel, searching his hard face for some sort of guidance. He had faced the Crimson Devils on the battlefield many times before. He would know what to do. He had to.

Fendrel drew a long breath through his nostrils. "Du Visgarus will try to stop us from pursuing our quarry," he said. "If we try to go around him, he will harry us from behind and from all sides, picking us off as we go. We had better meet him head on and put an end to this devil."

THEY TOLD ME I WAS SPECIAL.

Can you imagine what that meant to me? The little orphan girl, always shuffled from one doorstep to the next by relatives who preferred to pretend she didn't exist? After years of neglect, years of abuse, years of fear that finally melted away to silent numbness . . . now I was special.

Because of my mother.

And her mother before her.

Because once upon a time, long ages ago, my family had wielded great power and influence, changing the face of the world.

Now I, the last of my name, was also the last hope of the Order of Saint Evander. Only I could wear the Eitr Crown. Only I, by virtue of the blood flowing in my veins, could survive the power trapped in that living metal and learn to control it for myself. Learn to control it and to save souls and bodies alike.

So they told me, feeding me legends, feeding me myths. I lapped up their words like sweet honey and became glutted on notions of heroism and hope. But first, they told me, I had to train. I was old for an initiate—fourteen and already come to my womanly cycle. But none of the other children had my desire to please.

None of the other children were . . . special.

CHAPTER 3

WHILE TERRYN'S BODY FROZE ON THE BANKS OF THE Holy Lake, his spirit stood alone in the barren world of his mind.

It was a landscape devoid of any feature other than the deep crevices in the stone-hard earth. Nothing green or growing could survive in this place. It was a desert . . . worse than a desert, for it had once flourished with life. In some distant part of his memory, he half remembered that it had once been green and thriving, a sweeping vista of fertile hills and many-colored flowers under a cloud-wisped sky. But that was long ago. Back before . . .

Before his shade took possession. Before the overwhelming light and power of the Arcane spirit blasted his mind and left behind nothing but wasteland.

Terryn turned his head first to the right, then to the left. No matter how he strained his eyes, his vision darkened, tunneled. The iron-gray sky overhead deepened to black, and soon he was left practically blind.

Somewhere far away, his mortal body lay dying. And there was nothing he could do about it. Nothing he could do about anything now.

He tried to form coherent thoughts . . . *Ayleth* . . . *Gerard* . . . *Fendrel* . . . but none would coalesce into anything solid. He turned slowly in place, seeing only darkness, expecting only darkness.

Then suddenly—light. A faint glimmer of silvery light, there on the horizon.

His spirit jolted with sudden hope and fear combined. Like a ship lost at sea steering toward the guiding gleam of a distant star, he turned and ran toward that glow. Perhaps it was nothing but his own life force shining in one last burst before it flamed out and he died. But perhaps . . . perhaps . . . He ducked his head and drove himself harder. Somewhere in the mortal world, his body trembled in the frozen lake.

The glow intensified as he drew nearer, an orb of light so brilliant that he could hardly bear to look at it straight on. At last, he stepped out of the darkness and into the sphere of brilliance. He blinked and squinted, his hand upraised to shield against the glare. Slowly, his dazzled vision clarified.

His shade sat before him. A tiny, gleaming being, scarcely larger than a housecat, made up of woven strands of pure white, pulsing light. Razor sharp scales coated its hide, and fronds of curled light spooled out from its spine. It sat upright, a long, sinuous tail wrapped in a circle around its haunches, and a pair of diaphanous wings wrapped around the front part of its body, as though concealing something within their folds.

It looked up at Terryn. Long lashes gleaming like white ember strands lifted from a pair of eyes like multi-colored fire opals.

Terryn took a half step back, almost retreating out of

the sphere of light back into the darkness. He'd never encountered his shade like this, unfettered in his mind. Since the moment of his possession, he had always sought to suppress this being, keeping it wrapped under layers of song spells and stone.

"*What . . . what are you doing?*" he asked at last.

The dragonet blinked, its long lashes fluttering softly as translucent eyelids slid down over those polished orbs, then lifted again. It said nothing, but its gaze was searing.

Terryn squared his shoulders and clenched his fists. His last memories of the waking world were confused. The only thing he remembered for certain was bone-freezing cold closing over him. Cold no mortal body could survive. He would die soon. He should have died already.

He gazed down at the silent being that shared this inner world with him. He'd always envisioned his shade as something vast, something ugly. To see it now as such a delicate, shining thing . . . it was baffling.

"*Has the paralysis poison reduced you to this size?*" Terryn asked.

I have no size, the shade responded. Its voice was as

bright and shining as its form. *But I am reduced, yes.*

Terryn nodded. In a way, he understood, though probably not completely. He sat down in front of the being, crossed his legs, and leaned his elbows on his knees.

"*I'm dying, you know,*" he said. "*My body won't last much longer. Then you'll be free of me.*"

Perhaps, the shade sang back. *Perhaps not. We do not know what will be, only what is.*

It was hard to argue with a statement like that. Terryn raised an eyebrow and tilted his head. "*I suppose you must hate me. For all those years of bondage.*"

Must I? The shade tilted its long, pointy face in response, and its wispy whiskers curled and uncurled.

"*Well, I wouldn't insist on it. But it would make sense, at least from my perspective.*"

How very sad. What a miserable life you must lead.

Again, he couldn't fairly argue. Terryn leaned heavily on one elbow, resting his chin in his hand. Of all the deaths he'd ever imagined for himself, he'd never pictured one quite like this. Trapped in his own mind, conversing with his possessing spirit as though the two of them were

. . . not friends, exactly. But not enemies either.

He had no sense of time in this place, for time had negligible meaning in the realm of spirit. It could have been mere seconds since he lost consciousness. He might have mere seconds left to live. But it all felt so far away. He couldn't feel rushed or anxious, not now.

But he couldn't deny the heaviness in his spirit. The sorrow for all he had left undone, all he had wished he might do. Once more, he tried to think . . . *Ayleth* . . . *Gerard* . . . but the thoughts refused to form.

His shade watched him closely, saying nothing.

At last Terryn sighed and shook himself slightly. *"You were an accident. Did you know that?"* His words seemed to frost the air before his face. When had it gotten so cold? The freezing of the mortal world was beginning to penetrate even here.

The shade's wings shivered softly, like candle flames in the wind.

"I was supposed to carry an Anathema shade," Terryn continued. *"I was trained for it. I studied all the Anathema lore, I learned all the prayers, and I knew every spell and variation. I knew what to expect. And when the time of my possession drew*

near, Fendrel himself went to find the right shade for me to carry. A venator in Nion died violently, and his shade escaped into a fox. Fendrel hunted it for months, determined to bring it back alive. It nearly killed him. But he knew it was the right shade for me."

He bowed his head, staring at the hard earth beneath his feet. *"When I entered my Ceremony of Possession, I thought I was prepared for what was to come. Only . . . something went wrong. It wasn't an Anathema that tore through my eye and implanted in my soul. It was you."*

His shade gazed up at him, silent and shining as a distant moon.

"You broke through every barrier, every carefully woven spell. I wasn't prepared for you. I didn't know what you were. I didn't have the songs or spells to withstand the sudden onslaught of your power. You blasted my mind." Terryn swept his arms wide as though to encompass the whole of his desolate mindscape in a single gesture. *"You did this to me. And you made my life a living hell all these years. Perhaps I was cruel to bind you, but was I wrong? I used those spells to survive. You would have killed me if I'd not held you back."* He shook his head. *"You might kill me still."*

The long, fluttering lashes fell and rose again. *I suppose you must hate me,* the shade sang.

He had. For years now, he'd hated this being with every fiber of his spirit.

Terryn sighed and bowed his head into his hands. He was so tired. The cold must be finally getting to him. He would be dead soon.

"I don't hate you," he whispered. *"Not anymore. But I do wonder . . . what might I have been if not for you?"*

As the words slipped from his lips, a face seemed to appear before his vision. A lovely, stern face. Black eyes glaring at him from beneath dark brows. A soft, full mouth slowly transforming from a frown to a smile. In memory he still felt the warmth of that mouth pressed against his, responding to the pressure he applied with an eagerness as surprising as it was enthralling.

That same tempting mouth had whispered strange new ideas into his ear. Her words lured his mind to heresy even as her kisses lured his body to sin. She, and not this shining being, was the true instigator of his ruin. Were it not for her, he never would have strayed from the teachings of Evander.

And yet, he wouldn't take back a moment. If that

meant the Goddess must forsake him—if that meant he must end his life now, frozen to death on the shore of Loch du Nóiv—if that meant he must face the awful eternity of the Haunts that awaited him, a heretic shade-taken—so be it.

A silken rustle brought Terryn's gaze up. The filmy unknown of light that made up the dragon's wings fluttered. His shade was struggling, he realized. Its power was sapped to almost nothing by the paralysis poison, and it was channeling everything it had left into those wings. The rest of its body darkened, hardened. Its long tail and haunches were again encased in suppressing stone.

"What are you hiding under your wings?" Terryn demanded.

The shade blinked. Then, very carefully, it raised a shimmering wing, and Terryn saw a little green stem. A sapling, one frail leaf unfurling from its end. An oak with tiny roots clutching at the dry, lifeless ground.

With a lurch of horror, he realized what it was: his life. In all this barren place, only this one little sapling held on, green and growing. And the shade protected it, wrapping its magic and power around it. Otherwise, Terryn would be dead already.

For some moments, he could only stare. His shade wrapped its protective wings around the sapling once more, shielding it from the deadly darkness and cold. Terryn reached out one hand, his fingers trembling beyond his control. But he didn't flinch as he placed his palm on the head of the light-being. It shivered beneath his touch. Then it spoke again in its strange, singing voice.

The Goddess sent me to you.

Terryn blinked. Then he whispered, "*How can that be? You are a shade. Shades are abominations in the Goddess's sight.*"

As are humans, the spirit replied. *All beings who turn their gazes from Her Light lose the ability to see Her. So they fall and are lost, and the Goddess cannot look upon them in their degradation. But everything lost may be redeemed. Even the* Ildrir—*the shades, as you call us.*

Terryn shook his head and looked away. He could feel the being's gaze on the side of his face, but he dared not turn to meet it.

We have a purpose to fulfill in this world. The words were a small symphony of delicate sound and light. *Your body is the vessel through which we will accomplish Her will. Together, and only together, we will do what must be done.*

"*And what is that?*" Terryn asked. "*My purpose is to drive shades from this world. Is that why the Goddess sent you here?*"

The shade shook its head, the frond-like spines along its neck floating delicately. *I am come to this world to seek those who are lost. I am come to this world to sing them home to the Light.*

The world lurched. Terryn, unprepared for the sudden shift of ground beneath him, fell on his side. Stone broke beneath him and fell away into shadow, crumbling under his hand. He backed up just in time to avoid tumbling after it.

Frost crept up out of the darkness, knife-like shards of pure cold eating away at the world, encroaching on his hands, his legs. Terryn leapt upright, but the frost swarmed closer. He knew what this meant. His mortal body was succumbing. He was about to die.

Nisirdi lifted a wing. Terryn looked, saw that space where the little green sapling huddled, sheltered in the shade's warmth. Opalescent eyes gazed up at him with wordless entreaty.

Refusing to stop and think about what he did, Terryn

dived under that wing, into the embrace of his shade's power. Magic surrounded him as the wing swept him close. All over again he realized the horrifying power of this being that indwelled him, this spirit he had so desperately feared all these years. Now that it was unsuppressed, it could easily pluck his soul loose from his body and cast him out, and there was nothing he could do to prevent it.

Yet here he was, taking refuge under the wing of this profound soul even as death itself passed over him in an icy wave. Like a child, he tucked in close to that warm center, placing his head where a heartbeat pulsed with fire and comfort.

He realized suddenly how old Nisirdi must be. Old and not old, all at once. More like . . . *ageless*. As though, having lived an eternity outside the bounds of time, when it stepped back into this time-bound world, it brought with it the lingering traces of forever.

It held Terryn's soul close, hiding him and the little green tree that was his life as the cold closed overhead. The glow of its wings shuddered dangerously. At any moment, Terryn expected to see the frost creep in, crawling through the cracks, knifing up from the ground itself. But in this sheltered place, the cold could not penetrate.

Nisirdi's elegant head sank down beneath the wings, eyes full of fire. *It is time, mortal,* it said. *Wake now.*

Terryn's eyes opened. Not his spirit eyes in his mental world, but his physical, mortal eyes. A film of ice broke as his lids cracked open, and he gazed up into the frigid sky and saw dawn light glowing on branches overhead.

He was alive. Somehow, miraculously, alive.

Consciousness hurt, but that hurt was good. Pain meant a return of feeling. His body was still frozen, yet pain flowed out from his heart as his senses slowly reawakened. The paralysis poison took time to wear off— he knew that well enough from recent experience. But already the pulsing heat of his shade warmed him, filled him with unexpected energy and strength.

Terryn reached down inside his soul and drew on the power crouched there, summoning up more. His limbs screamed as his frozen blood heated and began to flow again. He gasped, and cold air lanced his lungs.

With a strangled cry, he flung out an arm, breaking through the icy water, and caught hold of the stones and wintery grasses and turf of the lakeshore. He firmed his grip and pulled. His other arm obeyed him next, surging out from the water and gripping a handful of dirt and rock. His leg muscles seized up, then moved, and he crawled up onto the land, dripping water and small icicles in his wake.

He was so cold, he couldn't even shiver at first. Then his body began to quake, and the pain of returning sensation increased. He tried not to fight it, tried to lean into it. To let the pain remind him that he was alive, *alive*, and he still had some fight in him.

"Nisirdi!" he called down inside his head. *"Help me!"*

The paralysis was still keeping his shade at bay. But a surge of magic in his core told him Nisirdi fought against it. Heat swelled, flowering from his heart, and the poison melted away.

"More, Nisirdi, more!" he begged.

The heat intensified. The ice filming his clothes, crusting his hair and skin, began to melt and stream.

Vapors rose from his body. He managed to push up onto his elbows, his knees, to lift his torso and throw back his head. He stared at the gold-streaked sky through the delicate interlacing of wintery branches. Still the warmth grew, glowing in his veins, shining out from under his skin, through his clothes.

Then he began to burn.

Terror seized him. Another few seconds and it would be too much, too late. He would disintegrate into a cloud of ash.

"*No more! No more, please!*" he cried desperately. The heat flared brighter, so bright he knew he could not take any more. But before it truly became too great, before it melted him from the inside out, it faded.

Terryn breathed out a huge gasp and sagged back onto his heels. His arms hung limp at his sides, and his racing heart slowly eased its frantic pace.

Are you well?

The voice appeared in the space inside him where usually only his own consciousness dwelled. Terryn felt rather than saw the shimmering contours of a dragon-like being, its wings upraised and unfurled, its eyes bright with inner fire.

In all his years as a shade-taken, Terryn had never truly shared his body. Was this what Ayleth experienced with her dangerously ascendant shade? That sensation of two souls in the space meant for one, distinct and yet indivisible?

Terryn closed his eyes and let his awareness step back into his mindscape. Nisirdi waited for him there, looming large, too beautiful and too brilliant to look at directly. It stood beside a young tree, an oak with many slender branches covered in green knobs of leaves ready to unfurl.

Are you well, mortal man? Nisirdi sang.

He nodded, unable to find words to speak. Then he opened his eyes and returned to the winter wood beside the lake. His clothes steamed, but when he checked, his scorpiona string was unbroken and his knife and his pipes—for whatever good they would do him now—were still in their sheaths. His quivers were almost empty, but that didn't worry him overmuch. He had power. More power, ready and willing at his beck and call, than he had ever before known.

If he could only keep it from inadvertently killing him.

Terryn gazed across the cold gray waters of the lake to the tall turrets of Dunloch Castle. How many hours had passed since he dove from those high walls? And what had Fendrel done in his absence?

He couldn't find out by standing here.

Though he ached in every bone and joint and muscle, Terryn squared his shoulders. "*All right, Nisirdi,*" he said. "*We're in this together now.*" He drew a deep breath, closed his eyes, and whispered, "*Come out to me.*"

A stream of white light poured out of his head into the world beside him. It whirled and coiled and coalesced at last into the magnificent image of his shade, towering over him, its mighty head high, its elegant neck arched. It was impossible and glorious, and invisible to all but Terryn.

The shade looked down at him, and its opal eyes seemed to smile. *Together?* it sang softly.

"*Together,*" Terryn repeated. Then he set out at a run along the shores of the lake, the light-dragon keeping pace at his side.

I TRAINED AT THE CASTRA FOR FOUR YEARS BEFORE *they deemed me ready to receive my shade. The Ceremony of Possession is a special rite, and only those initiates deemed worthy are permitted to endure it.*

I'd seen others, younger than myself, enter the Praetorum to undergo their Possession. I'd seen them bright-eyed and eager, boasting of the powers that would soon be theirs. I'd seen them stride off with pride, their new red hoods as vivid as blood while the priestesses and phasmators and venators and domini made prayers over their heads and anointed them with sacred oils.

I'd seen them enter the Chamber of Possession.

Most of them never returned.

To take a shade into one's body is to risk everything. Not everyone can master a possessing spirit in the first few moments of taking. Those who could not prove their mastery were shot down before their powers got out of control. Their souls were driven on to heaven, their shades either contained or sent to the Haunts. Then the Order would begin again with new initiates, devoting time and resources to shaping more weapons for Saint Evander.

Was I afraid when they told me my time had come? Of course not. I was special. I would survive my Possession, and I would master the Elemental they gave me. I would master the oblivis.

Then I would receive my crown. It was my destiny.

CHAPTER 4

AT FENDREL'S BARKED COMMAND, ROUGH HANDS reached up to pull Ayleth from her horse.

"No, no, no!" she pleaded, but it was no use. Her hands were jostled, and the spikes in the iron mitts pierced her skin. One moment she was in her saddle with Red Hoods surrounding her, her mouth open to utter a stream of curses . . . the next moment pain overwhelmed her, and she lost consciousness.

When she next became aware of her surroundings, she

found herself propped against a tree trunk several yards from the road, shielded by a swathe of evergreen boughs. Fendrel stood close by, speaking in a low voice to a venatrix.

"Oi," Ayleth cried. When he didn't acknowledge her, she tried again but louder, "Oi! Bastard!" He turned her way, his expression blank, almost bored. She carefully raised her shackled hands. "You're leaving me behind? Like this?"

He blinked slowly. Then, addressing himself to the venatrix, said, "Remember, she is a witch like the rest of them. Don't trust her for an instant. But she is also our most valuable asset. If she dies, we are lost. You must protect her at all costs."

Ayleth sat up straighter, shifting her position with care so as not to let the spikes drive into her skin again. Nausea whirled in her head and her gut, but she snarled viciously through it, "Let me fight! You brought me along as a weapon, didn't you? So take these Haunts-damned mitts off of me and let me do what I'm here for!"

He turned to go, pushing through the curtain of pine boughs and making for the road. Desperate, Ayleth screamed at his back, "You don't want me dead before I can kill her, right? I can't even defend myself like this!"

Fendrel paused. Ayleth held her breath, caught in the despairing balance between hope and dread. The wind stirred his hair, and light filtering through the pine needles played strange shadows across the dominus's shoulders.

Then he turned, his eyes hooded, and strode back up the incline to where she sat beneath the tree. His hand fished into one of the pouches slung from his belt and produced a bent brass bar. Taking care to touch the iron mitts as little as possible, he inserted the bar into a slot and, with a vicious twist, brought it round in a full circle.

Ayleth gasped as the iron clasps sprang open and the mitts fell away. Her hands were riddled with small wounds, bleeding and raw. But for the moment she could not see or feel any of that, only the profound relief of being able to flex and stretch her fingers and rotate her wrists.

Fendrel began to rise. "Wait," she said quickly. "What about these?" she demanded, and rattled the iron shackles still gripping her wrists, only a six-inch chain between them.

The look he gave her was so venomous, she half feared he would slap the iron mitts back on her hands and leave her. Instead, he swept up the evil objects in a fold of his cloak and, without a word or another look her way, rose and strode away. He shoved the iron mitts into the venatrix's unwilling arms, growling, "Arm your scorpiona with Feral poison. If she gives you any trouble, take her down and put these back on. But no matter what, keep her alive."

The venatrix managed to offer her dominus a hasty salute while juggling the iron mitts. He returned it and strode on down the shallow incline, back to the road where the other Evanderians waited.

Ayleth spat at his retreating back. A useless, stupid gesture, but it made her feel better anyway. She craned her neck to one side and the other, peering out from among the thick-hung boughs, and watched as Fendrel mounted his horse and led the way toward Camon village.

One of the horsemen hung back a little after the rest. He lifted his gaze, looking to where Ayleth and the venatrix were hidden. From her angle, Ayleth could just discern Kephan's square face wreathed in worry.

She hardened her jaw, hardened her heart. He could look as concerned as he liked—he'd chosen his side. He stood with the Venator Dominus and the Order. That made him her enemy. Ayleth tucked back against the tree trunk again, pulled her knees up, and rested her elbows on them so that her shackled hands hung between.

Now that the initial relief of being free of the iron mitts had passed, she shuddered at the wounds left behind. Looking at them made it worse, so she tried to look anywhere else—at the branches interlacing overhead, out to the road, down at the red pine straw on which she sat. At last she settled into watching the venatrix, her guard. The woman took a position a few yards away, standing where she could see the road while maintaining a clear shot at Ayleth should her captive make a wrong move. So long as they remained in place, they were invisible to any travelers passing below.

But they were not invisible to shadow sight. Any shade-taken would be able to detect their souls shimmering behind the sheltering branches easily enough.

The venatrix watched her fellow Evanderians ride out of sight. Even then she didn't turn or look Ayleth's way.

They didn't speak. Ayleth hadn't heard the woman's name. She was a hard-looking individual with a face so freckled, scarcely any pale skin showed between the golden spots. Ayleth couldn't sense the variety of shade she carried, but she could feel magic emanating from the woman's core. Ascendant, lethal magic, only just bound back by straining spell songs.

Ayleth leaned her head back against the trunk and drew a long breath. Then she closed her eyes and, as much as possible, let the world around her melt away—the cold air biting at her cheeks, the scent of autumn rot, the pain in her hands, the nauseating iron binding her wrists—and stepped into the world of her mind. The pine forest was full of glaring red light, and the shadows were darker and deeper than before. As though her own mind hid secrets from her.

Manifesting in human shape, Ayleth braced herself, cupped her hands around her mouth and called, "*Laranta!*" Her voice echoed through the trees once, twice, before fading to nothing. "*Laranta!*" she tried again. "*Come to me!*"

No answer.

Ayleth cursed. It was the Haunts-damned iron shackles. While they were not as painful as the spiked mitts, the direct touch of iron on her skin drove Laranta deep down into her soul. For the shade to rise any higher in ascendancy would be to experience pain—pain even worse than Ayleth experienced, pain that went far beyond physical sensation.

She ought to leave her shade alone, ought to let the poor spirit hide. But without Laranta's strength, she was helpless. Helpless in a world suddenly bereft of friends and allies, a world peopled entirely with enemies.

"*Please, Laranta.*" She bowed her head, no longer shouting. She didn't need to shout here, not really. She and Laranta shared a soul. There was no real distance between them, and a whisper could serve as well as a shout. "*Please, Laranta,*" she said again, scarcely more than a breath. "*I need you.*"

Mistress?

Ayleth's heart lurched. Her mortal eyes squeezed tighter as she concentrated her gaze through the shadows of her mind. "*Laranta? Is that you?*"

The bark sounded so far away, muffled, strained,

frightened. But its deep, growling edge was unmistakable.

Mistress . . . I come . . .

Ayleth's mental projection held out both arms, reaching. *"Good girl, Laranta, good girl. Come on, now!"* The shadows seemed to shift, move, and begin to take shape—

A hard impact in the side of her boot sent Ayleth's leg sliding out in front of her. She unbalanced, twisted, and her shackled hands came down hard to catch herself. Her eyelids fluttered as she struggled to regain proper awareness of the waking world. The images of her mindscape flashed in the darkness of each blink, and for a few moments the two worlds battled for dominance. She pulled herself back into reality and glared up into the fierce, freckled face hovering over her.

"If I catch you playing tricks like that again, witch, I'll shoot you," the venatrix growled, and raised her armed scorpiona for emphasis.

Ayleth bared her teeth. She pulled her leg back up and rested her elbows on her knees. The venatrix reclaimed her position a few yards away, watching the road. Her ascendant shade must have sensed Ayleth's call to

Laranta.

Still, despite the venatrix's interference, Laranta was nearer. She couldn't climb to any real ascendancy due to the iron, but Ayleth no longer felt empty inside. Something powerful prowled back and forth in the deeps of her soul, like a caged beast. If she tried—if she really tried—she might even be able to access some of Laranta's strength.

But she wouldn't dare with that venatrix so near. The woman wasn't exaggerating her threat, and the iron mitts lay in a pile only a few feet from Ayleth's position. If she woke from paralysis to find those grisly things binding her hands again, she might as well die.

The venatrix kept her gaze fixed intently on the east road, while Ayleth kept her gaze fixed on the venatrix. They remained thus in silence for at least half an hour, judging by the movement of shadows. Then Ayleth saw the venatrix's eyes widen. Just a fraction, almost imperceptible at that distance. If Ayleth hadn't been watching so closely, she would have missed it.

Ayleth twisted her shoulders and craned her neck, trying to get a better view of the road and the horizon.

She didn't need shadow sight to see the smoke rising black and billowing into the morning sky. The battle in Camon village had begun.

A flurry of wings drew her eye. She looked up and saw a black bird, a crow, settle into the bare branches of a tree standing not far from her current position. It turned a bright eye her way, each movement sharp and jerking. Ayleth frowned as she peered through the interlacing pine needles at that bird. Something wasn't quite right about it. When it turned toward her, its head flopped oddly to one side as though the neck had been wrung. But it clung to its branch, its head dangling, its eye staring, and watched her.

"Venatrix," Ayleth said slowly.

The venatrix started, and her scorpiona rose to firing mode as she glared Ayleth's way.

"Venatrix." Ayleth pointed. "Can you . . . can you see a soul?"

Turning in the direction Ayleth indicated, the venatrix peered up at the bird. She studied it in silence, and Ayleth felt her heart thud in her throat five times.

Then the venatrix braced her feet and raised her right

arm, crossing it across her left for support. She sighted along her scorpiona and took the shot. The dart sped through the air, struck the bird in the head, and stuck.

The bird shook itself, wings flapping, and the dart fell to the ground.

A living bird would have dropped dead on the spot when struck with a venatrix's poison.

Grabbing hold of the tree trunk for support, Ayleth scrambled to her feet. She knew what this meant. A dead bird flying, studying them. The Corpsewitch was controlling it, peering through its dead eyes. He must have realized that Ayleth—Fendrel's one weapon against Dread Odile—wasn't at the battle in Camon, and sent a scout searching for her.

"Come on," the venatrix growled. She had already reached the same conclusion and leapt up the incline, catching Ayleth by the elbow. "The horses are this way, hidden. We've got to get out of here."

The bird flew off, its head lolling as its wings pounded the air. Ayleth let the venatrix drag her down the slope. They ducked away from low-hung branches and crashed through autumn-bare underbrush. She saw the horses not far off, tied to a tree.

Beyond the horses, figures moved. Five figures. All men.

All dead.

They wore only their long linen shirts, as though their deaths had come upon them while they lay sleeping in their beds. Each man carried a tool of his trade—she saw a scythe, a pitchfork, knives, tanner's implements. One man bled from a gaping wound in his gut. Another's head was partially severed at the neck. But they lumbered on, awkward in their motions and yet strangely powerful as well, guided by their unseen puppet-master.

The horses, scenting death in the air, screamed. One of them broke its tether and crashed through the underbrush and away. The other kicked and pulled and squealed as the five figures moved past it without pause or interest.

The venatrix leapt in front of Ayleth, flinging out a protective arm. "Back!" she urged, and Ayleth didn't wait to be told twice. She turned to scramble through the forest grove, back the way they had come. Instinct told her to regain the high ground, a more defensible position.

But when she took a step toward the slope where they had hidden minutes before, the venatrix caught her elbow. "No. To the road," she said. "We need to get to the Dominus."

Ayleth opened her mouth to argue, but the dead men were just behind them, and there was no time. Gritting her teeth, she staggered after the venatrix, pushing out from the trees and up onto the open road under the incongruously bright sun. More dead lumbered toward them along the road. Men and women. Children too.

The witch was using children, Haunts damn him.

"Venatrix, give me a weapon," Ayleth said, and held out her shackled hands.

Before the venatrix could respond, the dead surged toward them, moving with a sudden burst of simultaneous speed, driven by a single impulse of will. The venatrix pushed Ayleth behind her again, drawing her long bone knife. If these were living mortals, her poisons would bring them down, but what use was the Gentle Death on those already dead?

The first man reached them a few paces ahead of the rest. He carried no weapon, merely grasped at them with curling fingers. The venatrix knocked his hands aside and drove her knife straight into the eye-socket.

The man did not pause or flinch. One hand caught hold of the venatrix's knife arm while the other went for her throat. Ayleth knew how this worked—the Corpsewitch planted his curses deep inside his chosen vessels, and only a direct blow to the curse anchor itself could bring one of these corpses down. Otherwise, they could be decapitated and all their limbs removed, and still they would keep coming by whatever means possible, driven by the will of their master.

The venatrix yanked free of his hold and pulled her knife out from his skull. She kicked him hard in the stomach, and he fell back into the man behind him. A woman reached them next, her hair long and gray and thickly snarled with blood. The venatrix deflected her grasp, turned her around, and drove her knife into her neck.

The woman didn't fall.

The first man was getting up again already, crawling on hands and knees, stretching out his arm for Ayleth. She kicked him in the face but staggered back into another man behind her. His arms wrapped around her. She doubled over and heaved him across her back and down on the ground. She stomped her boot in his face so hard she felt bones break. But the arms came up and grasped her leg, pulling her off her balance. She landed flat on her back, the wind knocked out of her.

Another dead face loomed over her. She got her hands up, catching the reaching forearm, and twisted in such a way as would have caused excruciating pain in anyone living. But the corpse didn't react, not even when the bone cracked. Another pair of hands caught her by the feet, and she kicked wildly to free herself of its hold. Strong fingers pinched down into the flesh of her arms, gripped the front of her jerkin, pulled her up from the ground. There were so many hands, so many dead faces, all ready to tear her to pieces.

"*Laranta!*" she screamed in her head.

Her wolf shade responded, surging up. But the iron poison knocked her back, and she cried out in pain inside Ayleth's head.

"*Laranta, come!*" Ayleth screamed again, desperate.

Her shade rallied and, despite the blow she'd just

received, flung herself forward again, offering whatever strength she could. It wasn't much. But it was something. Magic buzzed in Ayleth's veins, faint but real.

With a cry of rage and terror, she broke the hold of the man gripping her jerkin, tore free of the hands holding her braid and her shoulders, and flung herself at the gruesome figure directly in front of her, using Laranta's strength to hurl it into the oncoming corpse behind.

A flash of bone whirred passed her eye. The venatrix appeared in her vision again, her arm extended to full length, knife point burrowing up through the ribcage of one corpse. She whipped it free again in a gush of blood, and the corpse collapsed. Ayleth, her shade senses faint but present, felt a snap of tension as the Corpsewitch's curse broke.

The venatrix elbowed another man, whirled and stabbed a third. Ayleth dodged the grasping arms of yet another, and when she came upright, she saw the venatrix take him down with another well-aimed blow to the heart. Broken curse threads shimmered on the edges of her shadow vision, and dead bodies lay strewn across the ground. But more dead walked right over them.

A scythe whirred passed Ayleth's face. She bared her teeth in a ferocious grin. A weapon! And now that she knew where the curse was planted, she could do something about it. Her hands still shackled, she leapt at the dead man and wrenched the scythe from his grasp. With an agile spin, she hacked the sharp blade into the next nearest corpse's chest.

It didn't stop it. Her blow, though it would have killed a living man, didn't go deep enough to break the curse. She yanked the scythe free and hacked it into the next man, not anywhere near the heart, but hard enough to knock him over. Her bound hands slipped, and she lost hold of her weapon. She ducked and darted to catch it by the handle.

A thick-sounding thud filled her ears, followed immediately by a horrible, gasping cry. Ayleth turned on her knees, her hands gripping the scythe's handle. She saw the venatrix, a pitchfork driven into her side. One of the prongs pierced through her leather jerkin.

The venatrix went down on her knees.

With a savage cry, Ayleth leapt up and swung her

scythe again, smashing it into the chest of an approaching corpse. It fell but started to move again at once, its curse unbroken despite the ugly wound.

The venatrix still held herself upright by some miracle of stubborn strength. Corpses closed in on her. Ayleth swung, kicked, tore, hacked, tried to keep them off, tried to keep them away. Hands grabbed her from all sides, caught her arms, her legs. She dropped the scythe, and this time she could not reclaim it.

Through the mayhem of the dead, she felt the loosening of a soul tether, the break. Then a violent burst, as a shade soul sprang free from the venatrix's body. Ayleth just had time to think—stupidly, distantly—that if she could only reach the pipes strung from the venatrix's belt, she might be able to save her mortal soul.

Then her vision crowded with too many grasping hands.

IT TOOK TIME TO MASTER CONTROL OF MY SHADE. I *suppressed it at once, but learning the complexities of the spell songs, learning how to release just enough power to manipulate but never so much that I risked my own safety . . . that did not come easy.*

I hated those suppressions. I hated anything that got between me and the power I knew I was meant to wield. But if I wanted that crown—if I wanted to fulfill my purpose for existence—I had to demonstrate control and restraint as well as might and mastery.

Another two years passed before Venatrix Domina d'Arcand—the same venatrix who had found me at my cousin's house eight years earlier—told me that I was ready. That I would be presented to the Council of Agla to make my bid for the crown.

My moment was finally at hand. Or so I believed . . .

CHAPTER 5

GERARD PACED FROM HIS OFFICE THROUGH TO HIS private receiving room. From there he moved on to his dressing room, then to his bedchamber, leaving the doors open behind him. His office window looked out over the waters of Loch du Nóiv and on to where the rising sun cast a golden glow across the frost-laced world. His bedchamber window afforded a view of the bridge to the mainland. An hour ago, Gerard had watched his uncle and a company of eight red-hooded Evanderians ride across that bridge and disappear into the grounds beyond.

An hour. But it felt like a year.

He returned to that view again and strained his vision as far as it would go. But it was no use. Fendrel was long gone.

"Haunts damn," Gerard whispered and marched back through his suite of rooms to his office window, skirting around his large desk. He stared through the glass, studying the lake's far shore, studying the dawn-stained sky. Was that smoke he saw rising above the tree line? Camon village lay that way, the home of bakers and wheelwrights and candle makers, all living snug in the knowledge of their prince's proximity and protection.

They weren't prepared for witches, for war.

"Haunts damn!" Gerard hissed again. Though he knew it was useless, he strode to the door of his office and tested the latch. It was locked fast, just as it had been the last dozen times he'd tried it. He rattled it anyway and shouted, "Hey! Traitors! Villains! Let me out!"

No answer came. He put his ear to the panels but discerned no sound, no sign of life. There might be a half dozen guards standing in the passage on the other side, or none at all.

And what right had he to call them traitors? If they chose to obey the Venator Dominus instead of their unproven young king, could he blame them? In their shoes, he probably would have done the same. He'd always obeyed Fendrel with the same predictable obedience by which the tides obey the moon. One doesn't cross a force of nature.

He'd allowed Fendrel to imprison him in his own house. He'd let Fendrel . . .

His throat thickened painfully. Gerard turned away from the door and returned to the office window and its view of Loch du Nóiv. Why his gaze searched along the far shore with such care, he couldn't guess. It was as though some instinct beyond his understanding urged him. He half expected to see a tall figure approach through the trees with that long-legged, purposeful stride he knew so well. Terryn. His protector, his champion. Coming to his rescue.

But Terryn was dead.

A groan like a knife's blade sliding up his throat tore through him. Gerard pounded the window casement with a fist, then pounded it again, rattling the glass. "Haunts damn. Haunts damn, Haunts damn, Haunts damn." His voice was so raw, he almost expected the words to spatter blood as they burst from his lips.

At last his fist uncurled and pressed, open-palmed, to the glass. He bowed his head. "Goddess," he breathed in a tortured gasp. "Goddess, I have sinned against You. Not by what I have done, but by what I have left undone." He sagged to the floor and turned to put his back to the wall. His elbows rested on his drawn-up knees, and his head hung to his breast.

"I swore at Your altar," he whispered, "that I would stand as a banner of protection over Your people. All of Your people. Yet what have I allowed to take place? What have I sanctioned and supported? The murder of the shade-taken . . . those whom You have made our brothers and sisters, I have suffered to be hunted down like animals."

His words trailed off into silence for some while. At length, his limp hands curled back into fists and his mouth twisted in a grimace. "I thought it was by Your will that I stood in authority over other mortals. But it is only by mortal will that I rule. Even as it is by mortal will that I am now imprisoned. Helpless. Useless. A failure."

He tilted his head back and gazed at the ceiling. But his eyes seemed to penetrate plaster and stone, to see all the way to the heavens themselves. As though he sought the throne of the Goddess, as though he sought one desperate glimpse of Light.

"I don't know if You can hear me," he said. A tear trailed from the corner of his eye—just one tear, racing fast then gone. "I don't know if You're even there. It's all illusions. Everything I once thought so sure and certain? All illusions crafted by clever men. Perhaps even You, Goddess. Or perhaps You are real, but in Your divinity, You simply cannot hear the prayers of this doubter, this son of a liar. Whatever the truth is, I swear . . ."

The prince's words were so softly spoken, they might as well have been silent. He grimaced and spoke again, firmly this time. "Hear me or ignore me. Use me or reject me. It doesn't matter anymore. I swear by your holiness, Heart, Head, and Soul—I will atone for my sins and the sins of my father."

He let his head drop to his breast again as though it

had suddenly become too heavy. Despite his bold words, his bold vows, he sat there against the wall with his knees drawn up, a picture of utter wretchedness mingled with utter helplessness. The weight of his vow threatened to crush him.

Silence fell again. A silence so profound that mortal ears might begin to play tricks on mortal minds. A man might even begin to believe that through the silence he heard the chaos of the Haunts beckoning him through the veil of worlds. Gerard squeezed his eyes shut, trying to tell himself he didn't hear those tortured screams—

Small fingers touched his hand.

He jerked his head up so fast it hit the wall. His vision swam, and he saw—but didn't believe he saw—a little figure scurry away and bare feet disappear under his desk. He sat a moment more, blinking, letting the throb in his head subside. Then he shifted to his hands and knees and peered between the legs of his chair and under the desk.

Pale eyes stared back at him through a snarl of limp hair.

"Who—? What—?" Gerard blinked hard. Was he hallucinating? He shook his throbbing head, but the little urchin didn't disappear. "Who are you? How . . . how did you get in here?"

She blinked at him, her tiny frame trembling visibly. "*Blood to blood,*" a soft, lisping voice just reached his ear. "*Bone to bone . . .*"

Gerard shifted position, trying to make himself look less threatening. She must have ducked in here to hide during the mayhem of the attack. But he didn't recognize her. She was too young to be a scullery maid. Was she the daughter of one of his servants? Surely not; her ragged garments and dirty face were out of place among the denizens of Dunloch. How had she gotten through the castle gates unseen?

"It's all right, little one," he said, reaching out a careful hand. "I won't hurt you. Come on out from there and—"

She lunged suddenly, like a cat lashing out. Her small hands caught hold of his, her fingers latching with unexpected force. Her mouth opened, and words poured out. Strange words, unnatural words, in a voice that did not belong to that child: "*Blood to blood. Bone to bone. The Queen will rise to claim her own. Blood to blood. Bone to bone. The Queen will rise to claim her own. Blood to blood—*"

"Stop!" Gerard cried, trying to pull his hand back. Her grip was like iron. "Stop, let me go!"

Then—

He stands at the top of a dark, narrow stair, gazing out into an open balcony. A strange balcony, shaped by some extraordinary craftsman into the palm of a huge hand, pillars arching like perfectly sculpted fingers overhead.

A woman stands in the center of the palm, a blazing crown burning her head. Blue flames surround her in an aura, and her hair streams out from her on all sides like the rays of a sun. She screams in pain, reaching up to touch the crown but unable to grasp it.

He grips a sword in his hand. And he knows what he must do.

"Ayleth!" he cries.

She turns. And it is Ayleth. Ayleth, tortured, overwhelmed by a power that consumes her from the inside out, like a volcano erupting in her very soul.

"I'm so sorry," he gasps, striding toward her, lifting his sword. "I'm so sorry, Ayleth."

He swings for her neck. He feels his blade connect with bone, feels that bone give and break. He feels the spurt of hot blood on his face—

Gerard broke away with a cry, hitting his head against the shelf of the desk in his haste. The child huddled into a ball of misery, pressed to the backboard, her face buried in her hands.

She was shade taken. Gerard gaped at her, trying to bring his reason into the present, trying not to see the vision so violently implanted in his brain. Trying not to feel that hot blood on his face. The child was some sort of mind manipulator. The ascendant spirit was certainly no child but an ageless being, powerful, dangerous. Yet . . .

Yet when the girl peered at him between her fingers, there was no malice in her gaze. Strangeness, yes. Something otherworldly, something he didn't understand. But not evil.

"What . . . what was that?" he whispered. "What did you do to me?"

"*Forgive me*," the ageless voice spoke through that little mouth. The words were certainly not those of a child. "*The visions come upon us suddenly, and it causes my Nilly pain if*

I do not expel them at once. I did not mean to hurt you, mortal."

"Your . . . your Nilly . . ." Gerard shook his head, his hair falling into his eyes. He pushed it back, staring at the child, hardly believing what he saw, what he heard. He knew that name. "You are Nilly du Bucheron. The inborn. The Seer."

"She is here, yes. And she is safe. With me. I protect my Nilly."

A shade protecting its host's spirit? How could it be? Shades possessed bodies and ousted the original souls, unless those souls proved strong enough to resist. Or so he'd been taught.

But then again, so much of what he'd been taught had proven false. Why should this new revelation surprise him?

"And . . . what is your name?" he asked.

Something flashed in the girl's face. Gerard possessed no shadow sight, could not perceive the spirit world with his mortal senses. But he thought maybe his question pleased the being before him. *"I am Rasanala,"* it said. *"I am Nilly's. And she is mine."*

Gerard nodded. The name felt weird on his tongue,

but he gave it a try anyway. "Rasanala. Can . . . can you tell me the meaning of the vision?"

"*It is your future.*"

"My future?"

A recent memory appeared in his head—a memory of Ayleth crouched on the floor in her prison room, gazing up at him with those dark, dangerous eyes of hers. A memory of her voice, husky and full of terrible emotion: "*Nilly du Bucheron, the inborn child. She gave me a vision. I saw you with your sword drawn. You were sad, but you didn't hesitate. You cut off my head and . . . I was grateful to you.*"

"My future," Gerard whispered again, horror coiling in his heart. He saw again the vision. The night sky. The crown wrapped around Ayleth's brow. The Eitr Crown. It had to be. Possessed of a soul more dangerous even than Dread Odile herself.

And what of Ayleth? She was Odile's blood, the blood of Mauval himself. She could wear the crown and survive, and the spirit indwelling it could exert its will and power through her.

Was that Ayleth's fate? To become the vessel of the Eitr Crown? Was that the doom she and all Perrinion would face . . . unless Gerard himself took action?

Must he cut off Ayleth's head even as his father had cut off Odile's?

He had made a vow. He had promised the Goddess to atone for his sins, even unto his dying breath. She had heard him. She had answered his prayer by sending this child, this spirit, with a vision too clear to misunderstand, to ignore.

Little Nilly watched him. He could see the mortality in her face now and knew that both spirits were ascendant, side by side within that host. She rocked slowly back and forth, her arms wrapped around herself.

Gerard reached out his hand and placed it gently on her shoulder. "It's all right. You did well to share with me. Thank you, Nilly. Thank you, Rasanala." He drew a long breath and let it out slowly. "I know now what I must do. Goddess, grant me the strength!"

SHE IS NOT WHAT WE NEED," THE GRAND VANDERIAN
said. *She said it to my face, looking me straight in the eye but
speaking to others and not to me.*

*I stared at her, aghast. Even now, the enormity of the power I'd
summoned up burned in my fingertips. I controlled* oblivis—*an
element unlike anything in this world, almost infinite in its potential
and power and possibilities. And I controlled it. I. Me. The special
one they needed.*

*I had just demonstrated my abilities. They brought in captive
shade-taken, beasts and men alike, brimming with unsuppressed
power. I took them down one after another, binding them in* oblivis
*chains I crafted from thin air, then piercing them with darts and
driving out their souls. And when the battles were through, I had*

shown them my creative potential, sculpting a perfect likeness of the Grand Vanderian herself in pure, polished oblidite.

They applauded my efforts. As though I were a good dog performing some trick.

Then the Grand Vanderian said, "She is not what we need," and my world seemed to tilt on its axis.

"What can you mean?" Domina d'Arcand demanded. "She is of the du Mauval line. She is skilled beyond her years, more skilled than many of you in this room. The power she controls is unlike anything any of us have ever seen, and she makes it look easy! More than that, she is wholly devoted to the Order and will use whatever gifts we bestow upon her to further the cause of the Goddess here in the mortal world."

"I do not doubt her abilities. But as to her devotion . . ." The Grand Vanderian shook her head. "It is the devotion of a child. Untried, untested. She has not seen what we have seen. She does not know what we know. She cannot will this for herself."

"I do will it!" I declared, hot with wrath. "I can wear the Eitr Crown!"

The Grand Vanderian looked at me again but still spoke only to my domina, refusing to speak to me. "Her ardor is the ardor you have bestowed upon her. Until she has lived, until she has lost, until she has suffered . . . she cannot know. Not truly. Not wholly. Until her ardor is her own, I will not give her what you ask of me."

I shut my mouth. Though my domina continued to protest, to argue, I said nothing more. I saw in the Grand Vanderian's face the end of all my hopes, all my work, all my striving. In the end it did not matter that I was special.

Special wasn't good enough.

.

CHAPTER 6

THE SHADOWS WERE SO DEEP, AYLETH WONDERED IF she was dead.

But no. A scent of pine filled her nostrils when she breathed. Was she in her mind forest? Curled up tight in the darkness but still alive somehow?

She couldn't remember her last moments in the waking world. She thought they were violent. If she allowed her conscious awareness to drift out from this safe dark space, she would have to encounter all the pain of her body torn apart limb from limb.

"*Wake up, Venatrix.*"

Terryn?

Despite every instinct telling her to curl up tighter, to make her consciousness smaller, to hide so deep in this place of pine-scented darkness that she became almost nothing, she couldn't help lifting her awareness. Her mortal senses quickened, becoming aware of her physical body, becoming aware of the world beyond her head. She smelled musty straw, rotten wood. She felt the shift of a body beside her.

"*Come on. It's time to wake.*"

It couldn't be Terryn. Could it? No. No, he was dead.

But he couldn't be dead. She couldn't accept it. Not Terryn. Not without her seeing him one more time. That last moment in the pillared hall outside the gallery in Dunloch, standing across from one another, the body of the dead king lying between them . . . She refused to believe that he walked out of that room, out of her sight, and then simply ceased to be.

"*Venatrix.*"

That voice. It sounded like Terryn's. But also . . . not.

It didn't matter. Her consciousness rose swiftly now. The darkness just behind her own eyelids replaced the darkness of her pine forest. Pain roared through her body from multiple small wounds, and when she drew a breath, worse pain stabbed through her torso. One of her ribs was broken, possibly several. Blood trickled from small cuts, including one on her temple, warm and sticky on her skin.

Memory returned—memory of grasping hands and dead eyes and gaping mouths and blood. The dead closing in upon her.

"Venatrix." The word struck like the crack of a whip. "Open your eyes."

She obeyed at once. The darkness in her head filled with painful daylight, and the rest of her mortal senses rushed back to full wakefulness. She stared up into a dark face with sharp cheekbones, a long nose, and black hair falling over his forehead. For a heart-stopping moment she believed it really was Terryn.

But this face bore no disfiguring scar. And the eyes staring down into hers were black, not blue.

"Ah. There you are."

A hand caught her by the front of her jerkin, yanking her up from the ground. She cried out at the pain stabbing through her ribcage, and when she tried to catch her balance, she realized her hands were still caught in those Haunts-damned iron shackles. The man let go of her, but long fingers immediately reached out from either side and caught her by the shoulders. Two dead men crouched over her, their vacant eyes gazing off into nowhere. Their jaws sagged and their tongues lolled over their teeth, but their dead hands dug through the cloth and leather on her shoulders, pinching skin and bone.

The man with Terryn's face stood and stepped away from her, motioning with one hand as he did so. The corpses dragged Ayleth to her feet, deaf to her cries of pain. She stood suspended between them, the one a young man, scarcely more than a gangly youth, the other old, with a blood-matted beard frothing down the front of his tunic. They stood in a dilapidated barn. Part of the roof had caved in, and the door lay broken on the floor, allowing an easy exit if she could only reach it. Through that door she glimpsed open countryside, rolling fields.

Panting hard, Ayleth lifted her head and glared at the

living man before her. The Corpsewitch. Gillotin du Visgarus. Standing there in a host body so much like Terryn's, it made a lump of horror rise in her throat. For the moment, he didn't look at her. He stood with a far-off expression on his face, presenting her with his long-nosed profile, both hands upraised, each finger moving as though plucking at the strings of an instrument. Ayleth didn't need her shadow sight to know that he played with curse threads, manipulating the many corpses currently under his control.

How many could he manage at one time? There had been half a dozen at least sent to take her and kill her venatrix guardian. But none of that mattered right now. What mattered was that his attention was temporarily diverted . . .

Ignoring the shocks of pain through her body, Ayleth ducked suddenly, wrenching her shoulders free of the corpse hands, and turned. Agony cracked through her ribs, but she swung about, driving both fists up directly into the heart of the old man's corpse. It wasn't a strong-enough blow to break the curse holding the corpse in thrall, but it was strong enough to make him fall. She spun again, this time striking the youth's corpse in the side of the face, hard enough to spin him around.

A split second of decision hung before her—leap for the door or go for the witch?

But there really was no decision. Not for Ayleth.

She sprang at the Corpsewitch, hands reaching for his throat. Shackled or otherwise, it didn't matter. She would catch hold of him and hold on till she strangled the breath out of him. She would end this monster, she would—

Her feet rooted themselves to the hard dirt floor.

Ayleth lurched to a stop, her eyes widening, and stared down at her legs. Without shadow senses she couldn't see or sense a curse, but somehow she *felt* the threads wrapping around her legs, extending between her and Gillotin.

Hollis had taught her of the Corpsewitch's powers. He'd gained his title because of his preference for corpses, which he found easier for his Anathema powers to control. But he could and did, upon occasion, implant curses in living hosts as well.

A scream of rage sliced through Ayleth's clenched

teeth. She lifted her shackled hands, longing to reach and throttle her captor. But she couldn't take a step.

Still gazing off into some faraway space, the Corpsewitch smiled. It was a slow-coming smile, at first little more than a slight twitch at the corner of his mouth. But it stretched to cover the whole of his face, revealing a deep dimple in the cheek. Slowly he lowered his arms, letting go of his corpses for the moment, and turned toward Ayleth. Although he stayed out of her arms' reach, she could see mottled patches on his skin where the poisonous effects of the Witchwood had influenced his stolen body. Somehow he had escaped the tumorous growths that had afflicted his brethren, leaving his host body still strong, upright, and beautiful. But weakened. Definitely weakened.

If she could just reach him, she wouldn't need Laranta's strength to end him. She could do that all on her own.

He looked her up and down, that horrible smile still in place. "You are very like her," he said at last. "Beautiful. And ferocious. If I didn't know better, I would mistake you for her at first glance."

Sickness twisted in Ayleth's gut. She coughed, then spat at the witch's feet.

He took a half step back, the smile vanishing from his lips, and one eyebrow slid up his forehead, an expression so like Terryn's, it hurt her to see. He turned his head slightly, as though to study her from a different angle.

"I want . . ." he said, his voice deep and rich and dreadfully familiar. He shook his head, his mouth curling ruefully. "I want so much to kill you." He took a step nearer and, keeping a wary eye on her hands, reached out and stroked her cheek softly with his fingertips.

Ayleth snapped, trying to bite him. She wasn't fast enough. The Corpsewitch chuckled and moved back out of reach by several paces. "Perhaps I will," he mused. "I'll suffer for it. She'll destroy me; she'll damn me. She'll give me pain beyond endurance and then blast my soul to the Haunts. But if in this way I can protect her . . . even from herself . . ."

He turned away, his shoulders heavy, his head bowed so that a curtain of his long dark hair fell over his shoulder, hiding his face. Then he threw it back, tossing head and hair like some coquettish girl. "But no," he said, his teeth flashing, not in a smile but in a determined grimace. "Have I worked so hard to bring my goddess back that my first act will be to disobey her?"

Was he talking about Odile? He must be, but it made no sense. Surely Odile would have given orders to kill Ayleth outright. If Ayleth was indeed, according to the workings of the *Cravan Druch*, the only one who could slay her mortal body, it was in Odile's best interests to see her only real threat put to death. So why was she still alive?

The Corpsewitch turned away from her again, cursing viciously. He marched to the open door and gazed out into the bright countryside beyond. Then, lifting a hand, he beckoned. Ayleth's legs moved against her will, following him. The two corpses fell into step on either side of her, their heads lolling, their limbs shambling, their hands gripping her elbows.

"*Laranta!*" Ayleth cried out inside her head, desperate to find some sort of power.

The Corpsewitch stopped. He didn't turn, didn't look at her. But his voice was clear in the open air when he spoke: "If you reach for your shade again, Venatrix, I swear by my goddess's blood, I'll rip your arms from your shoulders and deliver you alive along with your bloodied stumps."

I RETURNED TO THE CASTRA AND SOON AFTER WAS sent to serve in a borough. I had hunt brothers and hunt sisters, and we rode the circuit trails, sometimes together, most often alone. I faced my share of monsters, both great and small, and each one I brought to ground with precision.

Even so, sometimes I thought of the Grand Vanderian and her words. My ardor must be my own . . . but what could that mean? There couldn't be a more ardent servant of the saint than I! Like all my hunt brothers and hunt sisters, I pursued my quarry and performed my prayers, and I offered up thanksgiving to the Goddess for each soul saved. What more could she want from me?

The question gnawed away at my insides, but I discovered no answer.

Within two years I left my first borough and moved on to a better post. Three years after that, I was given a position in Heulon City, hunting shade-taken through the streets and the slums and the alleys and the gutters, all the while seeing to it that the priestesses in their holy citadel were kept safe to live their pristine lives of prayer and piety. All this I did without complaint, without question, and soon the shade-taken of Heulon whispered my name with dread.

And yet I was unworthy to wear the crown? The crown which, should they give it to me, would enable me to save as many lives as I slaughtered?

CHAPTER 7

THEY DROVE THEIR STOLEN HORSES HARD ACROSS
the rough terrain, and Inren tried not to let herself look
back over her shoulder. She tried not to let herself watch
for the flash of a red hood or the gleam of scorpiona
fastenings. But sometimes the temptation was more than
she could resist.

Had Gillotin done his job? Had he stopped them or at
least slowed them down? In his day he was formidable,
his control over his Anathema unequalled among the

Crimson Devils, surpassing even Ylaire's abilities. But he had breathed too much *oblivis* over the years. He wasn't what he had once been; none of them were.

While Fendrel . . . he was still the same hardened monster of a man. He had orchestrated Odile's downfall even when she was at her strongest.

Inren looked down at the little figure riding before her on the saddle. Odile was too weak to ride on her own, so Inren encircled her with her arms, holding her close like she would a child. The stench of rotten, burned flesh filled her nostrils, more than once making her gag.

Her heart sank with hopelessness. This was not Odile. This sad, broken, decayed thing. And yet, what other hope did they have?

Inren could find no answer, so she pressed Odile closer and bent over the saddle, urging her horse faster along the hillside road. Deep inside her host body, she felt the mortal spirit of Fayline stirring, grasping hold of Inren's hopelessness, and using it to lever herself up, eager to regain ascendancy.

Inren snarled. Whatever else happened, she would not let herself become suppressed under that vain, petty, heartbroken little creature again. She'd be damned first!

They reached the top of the rise, Inren first, Zarc and Zilla behind her, and they stared down into the valley where Cró Ular had once stood, proudly guarding the magnificent Queen's Highway. Odile did not raise her head, did not look at the ruins of her once mighty tower. Perhaps she had swooned. If so, let her rest, Inren decided. She'd suffered enough shocks in the hours since her reanimation. Let her be spared this one.

Inren turned in her saddle to scan their back trail again, hoping for some sign of Gillotin, dreading to see signs of their pursuers. But the landscape was desolate and still.

"Come on," Zarc urged. "We'll get nowhere dawdling like this."

"Are you certain this is the right course?" Zilla interrupted. It was strange to hear the Windwitch speak with so frail a voice. Zilla had only ever possessed strong young bodies. She turned her wrinkled face to Inren. "I don't like it," she said, "taking our goddess into the Witchwood. You know what it will do to her."

Inren shuddered but steeled her face. "What do you

propose then, Zilla? Will you march into Dulimurian yourself and fetch the crown?"

The Windwitch bowed her head. She knew it was impossible; they all did. Not one of them could touch the crown and survive. Their host bodies would disintegrate on contact, and their souls would fly screaming to the Haunts.

No. There could be no bringing the crown to Odile. They must bring Odile to the crown.

So they kicked their horses forward and descended into the valley. While riding past Cró Ular's broken walls, they spared it hardly more than a glance. It was too dreadful to think of the final battle waged there. Of the friends they'd lost, the deaths they'd suffered. When the Tower of Blood and Eyes fell, they'd known the end was near.

But the end wasn't the end after all. Perhaps it might still be made into a beginning.

Inren led the way to the broken remains of the Queen's Highway. The oblidite paving stones were gone, but the scar of the road remained. They followed it into the fringe forest. In single file they passed under the canopy of winter-bare branches, riding east with their faces toward distant Dulìmurian.

Not far ahead, the Great Barrier hummed with power. Inren's heart shuddered at the sound of the spell song ringing through the trees.

A moan startled her, and she looked down to see Odile's head turn slowly back and forth. Another moan, and her head tilted up, just a little. One of her emaciated hands fluttered and caught hold of Inren's arm. "What . . . what . . . ?" Her tortured voice broke over the words.

"My Queen," Inren said, trying to make her voice soothing, "we are taking you to your city. We are taking you to your crown."

"My road," Odile said. Then, in a thin wail, "My road!"

The next instant, she slipped out from under Inren's protective arms, down from the saddle, to collapse on the scarred ground where her road ought to be. She fell over, weeping, her hands clutching at the dirt.

Inren hastily dismounted. Zilla and Zarc both did the same. All three of them gathered around their queen, none of them speaking, none knowing what to say. They cast each other uncertain glances. What could anyone do for a weeping goddess?

Odile's fingers, scrabbling in the dirt, pulled something free—a sliver of gleaming black rock. A shard of oblidite, Inren realized. The queen clutched it to her heart, rocking back and forth. Her weeping eased away, replaced by deep, agonized breaths. Her lungs labored, a sound painful to the ear.

But . . .

A little whorl of darkness spun out from Odile's slowly opening hands. The sliver of oblidite melted away, becoming pure *oblivis* once more. Shadow-light flared in Odile's eyes, and she opened her mouth, breathing in the *oblivis*.

Inren blinked. She blinked again, certain her eyes deceived her. A change had come over Odile. Her skin, though raw and red, was no longer blackened and flaking away. Her neck was stronger too and supported her head without visible effort. Even her hair was thicker somehow. Patches of bald scalp still showed through in places, but they were smaller, less noticeable.

Odile stood, swaying. Without a word or a look for her lieutenants, she progressed on foot down the center of the broken road. The witches exchanged glances, then left their horses behind to fall in behind their queen, following as she led. They passed through the fringe forest, every step bringing them closer to the Barrier. The humming of the song spell increased, growing in both depth and complexity until Inren felt it down in her very bones. She shuddered, and her feet hesitated over each step. But Odile continued resolutely onward.

At last, they came to the break in the trees where the fringe forest shrank back from the Barrier and the Witchwood waiting beyond. To shadow sight, the woven strands of the Anathema magic stood out glaring and red and raw. Fendrel du Glaive was a true master despite his Evanderian limitations.

"What . . . what is that?" Odile said, pausing on the edge of the fringe forest.

"When you were gone," Inren said, "the crown was left behind, empowered by the spell the Evanderians fed it. It pulled *oblivis* from the Haunts and created this forest, which—"

Odile put up a silencing hand. "Hush," she breathed. "I'm listening."

Inren shut her mouth. She, Zarc, and Zilla watched uneasily as their goddess stepped out of the forest and approached the Great Barrier. She was no longer unsteady on her feet, but she looked thin and frail, standing there in the light of the winter sun. Her body swayed gently as she crossed the empty grass and drew closer to the massive song spell. Turning her head this way and that on her thin neck, she surveyed its proportions.

Suddenly, she stretched out both hands and caught hold of the spell threads. They flashed with magic and dug into her skin, drawing blood.

"My Queen!" Inren gasped. She and the other two witches lunged forward, reaching out to their goddess. But before any of them could touch her, Odile barked, "Back!" They obeyed at once, cowering like well-trained hounds. Inren watched with shadow sight and saw the spirit inside Odile reach out from her core. Reach out through those spell threads and into the Witchwood beyond.

She saw the *oblivis* respond to the call of the Elemental shade.

It gathered on the far side of the Barrier, a thickening haze of dark-gleaming motes. It obeyed the shade even as the shade obeyed Odile. Fendrel's barrier spell flashed hotter, fiercer, drawing more blood from Odile's clutching hands. Not once did the queen flinch.

The cloud of *oblivis* writhed now, more and more of it streaming out of the forest and hurling itself at the Barrier. It wanted its mistress, wanted to answer her summons. The Barrier buckled, bulged. The pressure mounted.

Inren looked at Zarc and Zilla. They looked at her.

Then, moving as one, they flung themselves on the ground at Odile's feet.

And not a moment too soon.

The Great Barrier burst—an explosion of ruptured magic threads. After twenty years of reinforcement, Fendrel's spell song shattered, and *oblivis* surged through, blasting the world. The wave of darkness flowed over Inren's head. She couldn't even feel afraid. All ability to feel had left her; her mortal senses were frozen. Her shade screamed and ducked down inside her, and the other spirit—the little parasite—cowered in terror in the very depths of her core.

The wave crested, broke, and eased. With its easing came a return of perception, and Inren found herself lying with her face in the dirt, hands over her head, every limb shuddering. With an effort, she propped herself up on her elbows and looked back over her shoulder.

"Haunts devour us!" she gasped.

The fringe forest was gone. In its place was a petrified wood of pure oblidite, frozen in perfect black stillness for all time.

Gasping, choking on her own pounding heart, Inren turned her gaze up to the woman standing above her. That frail creature . . . Only she wasn't frail anymore. Her arms were outstretched, strong and commanding. Her head was high, her thick black hair flowing. Her skin was renewed: soft, supple, glowing with vitality and magic. Small bolts of darkness shot from her eyes, and her mouth flashed in a terrible smile.

"My queen," Inren breathed. "My goddess."

Odile uttered a groan and sank to her knees. Her dark

hair covered her face in a thick curtain, and she curled over, arms wrapped around her stomach.

Boom . . .

. . . boom . . .

. . . boom . . .

The ground beneath her hands shook. Inren's eyes widened. She knew what that sound was.

The Witchwood. The Witchwood was awake. Aware.

It was coming.

Inren shot up, her eyes rounding as she watched the parasitic vines crawling along the ground, coiling from trunk to trunk, swarming across the branches. A dark mass of writhing tentacles hurtled out from the heart of the Witchwood, making for that broken barrier and the world it longed to devour.

"My Queen!" Inren cried, clutching at Odile's torn skirts. "My Queen, my Queen, help us!"

Odile didn't move or speak. She remained in her fallen position, her arms wrapped tight as though she sought to keep herself from breaking in two.

"Quick!" cried Zilla, leaping to her feet beside Inren. "We must protect her!"

Zarc scrambled upright as well, and the Windwitch and the Stormwitch took up positions in front of Odile. Just as the vines poured out into the clear space between the Witchwood and the petrified fringe forest, a great blast of wind throttled them, driving them back. The hair on the back of Inren's neck stood on end, and the next instant a bolt of lightning struck not ten feet away. Vines sizzled, others pulled back, hissing softly.

The Windwitch, her frail old arms flung wide, shouted a command. Her Elemental magic surged through her thin host body, and another gale surged, ripping vines up by their roots.

But this time several vines made it through the blast, slithering along the ground to wind up Zarc's legs and pull him off his feet. With a scream of surprise, the Stormwitch hit the ground and was dragged into the writhing mass. He disappeared only to reappear a moment later, high in the air over their heads. He screamed again, this time in pain, as more vines caught him by his arms, wrapped around his neck, his torso.

"Zarc!" Zilla cried and sent a slicing blast of wind. Vines broke and fell, but others took their place. Zarc's screams intensified, then abruptly broke off.

Blood rained from the sky.

"*No!*" Zilla shrieked. Her hands moved, magic twisting at her command, and the winds gathered around her, churning the air and the ground in a violent tornado of destruction. When she flung out her arms as though hurling a missile, a blast of wind funneled out from her and struck the Witchwood, tearing up trees and vines and soil.

But *oblivis* whirled up, caught in the winds, and choked out the Elemental magic. Zilla staggered, her spells breaking. The vines of the Witchwood swarmed, prepared to descend on her, to tear her limb from limb as they had torn her brother.

Inren reached for a curse anchor. It was time to get out of here, time to take Odile and—

A hand closed down over her wrist. "No."

Inren looked up. Odile's eyes burned into hers, black fire roiling in their depths.

"No," her goddess said, rising to her feet. "We do not flee." With three long strides she placed herself between Zilla and the Witchwood vines. The vines lashed out to take her instead, but Odile lifted one hand. Her shade burst up from inside her, magic brimming, and the *oblivis* in the air responded to her command. It whirled in a hundred million glinting motes, an impenetrable wall.

The Witchwood stopped. The vines seemed to hiss and screech as they pulled back.

"Oromor."

Odile's voice was soft, yet it seemed to thunder in that atmosphere. The Witchwood tensed at the sound.

"I am coming for you, Oromor."

The vines shuddered. Then, as suddenly as they had appeared, they slithered in retreat, racing back through the trees, scuttling along the ground, threading between branches, pulling back farther and farther. Soon the forest was bare. Inren could even see patches of sky through the canopy.

Something else became visible as well. Inren gasped, taken completely by surprise. The Queen's Highway! It was still there, its mighty paving stones of oblidite gleaming. It led straight and true through the Witchwood, plunging onward for miles. If they were lucky—if their goddess was indeed what they hoped she could be—that road would take them all the way to Dulimurian.

Odile didn't turn to look back at her two remaining lieutenants. The moment the road was revealed, she started moving, walking down its center into the Witchwood. Fearless and ferocious. A true queen returned to her kingdom.

Inren got to her feet. She turned to Zilla, who knelt in the dirt, sobbing. "His soul!" the Windwitch choked. "His soul! His soul! I did not see his soul! Where did it go? Where is my brother's soul?"

"Pull yourself together," Inren snarled. She grabbed her sister witch's scrawny old arm and hauled her to her feet. "Zarc will find a fresh host. And if not, he's served his purpose. Now you must serve yours." She gripped Zilla's shoulders hard. "Return to Cró Ular. Wait there for Gillotin. If he did not stop Fendrel du Glaive, you must kill him yourself."

Zilla wiped her face with her hands and nodded, shadow-light flaring in her eyes. "Guard our queen, Inren," she said, her voice trembling. "Guard her well."

"With my life," Inren replied.

With her promise still echoing in her ears, Inren

turned and hastened down the broad road after Odile. For the moment, the parasitic soul inside her was quiet. For the moment, the Witchwood itself was on the retreat.

For the moment, Inren allowed herself to hope.

WORD CAME TO MY CASTRA OF AN INFESTATION IN *the Skada Mountains. Rumor had it that shade-taken men and women had gathered in a hidden valley, established a colony, and begun to breed, propagating inborn children and raising them in their unholy powers. Back in those days, such rumors were not uncommon, and the Order was always quick to investigate and, where necessary, to stamp out these infamous colonies.*

I was summoned to participate in this particular hunt, called away from the streets of Heulon and sent with a company of hunt brothers and sisters across Perrinion and up into the mountains. By this time, I thought I had hardened my heart to all that my Order required of me.

But the truth was . . . I had yet to participate in the ritual purification of an inborn soul. Thus far, all the inborn I had encountered were either adults or animals, and in such cases, we did not bother separating their souls but simply banished the conjoined human and shade spirits to the Haunts together. Children, however, did not merit such a fate and therefore must be saved.

The prospect was a grim one. I wondered if I'd have the stomach for it.

The thought plucked at the back of my mind: Was this the final test? Was this the moment when I proved my ardor? Could it be that after this mission, the Council of Agla would receive me again and see before them one worthy of their great treasure?

CHAPTER 18

CERINE LAY WITH HER EYES OPEN, AWAKE BUT NOT fully conscious. She was aware of a soft pillow under her head, aware of a light blanket thrown over her body. She was aware of a deep, abiding heaviness in every limb, like paralysis. But this wasn't true paralysis. She could move if she wished to. If she could summon the will.

How had she come to be lying on this bed? In her mind lurked vague memories, more like impressions, of strong arms carrying her, of gentle hands stroking the blood off her face and drawing a blanket up to her chest. But more than that she could not guess.

She closed her eyes. But the space inside her head was filled with violent images that felt more like nightmares than reality. She saw her arms breaking before her very eyes and reforming into hideous, many-jointed appendages. She saw Gerard gazing up at her in pure horror, one arm upraised to defend himself. She remembered the terrible compulsion to tear him apart raging through every vein in her body.

A little voice fluttered on the edge of her awareness. *Help us! Help us!* Like a ghostly breath, it brushed past her ear. Then it was gone.

Shuddering, Cerine shook her head, her eyes still closed. Where was Gerard? Was he still alive? She hadn't killed him . . . had she? She felt again the horrible pain of Ylaire's finger digging into her face, planting her sigil deep, where it wouldn't be seen. She remembered how Inren—still wearing Liselle's face—forced something into her mouth, closing her jaw and holding her nose until she had to swallow or suffocate.

Why had she not fought harder? Why had she not, at

the very least, forced them to kill her rather than comply? Her stomach and throat hurt, burning with the aftereffects of the magic she had vomited up the night before.

The soft fluttering returned again, close to her ear. *Help us! Help us!* it whispered. Then, once more, it was gone.

Cerine frowned. Drawing on what strength she possessed, she turned her head on the pillow, her gaze searching the room. All was dim, the tapestries pulled over the windows. She couldn't have told what time of day it was if not for the slit of light slipping through one window and sliding up one wall. The tapestry over that window moved softly. A sound like flapping wings moved near its top. A bird?

Help us! Help us!

Though a moment before she'd felt too lifeless to move, Cerine sat up. She couldn't have imagined that voice. It was too real, too desperate. Too strange. She swung her legs over the edge of the bed, letting the soft blanket fall in a puddle to the floor. Her bare feet cringed against the cold floorboards as she stood, padded across the room, and peered up at the shadowy thing throwing itself against the tapestry.

It was a bird. Or like a bird, but not quite. Even in the half-light, Cerine realized at once that it was more shadow than substance. She could see the pattern of the tapestry right through its body. Perhaps she was dreaming.

Help us! Help us!

"Who are you?" Cerine asked softly.

The little creature turned its beaked face down to her. As though her vision suddenly clarified in the gloom, she saw that it was much less birdlike than she'd first thought. The wings looked more like trailing fish fins, and the tail, split like a swallow's, was vaporous.

I am Hrelele, the thing sang to her, its voice like a hundred tiny silver bells all pitched in perfect harmony. *We are frightened. Help us! Help us!*

"How can I help you?" Cerine asked. Without waiting for an answer, she reached out and pushed the tapestry aside, then opened the window, thinking perhaps the bird thing wanted to escape to the open sky. But even as the glass swung open, the little being, rather than flying free, flitted down and rested on her wrist. She could see it sitting there, its delicate claws pressing into her skin. But she didn't feel a thing.

I was broken free from my host, it said, gazing up at her with earnest bright eyes. *Violently liberated. I was afraid. The Haunts would claim me. I cannot go back to the Haunts! I searched for a host to shelter me.*

"Who?" Cerine asked. "Who did you find?"

But the bird thing trembled all over, its shadowy wings vibrating in the air. *My host is in danger! The hunters—they are rounding us up. They will kill our hosts and drive our souls to the Haunts. You must help! Help us! Help!*

The voice broke into a language of pure song without words, but with a compelling meaning that shot to Cerine's heart. Frightened, she shook the bird thing from her wrist. It spread its wings and flew up, straight for her face—

She opened her eyes.

She lay on the bed, staring up at the embroidered canopy, a light blanket lying across her body.

Had it been a dream?

Cerine blinked several times. Then she groaned and moved her hands to her face, prodding at her jaw, her cheekbones, her nose. She felt all the places where her bones had broken and re-knit the night before, when the Warpwitch's curse took effect.

All was deathly silent. The room, the hall beyond her door. All of Dunloch seemed trapped in stillness. Then, as though echoing from far away . . . *Help us!*

Cerine bolted upright, her heart pounding in her throat. "The shade-taken," she breathed as realization dawned. The castle was attacked last night. Witches and Evanderians died, and their shades were violently loosed. They could have possessed anyone. Anyone!

The next moment, she was out of bed and rushing to her door. She fell against it, her breath tight in her lungs. Was she locked in? She tried the latch.

It gave at her touch. Her door swung open.

WE SEARCHED THE SKADA MOUNTAINS FOR THREE *months, living as wild beasts in a wild land. And yet we found no sign in all that time of a shade-taken colony. We began to doubt that these particular rumors were true, and several of my company urged us to turn for home.*

I could not bear to return unsuccessful. Something told me, some instinct of the hunt, which had grown inside me over the years, that we were close. It was as though a curtain had been drawn across our senses, obscuring our ability to see our prey.

But they were close . . . so close . . .

CHAPTER 9

THOUGH SHE'D SPENT THE LAST SIX WEEKS RIDING THE
circuit trails across Wodechran Borough, Ayleth
recognized none of the land the Corpsewitch now
marched her across. It was all hills, slopes, little valleys,
and more hills. They encountered no one, man or animal.
The only birds Ayleth spied were vultures wheeling
overhead in slow, lazy circles, their wings never flapping.
Were they merely interested in the walking carrion down
below, fanned out in formation behind the Corpsewitch?

Or were they dead as well, being used by the witch to watch the countryside from on high?

The only thing she knew for certain was that they were heading east. Toward the Witchwood. To rendezvous with Dread Odile and her remaining Crimson Devils, no doubt.

The Corpsewitch walked ten paces ahead of her. His attention was stretched far, she guessed, as he endeavored to control and manipulate his puppet corpses while he himself was in motion. How many could he maintain while on the move like this? For all she knew, he might still be battling Fendrel and the others a valley or two away.

Or he may have killed them already.

Ayleth watched her captor's back, watched the swing of his long black hair across his shoulders. She couldn't count on Fendrel to come to her rescue. She had to assume that they'd lost her trail and she was on her own. But no matter. She forced her tight lips into a grin. Her goal was to find and kill Dread Odile, wasn't it? Which meant she was going in the right direction.

Something *thunked* heavily to the ground. Startled,

Ayleth turned and saw a vulture sprawled not twenty feet away with a bolt through its heart. Even without her shadow senses, she felt the strange, sour twinge in the air of curse threads breaking.

The Corpsewitch uttered a startled cry and stopped short. His fingers tensed, curling slowly into fists. Off to one side, Ayleth saw movement. Corpses filed into view—many of them, more than she'd thought possible, appearing suddenly. They all faced in the direction from which that bolt had been fired.

One of them dropped. Ayleth saw another scorpiona bolt vibrating from its mark.

"Festering damn!" the Corpsewitch snarled. He turned, his attention focused on his soldiers, on that line of defense. Another corpse dropped, then a third. Gillotin motioned, and the figures dispersed, advancing in a silent onslaught toward their attackers, who were still hidden in a copse of firs.

Ayleth glimpsed a flash of red. Had the Evanderians come to her rescue after all?

Another bolt flew through the air, whizzed just passed her cheek. It struck the corpse holding Ayleth's right arm.

The dead man dropped at once, the implanted curse shattered.

"Run!" the Corpsewitch's deep voice roared in Ayleth's ears.

Her legs responded before she could think, acting on the impulse of his control. But he chose his route for her flight poorly. He sent her running straight toward him, intending to send her on past him so that he could stand between her and those who had come to take her from him. But with that choice, he sent her running within arm's reach of him.

Ayleth stretched out both hands and, lunging with the top half of her body, which still belonged to her, looped her arms over the witch's head. She had the iron chain of her shackles digging into his throat before he could blink, and yanked him off his feet.

The weight of him toppled her, and the two of them rolled in the dirt. She could feel curse threads snarling as his concentration was shattered both by his surprise and by the iron ripping into his skin.

"*Laranta!*" she screamed inside her head.

Her shade responded at once, bounding forward and

throwing herself against the iron poison holding her back. She couldn't give much, but she gave all she could, and Ayleth felt a fraction of her shade strength flow through her veins. It was enough—all she needed to hold on.

The Corpsewitch came out on top of her when they stopped rolling, his huge, muscular body crushing into her broken ribs. He flailed, jabbing with his elbows, and she cried out in pain as he dug into those ribs. But she didn't let go.

The iron hurt him; she felt the magic inside him vibrate in reaction to it. His hold on her wavered, and her legs were, momentarily at least, her own. She wrapped them around his body, squeezing tighter.

The Corpsewitch raised one hand. Her shadow sight partially restored, she saw it flare with red Anathema light. He twisted his wrist as though pulling at strings.

Two dark forms plunged from the sky—dead vultures, diving straight at her face with their talons and beaks. Ayleth rolled, pulling Gillotin with her, using him as a shield against the vultures' attack. They tore at her back and her neck. A talon sliced the skin along one cheek. She tried to keep rolling, but her body stuck in a rut in the landscape.

The Corpsewitch caught hold of her hands, somehow yanked her arms up, and slid out of her grasp. His throat was raw, red, and welted from the iron, but he crawled away and got to his feet. She lunged out to catch his foot, but another vulture tore at her. She gripped it by the neck and smashed the bird into the ground, snapping its neck. It didn't stop. The curse still controlled it, and it attempted to tear at her with its talons.

Cold, dead hands caught her by the hair on the back of her head and yanked her to her feet. Long arms wrapped around her neck and squeezed. Ayleth, her eyes bugging, stared at the Corpsewitch standing but a few paces away, controlling the dead man who held her. Seeing murder in his eyes, she knew that, regardless of his goddess's command, he was going to kill her.

A dart whirred through the air and planted itself in the bunched fabric of the cloak attached to his left shoulder, where it failed to reach his skin—an inch or two to the right, and it would have pierced him.

Still helpless in the corpse's strangling grasp, Ayleth strained to see where the dart had come from. From the corner of one eye, she glimpsed Kephan on the slope of the nearest incline just as he snapped a second dart into his scorpiona, took aim, and fired.

That dart just missed the Corpsewitch's cheek. At the last second, he whirled and ran, waving his arms in wild gestures as he went. A dozen corpses poured down from the slope, falling over each other but still moving at their master's control, covering his retreat. Kephan took another shot, and more darts followed soon after as other Evanderians appeared at the top of the slope. Many of these hit the dead men and women, producing no effect whatsoever.

The Corpsewitch reached the crest of the slope and vanished down the other side. But instead of following him, his corpses turned and lurched straight for Ayleth.

She managed to get her shackled hands up enough to wrench at the arm strangling her, and sucked in a few gasps of air. But as Laranta struggled against the restriction of the iron, the shade strength in Ayleth's limbs faltered. "*Laranta! More!*" she screamed inside her head. She felt her wolf shade hurtle forward, throwing herself at the iron barrier. But Laranta had already given so much—the iron tortured her spirit substance so cruelly that she fell back again, helpless, whimpering.

As the other corpses closed in, Ayleth could no longer see Kephan or the red hoods of the other Evanderians. Around her were only dead faces, swollen tongues, sagging heads, and stumbling feet. Ayleth faced a girl no older than sixteen, with soft round features and golden hair still neatly held back in plaits draped over each shoulder. The blood of her death wound had already dried on her neck, and she extended fingers curled like claws to tear Ayleth's heart out.

Darkness swarmed the edges of Ayleth's vision as she sank to her knees, defeated. The dead mounded on top of her.

ONE COLD DAY, WITH A HIGH WIND BLOWING DOWN *from the mountain and driving rain into our faces, we pushed a little farther into that obscuring curtain than before—and suddenly we were surrounded. Creatures in hideous masks arose from the rocks as though they had sprung suddenly into existence. Magic burst from their souls in deadly waves.*

Our shades were too deeply suppressed to fight back efficiently. Four of my brethren died within moments, their shades violently driven from their bodies, their souls left to fade into nothing.

CHAPTER 10

GERARD LANDED HARD, JOLTING HIS BONES DESPITE his attempt to roll with the impact. Grasping a blanket in both hands, he lay for a moment on his back, staring up at the stone wall he had just descended, watching the rest of his makeshift rope of blankets and curtains sway in the breeze. One of those knots had failed under his weight.

Nilly du Bucheron's head appeared at his office window, blinking down at him. He waved to signal that he was all right, then made a sharp, beckoning motion.

The little girl disappeared. A moment later, the top half of the rope jerked, spun, and finally fell in a coiled mass on the ground beside him. Nilly peered out again, her thin fair hair wafting about her small face.

Gerard regained his feet and located the sword and sheath he'd tossed down in advance of his climb. Strapping them to his back, he looked up at the window and waved again, this time motioning Nilly back into the office. He gathered the "rope" into a large bundle, trying not to notice how many of the knots had nearly come undone. Haunts, he should never have trusted his weight to such a flimsy thing!

But then again, what had he to fear? He'd seen his future. He knew he wouldn't die falling out a window.

After shoving the makeshift rope behind a low retaining wall where it wouldn't easily be spotted from the castle itself, Gerard looked up one last time. Nilly had pulled the window shut, but he could still discern her pale face through the diamond panes. He offered a hasty, reassuring smile.

It felt wrong to leave her behind like this. Fendrel had left at least two venators in Dunloch, and they'd be hunting for shade-taken. But he couldn't very well bring a child with him. Not into the Witchwood.

By skulking along the lakeshore behind retaining walls and bushes—desperately hoping no one happened to glance out one of those dozens of windows at just the wrong moment—Gerard skirted the edge of the island, making his way to a certain place on the north shore.

It was strangely silent down by the lake. The freezing wind cut through cloth and skin down to the bone, numbing one's senses to anything other than cold. Now and then he thought he heard a shout from inside the castle. But when he looked up, only the impenetrable stone walls looked back. The windows reflected the morning sky, revealing nothing.

Gerard cursed and moved on. He couldn't stop now. The Goddess had given him a mission, and he must fulfill it, come what may. No hesitation. No cowardice. No hiding behind so-called responsibilities.

He found the rowboat moored to a little dock and pushed it out into the frigid lake, breaking through a thin film of ice. Once out on the water, he could easily be seen from the upper-story windows, not to mention the towers. At any moment he expected to see Red Hoods appear or his own guards in uniform swarm out through the kitchen door to chase him down. But no one came.

Partway across the lake, he remembered the magic barrier Fendrel and Terryn had raised around Dunloch. Without shadow senses, Gerard couldn't detect magic, but he knew very well that the barrier, if still present, would prevent his passage. He kept glancing nervously over his shoulder, expecting, with every pull of the oars, to crash into an invisible wall.

But he reached the far shore of Loch du Nóiv without incident, and soon the prow of his little boat crunched on stones and ice. He stood, arms out for balance, and leapt from the prow into the dead grasses. After dragging the boat ashore, he hurried into the shelter of the trees.

There he paused for breath, looking back at Dunloch. The castle looked so small and calm and stately out on its island under the winter sun. Who could guess what turmoil took place within those stone walls?

A pang shot through his heart. He was abandoning his people. For a hopeless errand inspired by the vision of a shade-taken child. He had no horse, no weapon other than his sword, and he carried no supplies. He didn't even know the way to Dulimurian, only that it was through the impenetrable and inescapable Witchwood. This mission was suicide.

His gaze lingered a moment longer, searching out a particular window in the west wing behind which he knew a pale young woman lay in a stupor. He hadn't said goodbye.

Now it was too late.

He turned his back on Dunloch and set his face east. To the Witchwood. To Dulimurian.

To the end.

Cerine met no one as she crept along the passages of the west wing, heard no sounds of life or stirring behind the closed doors. She paused at the door to the prince's office and even moved her hand toward the latch. But she couldn't bring herself to touch it. Besides, Gerard wouldn't be in there. Not now. Not with shade-taken loose in Dunloch.

But where was he?

Help us! Help us!

Clutching her skirt with both hands, she hastened on down the passage, making for the gallery overlooking the Great Hall. The farther she went, the more voices she heard, always distant, echoing through many walls and doors. Always frightened. Were the witches still in the castle? Or had they gotten what they came for and fled? She had no way of knowing.

The passage opened up, and she saw the gallery rail up ahead. Sounds of murmuring voices and stirring footsteps rose to her ears. She knew before she looked that people were gathered in the Great Hall below.

Taking care to avoid being seen, she crept up behind one of the support pillars and peered down. A little hiss escaped her lips. There were so many! Household servants, some in uniform, some still in their nightclothes. There were two rough-and-ready-looking stable hands, and one little page boy. There were guardsmen, a dozen of them armed, but others who were stripped of their armor and wore only the under tunic of their uniform, looking uneasy.

But Cerine's gaze passed over all these to land on a

familiar face. In the center of the gathering stood her friend and Siveline sister Ducette, wearing the sky-blue hood of her Holy Order. Her hands were pressed together in prayer, her eyes closed, her lips moving. Over her head something . . . something flickered. Cerine frowned, uncertain what she saw. A little shadow with wings. There and then gone.

Most of the gathering stood with their backs against the south wall, facing the line of castle guardsmen and their lowered pikes. Were they all prisoners? Shade-taken? Surely not all of these people could have been possessed last night!

A flash of red caught Cerine's eye. A venator strode into her line of sight. For a moment she hoped it was Terryn du Balafre, Gerard's friend. But no, she didn't know this young man with his thin brown beard and his stooped shoulders. His face was pale, shining with sweat, and his right arm hung limp from his shoulder. Broken, Cerine realized. Judging by the grim expression on his face, he was in a great deal of pain. He walked up and down the line of people, studying them closely. But he made no move for the poisons strung across his breast.

These must be the eye-torn, Cerine guessed—people susceptible to possession but not necessarily possessed. When the violently liberated shades burst from their dead hosts during the night, they would have sought the nearest available bodies and dived down deep inside. Most newly taken hosts did not begin manifesting signs of possession for days or even weeks. It took time for a shade to secure its hold over its host, to feel safe enough to start climbing to ascendancy. Any one of the folk below could be possessed.

Cerine's gaze lingered on Ducette again. The poor girl was trying to be brave, trying to stand strong, but Cerine saw the tears pouring from the corners of her closed eyes. Did she believe she was taken? Did she suspect? Did she—

Help us!

Cerine's heart jumped. She grabbed hold of the pillar as if to keep herself upright. That voice . . . it had come straight from inside Ducette, but it wasn't Ducette's voice and it didn't speak with Ducette's mouth. It was a strange, musical, otherworldly voice.

"Hrelele," Cerine whispered. She had to do something.

But what could she possibly do? How could she possibly help?

"Last one. Found him hiding in the buttery."

A venatrix appeared below, dragging a miserable person by the collar. It took Cerine a second and even a third glance before she recognized Chancellor Yves, his handsome velvet robes stained and torn. The poor man sputtered a stream of protests, declaring that he came from a long, proud family of untorn, that he couldn't possibly be possessed, that—

"Silence," the venatrix growled. After pushing him in among the rest along the wall, she assumed a wide-legged stance beside her fellow Evanderian. From her angle above, Cerine saw terrible burns on the woman's head, trailing down the side of her face and neck. Fresh burns in a spattered pattern, like drops of water. She must have been caught in the Stormwitch's acid rain.

Where were the other Red Hoods? Ayleth and Terryn and the king's brother, Fendrel du Glaive? Why were these two Evanderians not being treated for their wounds? Were they the only ones still living? Had the rest been slaughtered by Crimson Devils last night?

Help us! the shadow voice whimpered in her mind.

"That one," the venatrix barked, her voice echoing in the high ceiling of the hall. Two of the armed guards lunged forward and grabbed a shivering, square-faced maid, dragging her to her knees before the venatrix. Moving with deft experience, the venatrix lifted a small silver vial, unscrewing the lid. She drew something out of the vial, something too small for Cerine to see. "Hold her still," she ordered, and the guards grabbed the maid's head. The poor girl whimpered a protest, then screamed as the venatrix did something to her eye, something too quick for Cerine to see.

The venatrix backed up to a small table Cerine had not noticed before. With her back to the captives along the wall, she performed some alchemy or magic, mixing different fluids into small glass bowls and thin bottles. At last she stepped back and, looking at the maid, waved one arm.

"She's untaken," she said. "Next."

The maid gasped a stream of grateful prayers, clasping and unclasping her hands as she was dragged away from the rest of the group and sent through the open front door. Another one, the little page boy, was brought forward next, made to kneel, made to endure whatever brief pain the venatrix inflicted on his eye. Then he stood, held between the pale, solemn guards, as the venatrix once more worked with her potions and dusts.

"Untaken," she declared again, and the page boy was released. "Next."

"Gerard," Cerine whispered, pressing closer to the pillar, watching as a third, then a fourth were tested and released. "Where are you?" Surely he would not stand for his people to be rounded up like this, like animals! Had the witches gotten to him after all? Was he kidnapped? Was he dead?

It didn't matter. He wasn't here.

And now the guards approached Ducette.

Help us! Help us!

Cerine blinked, trying to un-see the shadowy vision flitting just above the young nun's head, trying to tell herself she imagined that voice singing in her head, trying to will the truth to be anything other than what she saw taking place below.

The guards took hold of Ducette's arms. But before

they could drag her to the venatrix, the venatrix raised a staying hand. "Wait. I . . . I sense something."

The other Evanderian stepped to her side. "I do as well," he growled, his gaze fixed hard on Ducette, who shrank back from him. The guards gripped her harder, their fingers tight and unrelenting. The venator felt for the darts at his breast, slipping one free of its quiver. He didn't bother to load it into his scorpiona, for his broken arm couldn't fire the weapon. Instead, gripping the dart in his fist, he stepped toward Ducette.

Her eyes widened. She screamed. "No! Please, mercy! Don't kill me! I am the Goddess's servant, a sister of Siveline! Don't kill me, don't let me be damned!"

"You'll not be damned, Sister," the venator answered. "I'll save your soul, I swear it." He took another step, raising his arm.

Cerine sprang out from behind her pillar. She stood at the top of the staircase, swaying on her feet, her hands outstretched. For a terrible, jolting heartbeat she felt her utter helplessness.

Then, grabbing hold of the upper banister, she shouted at the top of her lungs, "Stop!"

Her voice echoed from the high ceiling, rang out among the pillars. The venator paused, turned. The venatrix looked up, her brow creasing. "What in the Haunts—"

A roar filled the hall, followed immediately by terrified screams. Cerine, still poised at the top of the stairs, watched in horror as the shadowy winged creature burst from Ducette's head and took to the air. Only it wasn't the delicate birdlike thing that had found her in her room. This was a leather-winged nightmare, its mouth full of fangs.

It swooped at the guards holding Ducette's arms. They screamed, dropped their hold on her and threw themselves to the floor. Another guard, a brave man in captain's uniform, hoisted his pike and struck at the monster as it passed him. But the weapon passed through the creature like vapors. The hideous body rippled and reformed, an untouchable illusion.

The monster banked in midair and hurtled itself at the venatrix, who stood beside her table of implements and bottles. The woman took a step back, then another, then braced herself, refusing to take a third. She lifted her head, and the bat-winged thing flew straight at her, hind feet outstretched, mighty claws eager to tear out her heart.

It swept through her. She swayed and grabbed at her chest, feeling for a wound she half expected to be there. Then she grimaced, plucked a dart from its quiver and jammed it into her scorpiona. Just as the nightmare tilted its wings, turning to make another attack, the venatrix raised her right arm and fired.

The dart struck Ducette between the eyes. The poor girl gasped, making a sad little mewling noise. "Please," she begged. "Please, don't—"

She dropped to her knees, sagged, and fell on her side. The monster that had sprung from her mind screeched in rage and pain and disintegrated in a cloud of silver sparks, which rained down to the floor and vanished.

Cerine held tight to the banister, staring in horror at her fallen sister. But, wait . . . She wasn't dead. Not yet. Evanderians used two poisons, didn't they? One to paralyze, another to kill. Ducette was still alive.

The venatrix drew a second dart from her quivers. This one fletched in black.

"*No!*" Cerine hurtled down the stairs, half falling, half

leaping. She was six steps from the floor when she grabbed the banister and sprang over, tumbling into the venatrix. The two of them hit the ground hard. The impact jarred Cerine's body, and her ears rang with the sound of the venatrix's curses. The Gentle Death dart rolled to one side. The venatrix lunged for it, but Cerine reacted just in time, kicking it farther away and managing to trip up the venatrix at the same time.

"What do you think you're doing?" the venatrix bellowed at her, snarling viciously as she pulled herself upright again. The burned skin on her face puckered, and her eyes were glassy with pain and rage.

Cerine pulled herself upright, every limb shaking as she got to her feet. Her body ached from the impact of her fall, and pain shot up her leg when she put pressure on her right foot, but she stepped between the venatrix and Ducette's fallen body.

"I am Cerine du Glaive, wife of the Golden Prince of Perrinion," she declared. "In the name of my husband, Gerard du Glaive, son of the Chosen King, Sovereign Lord of Perrinion, Guardin du Glaive, I command you to stand down." She swept her arms to each side, indicating the huddled folk of Dunloch standing behind her against the wall. "These people are under the prince's protection."

The venatrix stared at her as if she'd lost her mind. Her fellow Evanderian stepped to her side, holding his broken arm, his head tilted to one side. "Is she shade-taken?" he asked the venatrix through his gritted teeth.

"I can't sense a shade presence," she answered without taking her eyes off Cerine. "But that doesn't mean—"

Something grabbed Cerine's shoulders, pushing her down with a force of weight that sent her to her knees. She cried out, shocked, and looked up to see a flutter of velvet robes flying over her head and hurtling straight for the venatrix.

Chancellor Yves knocked the venatrix flat on her back and crouched over her. Scarcely did his feet and hands touch the floor before he sprang again, leaping ten feet to one side, avoiding the venator's retaliatory blow. He caught hold of one of the pillars, swung around to the far side of it, and began to climb, bare hands and feet grasping at invisible holds in the fluted stone. He scuttled up, fast as a spider.

"Haunts damn!" the venator shouted, grasping the other Evanderian by her shoulder and pulling her up to her feet. "He's got du Creadu's shade!" He looked up at the pillar, blurted a wordless cry, and yanked the venatrix to one side—just in time. A glob of green spittle struck the floor and burned into the stone.

Keeping a wary eye on the venators and the shade-taken chancellor, Cerine eased to Ducette's side. Her fingers shaking, she pulled the dart out and dropped it. To her surprise, Ducette's eyes fluttered and her mouth tried to move. She wasn't unconscious. Perhaps the poison dose wasn't quite right.

Something shifted in her eyes, and Cerine nearly screamed when a shadow suddenly burst from one iris, nearly taking bird shape as it struggled to pull free. Ugly threads like those of a spider's web seemed to pull it back down into Ducette's head again, but the shade inside her fought for all it was worth, resisting the influence of the poison.

What could she do? Desperately, Cerine looked back over her shoulder at the people still pressed against the wall. The guardsmen had shifted position now, standing with their pikes pointed out to protect their recent prisoners from the shade-taken threat. Cerine's gaze fell on a tall serving boy in a nightshirt. Something about him—she couldn't say what—made her think he might hide a shade as well.

"Help!" she cried, calling to the spirit inside him rather than to the lad himself. "Help your sister!"

He hesitated. His gaze swiveled to the guards, to the humans on either side of him.

"Hurry!" Cerine urged.

Shaking his head as though he didn't quite believe what he was doing, the boy lurched forward, stooped, and caught Ducette by one arm. Cerine grabbed the other, and between them they got the nun to her feet. Cerine gasped and nearly fell when she put pressure on her sprained foot. As soon she met the boy's gaze, he seemed to read her mind, instantly shifting Ducette's weight to drape her over his shoulders.

"Where to?" he demanded, his voice breaking.

"Upstairs," Cerine answered. She didn't have a plan, only a half-formed idea that she might hide Ducette in her rooms and bar the doors until she had time to think of something better. Without arguing, the boy nodded and started for the stairs. Cerine limped after him. The Great Hall rang with chaos as Chancellor Yves leaped from one pillar to the next, dodging darts and spitting more globules at the cursing venators. They were distracted, at least for the moment, and maybe . . . maybe . . .

They were only three steps up when the boy suddenly gave a cry and staggered; Cerine saw a dart in the back of his neck. The boy did his best to continue climbing, but his knees buckled, and his hold on Ducette weakened. He fell, and both of them landed hard just in front of Cerine.

She spun around to see the broken-armed venator approaching, a black-fletched dart in his fist. Cerine planted herself between the two shade-taken and the venator, her arms spread wide as if to shield them. His face twisting into a grimace of contempt, the venator kept coming without pause. He lunged at Cerine, swinging the dart like a knife, ready to kill her just to get her out of his way. She dodged to one side, but her injured ankle gave way beneath her weight, and she fell sprawling on the steps. The venator stepped over her, his gaze focused on the shade-taken. Cerine caught him by one leg, yanking him off balance.

With a growl, the venator turned on her, his Gentle Death poised to strike. Looking up into his eyes, she saw murder there. His good arm rose, taking aim with the dart.

He stopped. Choked.

A dart quivered where it had struck just behind the venator's ear.

Cerine turned her head, searching, and saw Terryn du Balafre standing in the open doorway of the Great Hall, his scorpiona upraised.

WE FOUGHT OUR WAY DOWN THE MOUNTAINSIDE *against foes both numerous and powerful. Our way had led up a steep gorge along a track almost too narrow for horses, and in our haste to retreat, several of our beasts lost their footing and plunged over the side. My own horse took a wrong step in her panic. I heard the bone in her leg break, and she fell, screaming and groaning.*

I sprang from the saddle before I could be crushed against the mountain wall and took shelter behind her body. A blast of fire went over my head, followed by a blast of sound that shattered rock and brought a small avalanche of stone down just to my right, overwhelming the comrades ahead of me on the narrow trail and carrying them over the edge.

I knew I had to call my shade to ascendancy, access its greater, darker powers, powers I'd had no need to summon in years. I pulled out my Vocos, put it to my lips, and began playing the Song of Unbinding, carefully relaxing the many chains with which I kept my shade constrained. The song poured deftly from the pipe heads, and I closed my eyes, concentrating on that work, blocking out the horrors, the screams, the cacophony of magic and mayhem all around me.

The song took mere moments to play—less than that. But even as the power rose inside me, even as I opened my eyes and peered from behind my horse, ready to fight, I found myself staring at a man—a man who hovered in the air above the gorge, supported on powerful winds.

He held out one hand and, before I could act, flicked his wrist.

I was plucked from my hiding place and sent flying out over the brink, spinning wildly through empty air.

CHAPTER II

TERRYN'S DART VIBRATED WHERE IT HAD STRUCK JUST behind the Evanderian's ear. A shudder passed through the man's soul, a sickly color visible only to shadow sight. His arm swung down, still trying to stab Lady Cerine with the Gentle Death, but his aim was off. He staggered, lurched, and dropped the poison. He turned, eyes wide, searching for the source of this new attack.

Across the cavernous space of the Great Hall, Terryn met the venator's gaze. He knew that face: Ragno du

Gontier. He'd been only a year behind Terryn at the castra. They'd served together on more than one occasion, though Terryn would hardly consider him a friend.

Ragno's expression shifted from fear to shock as he realized who had fired the dart. No doubt he'd heard that Terryn was dead, struck down by their fellow Evanderians hours ago.

"You," he breathed, his good hand fumbling among the darts across his chest, still eager to fight even as poison coursed through his system. But the pain he suffered from earlier wounds accelerated the paralysis. His broken right arm hung loose on one side, and his left arm, numbed, dropped. He took a step, stumbled, and fell headlong to the floor. The shade power inside him sank back into his core, suppressed and helpless.

Terryn looked from the fallen venator to Lady Cerine, who gripped the banister for support. What was she doing here, grappling with Evanderians? Beyond her lay the bodies of two shade-taken. Of all the sights Terryn had expected to see upon his return to Dunloch, this one had never even crossed his mind. The lady looked unharmed at least, but—

"Watch out!" Cerine cried, flinging up a hand as though to stop Terryn in his tracks.

Before Terryn could take a step, something flew past his face, missing his nose by inches, and struck the doorpost. A sizzle burned in his ears as stone melted and dripped to the floor.

Terryn whirled, his gaze scanning the walls and pillars of the hall, attempting to follow the trajectory of that missile back to its source. He was familiar with old Venator du Creadu's unique powers, but it wasn't du Creadu he identified climbing in a spiral up one of the hall's supportive pillars to scrabble spider-like along the ceiling.

"Chancellor Yves?" Terryn stared, his shadow sight revealing the glow of the shade whirling violently inside the dignified chancellor. For a moment, Terryn was too stunned by the sheer incongruity of the sight to react.

Terryn leaped to one side just in time to avoid being struck in the face by another glob of burning acid. As it hit the wall behind him, he rolled unharmed across the floor and came up in a crouch. Nisirdi flared brilliantly beside him, sweeping a shining wing in front of Terryn as though to shield him from physical blows. But those wings were spirit stuff and could not stop projectiles of the material world. Terryn felt his shade's power teeming in his soul, power he could use to blast the newly possessed Yves off the ceiling.

But no. He couldn't hurt the shade-taken. Not anymore. Not unless he had no other choice.

Movement drew his eye, a flash of red. Another Evanderian—Gildys di Javis, her face mottled with raw acid burns. She stood braced in firing stance, and she had him in her sights.

He would not fall under paralysis again. He'd rather die.

Venatrix Gildys took her shot.

Terryn raised one hand. The dart speeding across the space between the scorpiona and its target struck a wall of pure light.

It disintegrated to ash and drifted away on the air.

Terryn cried out as pain rippled along his arm. Nisirdi's power was there, ready for him to take and use, but that didn't mean he could balance or control it yet.

"*Pull back! Pull back!*" he barked.

His shade responded at once to his voice and his pain, reducing the amount of magic it offered before Terryn's arm could blacken and burn like the dart. Terryn blinked back into mortal vision and met Venatrix Gildys's gaze.

Her features went slack with dawning horror. His ascendant shade must shine like a star to her shadow sight. With a single bolt from his hand, he could blast her to oblivion. And she knew it.

"Venatrix, please," Terryn said, putting up both hands and taking care to angle them away from her. "I have not come to fight you. What's happened here? Where is Fendrel? Where is the prince?"

She reached for her Vocos pipes, drawing them from her sheath. Her shade was already called to high ascendancy, but if she loosened the suppressions still more, what kind of power would she wield? Not enough to match the ascendant Nisirdi, but enough perhaps to force Terryn to fight her for real, to hurt her. Even to kill her.

He had to stop her. Now.

With pipe song filling his ears, Terryn reached for his

darts. But no, he'd used the last of his supply on Ragno.

His head swiveled, his gaze latching onto the unconscious Ragno. He sprang across the Great Hall, ignoring the huddled, frightened figures crouched along one wall, ignoring Lady Cerine, who stood on the stairs, gripping the banister, even ignoring the scuttling of Chancellor Yves overhead. He fixed every sense entirely on the fallen venator.

He dropped to his knees, sliding the last foot to Ragno's side, and heaved the young man onto his back. His quivers were full, but . . . Terryn hesitated. What kind of shade did Gildys carry?

The spell song, hastily played, resolved in a mad flurry of notes. Terryn looked over his shoulder, saw Gildys drop her pipes to the floor and raise both hands. Magic gathered in her palms.

Terryn grabbed a handful of fletched darts from Ragno's quivers and cast himself to one side. Something struck the steps, which immediately crusted over in a thick dark sheet of ice. Well, that answered that question.

He ducked behind the sweep of the stair just as another blast of ice struck close by, instantly encasing the carved lion at the base of the banister. Terryn looked down at the handful of darts he held and, to his relief, saw a single Elemental poison in their number. He'd better not waste this shot.

Springing his scorpiona into firing mode, he loaded the dart, drew a breath, and then sprang up, aiming over the banister.

The venatrix was halfway across the hall, running straight for him, her hand upraised. She sent out a blast of ice, freezing his scorpiona and his hand to the banister. "Damn," Terryn growled. In his head he cried, "*Nisirdi!*"

Heat flared up from his bones and through his skin, melting the ice. But the heat, not fully under his control, burned right through the string of his scorpiona, which fell in limp, useless pieces to the floor.

Gildys was on him the next instant, her next dart gripped in one hand. She swung it straight for his eye. Terryn deflected the blow, but she twisted his arm and struck out again, this time trying to lodge the dart into the back of his neck.

Terryn warded off that blow, caught her arm with a swift turn of his wrist, and brought her in close, snarling into her maimed face. "I'm not your enemy. I don't want to hurt you."

"Heretic!" she spat, her eyes rimmed with icicles. "The Dominus warned us about you. You betrayed your brethren for witches!"

To take her down, he had to get the Elemental poison out of his scorpiona and deliver the dose manually. But he couldn't access it while maintaining his grip on her. She looked into his eyes, read his intention, and her face twisted into a furious snarl. Suddenly ice crusted up over Terryn's fingers, freezing his grip. He couldn't pull away. She flung her head forward, butting him hard between the eyes. He staggered, stunned.

A blast of burning spittle struck the ground at their feet. Terryn and the venatrix both looked up. Yves, his robes flapping, his bare, skinny legs fully on display, scurried across the ceiling and darted behind the ornamental moldings at the top of a pillar. He peered out, his dignified face transformed into an ugly mask. His jaw dropped, and he took aim again.

Terryn, his grip frozen to the venatrix's arm, hurled both of them to one side, avoiding the poison by inches.

Summoning Nisirdi's power, he heated through the ice, breaking his hold on the venatrix. She screamed at the burn, but he couldn't help that. She pushed herself up onto her knees, flinging a snarl his way as her ascendant shade flowed through her spirit. Her eyes were white and her skin tinged blue as she raised her hand, taking aim at his heart.

Terryn yanked the paralysis dart from his scorpiona. A bolt of ice streaked toward him, but a curtain of light blazed between it and him, melting the ice to mist in an instant and leaving Gildys dazed by the glare. Then the curtain parted, and Terryn lunged forward to plunge his dart into her neck just above the collarbone.

Gildys screamed. Leaping upright, she flung out her arms, and blasts of ice shot out from her core, whistling through the air and striking the pillars and walls. The people gathered on the edges of the hall crouched, screaming, and Cerine, up on the stair, ducked behind the banister.

Terryn grabbed the venatrix before she could shoot out another blast. Wrapping one arm around her neck and the other around her waist, pinning her arms, he pulled her close. All too well he remembered the helpless horror as the paralysis took effect, the terror of realizing there was nothing he could do to stop it. In those last moments, it was too easy to lose control, especially with a shade as ascendant as Gildys's currently was.

So he held her tight, radiating light through his limbs. Nisirdi's magic met that of Gildys's struggling shade, melting the ice even as it formed. Gildys struggled, both physically and spiritually, but Terryn refused to release her.

"I know you don't trust me," he said into her ear as she screamed with wordless rage. "But I swear on the Goddess's Head, Heart, and Soul, I will not harm you."

"Heretic," she hissed, the word bitter and slurred. "Your vows are nothing!"

Only the day before, she'd been his colleague. Only the day before, she'd been his sister under Evander's law.

A sister ready and willing to march Ayleth out to the pyre and stand by to watch as she burned.

Terryn hardened his jaw, his hold unyielding, and waited until her body went limp. Only then did he loosen his grasp and let her fall senseless to the floor, both her spirit and her shade suppressed.

A glob of spittle hit the ground mere inches to the right of the venatrix's face. Terryn looked up, blinking into shadow sight. The shade-taken Yves loomed overhead, gathering magic in his throat for another attack. Terryn grabbed Gildys's arm and hauled her around behind the sweep of the staircase, but Yves crawled up to the highest arch of the ceiling, angling for a better shot.

"*Nisirdi, can you speak to him?*" Terryn asked, his gaze following that crawling form. Yves's own spirit was too far reduced for Terryn to reach him, but perhaps the shades could communicate.

Nisirdi rose up beside him, its magnificent dragon form visible to his perception once more. Luminous eyes gazed down at Terryn, and the mellifluous voice which was already becoming familiar answered, *I will try.*

Turning its graceful head up to the ceiling, Nisirdi opened its mouth, and a beam of pure light shot out from its throat. No . . . not light, or not exactly light. This was magic; this was song. This was language felt with sensations beyond mortal hearing.

The language of the *Ildrir.*

The complexity of sound and sensation cut Terryn to the quick. He realized then, as though for the first time, how horribly wrong he'd been about everything he'd believed. He had been taught that shades were barely sentient, too malicious for true personhood—that whatever feelings they experienced were merely emotions stolen from their hosts. But this language ringing through the lofty arches of Dunloch's Great Hall suggested a world of emotions far more complex than those of mere mortality.

Yves—or rather, the shade indwelling Yves— responded to Nisirdi's song. It sent its host body creeping spiderlike down a pillar, winding as it went. Yves's robes pooled around him as he reached the floor, and he crouched there, knees up, head low, his old face sagging with exhaustion. The spirit gleaming behind his eyes didn't belong to the old chancellor at all, and Terryn could only hope that Yves himself hadn't been ousted entirely during possession. With Nisirdi's song resounding in his soul, Terryn took a step toward the old man.

Suddenly his mind exploded with tearing talons and raucous shrieks. Terryn cried out, his hands flying to his temples.

Cerine stared down at Terryn as he screamed, dropped to one knee, and gripped his head in both hands, writhing with sudden pain. She blinked once, twice . . .

Was that a flutter of shadow wings she saw around his head?

Whirling, she saw Ducette just propping herself on her elbows. Her head sagged heavily, but she fixed her gaze on Terryn. Her expression was ferocious and wild, demonic.

"Ducette!" Cerine cried, but either the young nun didn't hear her or didn't care. Shaking her head, Cerine tried again. "Hrelele!"

The nun started, shivered, and turned to Cerine—but it wasn't Ducette gazing out through those hazel eyes. Even without shadow senses, Cerine could feel the presence of a strange, unnatural soul.

"Hrelele," she said again, letting go of the banister and taking a careful step. Her swollen ankle wouldn't take much weight, but she continued despite the pain, sinking down on the step beside Ducette. She reached out and, after only an instant of hesitation, took the nun's hand. "Hrelele, don't hurt him."

He is one of them! the song-like voice of the shade rang through her head. *He is a hunter! He will kill this host and drive me out!*

"No." Cerine shook her head, taking care to hold that strange gaze, to not look away from that face. "He didn't hurt the other shades, did he? He saved you from the hunters. He saved me as well. He's on our side."

He is a hunter! He must die!

The voice broke off in a despairing shriek, and Cerine turned sharply in time to see Terryn rise to his feet. He'd fought off the invisible attack and now took aim with his scorpiona at Ducette.

"Get away from her, my lady!" he called out, his voice hard as flint. "That's an Apparition, a mind manipulator. It'll hurt you."

"Wait, please." Cerine extended one hand, palm out, motioning for the venator to lower his weapon. "She won't hurt me." She faced Ducette again, gazing at her with earnest entreaty. "You won't, will you? You called me to come to you. To help you."

This host had you in her mind. She thought you would answer if called.

A sliver of ice pricked at Cerine's heart. The shade had plundered Ducette's thoughts and memories. What else had it done to the young nun's soul?

"Is she . . . is she still there? Your host?" she asked, half afraid of learning the answer.

For a moment, Ducette's eyes cleared, like frost fading from a windowpane. The nun blinked and her hands flew to her face as though she didn't quite believe it still belonged to her.

Then she lunged at Cerine, gripping her arm frantically like a lifeline. "Help me!" she gasped. "Cerine, help—"

Before Cerine could respond, Ducette blinked again, and the shade was back, forefront in her mind. *She is here,* the voice sang. *I won't hurt her if you won't hurt me.*

Cerine licked her dry lips and swallowed with some difficulty. She was far out of her depth. One wrong move would certainly mean drowning in this new and wild sea. It was one thing to read the ancient documents, to pore over translations and reconstruct the words recounted by prophets and saints of old. It was one thing to theorize, to construct arguments in favor of the shades, to believe they were not all irredeemably evil.

But, evil or otherwise, they were *other*. This voice in her head was no mortal voice; if she let herself think too closely on what she heard, she knew she would be lost in those impossibly complex sounds and feelings. And that being, the inexplicable being now poised in a position of dominance over Ducette . . . after years of suppression in a venator host, it had been swift to take ascendancy in this new body, this new mind.

Was it evil? Perhaps not. But it was deadly even so. And it held Ducette's fate in the balance.

Cerine held out her hand, palm up. An invitation of sorts. The shade-taken looked at it sharply, then looked up at her face again.

"See inside my mind," Cerine said. "See who I am. See who I have become." She paused for a moment, mustering her courage, her conviction. "I am the wife of the Prince of Perrinion. Here in his house, I speak on behalf of the prince. And I swear to you that all shade-taken who dwell within these walls are under my protection. Do you understand me, Hrelele? You are welcome here. You are safe." She took a long breath before adding carefully, "But don't hurt Ducette. Don't harm your host spirit."

The being studied her for what felt like an age. Then, slowly . . . it nodded.

There was a flash of motion, something Cerine couldn't quite see or comprehend. It felt as though the birdlike shadow dived back through Ducette's wide-open eyes, vanishing inside. Ducette uttered a little moan and sank to the steps, bowing her head into her hands. Cerine placed a hand on her shoulder and turned to Terryn.

He stood at the base of the stair, watching her with a curious expression on his face. "Did you hear me, Venator du Balafre?" she asked, a slight quaver in her voice.

He nodded. "I heard you, my lady." He pressed a fist to his heart and bowed. "Your will is my command."

She could have sunk to the floor in relief. To have even one Evanderian on her side was a victory beyond anything she'd hoped for. Terryn's loyalty to her might only be an extension of his loyalty to Gerard, but she'd take it.

Terryn cast a wary glance at Chancellor Yves, still crouched froglike at the base of the pillar, then at the poor servants and guards still clustered along one wall. "What exactly has happened here?" he demanded. "Where is everyone? Where is Gerard?"

"Don't you know?" Cerine's brow puckered.

Terryn shook his head. Without waiting for another word from her, he strode up the staircase, brushing past both Cerine and Ducette, and around the paralyzed shade-taken lad still lying on the step.

"Stay here," Cerine whispered to Ducette, uncertain whether the nun even heard her. Gathering her skirts in both hands, she turned and tried to hasten after Terryn. But her ankle twinged painfully, and she almost fell. Biting out a curse, she gripped the banister and limped up the stairs as fast as she could, trailing after the venator, hard-pressed to follow his long-legged stride. She caught up to him in the hall just outside Gerard's office door.

Terryn pounded on the door, waited a breath, and then pounded again. "Gerard? Are you there?" He tried the handle, but it was locked.

A hundred questions piled up on Cerine's tongue. She still didn't know what had happened last night. Her memories were hazy, like images of a nightmare that are vivid while the dreamer experiences them but too bizarre upon waking to be believed.

Terryn hammered his fist against the door again. Then, suddenly, his right hand flared with brilliant white light. Cerine stifled a scream and took several steps back, her heart racing. Terryn gripped the door handle and melted it within a few seconds. It fell away, and something clunked on the other side. Terryn pushed the door open and disappeared into the room.

Pressing one hand to her heart, Cerine followed, but stopped in the doorway. The office was empty. She caught sight of Terryn disappearing through a door that led deeper into the prince's suite. Otherwise, all was still.

Instead of trying to follow Terryn, she hobbled across the room to Gerard's desk. As she leaned her weight against it, pressing her hands to its surface, a series of painful memories flooded her mind and threatened to sweep her away in their flow. She pictured Gerard standing here, almost exactly where she stood now. She recalled the look on his face when she told him of her findings. When she told him that his whole life was a lie.

Cold air blew on her face. Cerine looked up. The nearest window wasn't properly closed. Strange. Slowly she moved around the desk, favoring her ankle. The window stuck in its frame, but she caught the latch and pulled hard, yanking it shut. Then she looked through the glass at the landscape spread before her. The shining waters of Loch du Nóiv. The formal grounds along the lake's edge. She lifted her gaze higher, searching the horizon.

"Gerard," she whispered, her breath fogging the windowpane. "Where are you?"

"He's gone."

A startled thrill shot down Cerine's spine. She spun around, her eyes swiveling in her head as she searched the empty room for the source of that voice, a small, whispering voice that couldn't belong to Venator Terryn.

A flicker of movement drew her gaze down. Cerine sucked in a short breath. Then she crouched and peered into the alcove beneath Gerard's desk.

A pinched little face met her gaze, a face Cerine

immediately recognized, framed by locks of fair hair.

"You!" Cerine gasped, her voice a tense whisper. "How . . . how did you get here?"

The inborn Seer child hid her face in her arms.

Cerine pressed her lips together and swallowed hard. Then, with a shake of her head, she tried to make her face and voice as gentle as possible. "Did you see the prince?"

This time the girl nodded. Her grubby hand held out a folded parchment pressed with a red seal. After dropping it into Cerine's hands, she immediately retreated back under the desk, pressing as far as she could into the shadows.

The seal was Gerard's: the eagle and the sun. Cerine stared at it, unable to bring herself to break it, to read what he'd written. She knew what it was. She didn't have to read it to know.

It was his farewell. His final farewell.

"No sign of him." Terryn's voice sounded abrupt as he reentered the office. From her angle at the desk, Cerine could see him stride into the room, looming tall, his scarred face dark and forbidding. "He must be—"

"He was here," Cerine said.

Her voice drew his gaze to where she knelt by the desk. He frowned. "What? How do you know?"

Before Cerine could answer, the little Seer girl made a small squeak and scooted out from under the desk. At first Cerine thought she was attacking or possibly fleeing. But instead, much to her surprise, the child scrambled up, bolted across the room, and threw her little arms around Terryn.

Looking nearly as shocked as Cerine felt, he stared down at the top of the little head pressed against his legs, then looked at Cerine, his expression baffled. But when the child turned her face up to him, Cerine saw recognition dawn in his eye.

"Nilly," he breathed. He sank to his knees and let the child wrap her arms around his neck. She didn't say anything, just held onto him, burying her small face in his shoulder. Terryn looked . . . Cerine couldn't quite read his face. Relieved. And guilty. Frightened, almost. Yet he held the child with tenderness that seemed utterly out of place in the tall, stern venator.

Cerine could only stare in amazement, disbelieving her eyes. Was it possible . . . was it truly possible that change could be wrought in the hearts of Evander's followers? Was the Goddess's transforming work already begun?

At last the Seer child took a step back from Terryn, gazing into his eyes. She tilted her head to one side and opened her mouth. But the voice that came from her lips wasn't a child's voice at all. It was a strange, ageless, songlike voice speaking with an inexplicable combination of mortal and spirit language:

"Your brother is in danger."

"What?" The gentleness in Terryn's face vanished. "What did you say?"

"I have seen it," the voice continued. The girl lifted her small hands to cup Terryn's cheeks. *"What will be and what may be, all as one. I will show you."*

Something flashed between them, passing through the child's hands and into Terryn's head. Something Cerine could not quite perceive, but which she felt like a rumble of distant thunder.

She watched Terryn's eyes fill with horror.

I DID NOT WAKE. FOR DAYS, FOR WEEKS EVEN, I LAY IN *a stupor, trapped inside my own mind.*

My own mind, which now contained an ascendant shade.

It stalked me in the darkness. In the winding corridors of my unconscious it was there, behind every turn, around every bend. I would flee down a hall of doors, but no matter which door I went to, no matter which handle I tried, I would find it waiting for me on the other side—a being of pure darkness, without shape, without form. Wrath made manifest.

I felt its hatred of me pulsing in my blood. It had ascendancy, and I was unconscious, unable to fight, unable to bind it back with spell songs. Eventually it would catch me. And then it would uproot my soul and send me hurtling from this body, taking full possession of whatever was left behind.

But I would not give in easily.

So I slammed doors and ran harder and harder still. I wound my way deep through the labyrinth of halls that made up my mind, through all the secret chambers and hidden byways, always a single step ahead of that power.

At last, it drove me to a hall from which I knew there was no escape. The doors were all shut fast, and there were no stairs or side passages. Only a window at the far end, but no matter how I ran for it, it was always too far. My feet sank into the paving stones, and I fell to my knees, clawing my way forward.

The shade approached. Slowly, stealthily, like a panther stalking its prey. It was in no hurry but savored its moment of glory as it finally had me at its mercy. For the first time since the day of my Possession, I knew real fear.

I could move no more. The corridor faded around me, becoming only darkness. My shade was all around me, over me, under me, on either side. Only straight ahead could I still see that distant window, that gleam of light, of hope, too far to reach. I despaired.

Then suddenly, something stood framed in the window. The figure of a man. But that could not be. This was my own mind—no one else dwelled in this place.

He approached, shining like a torch, but with a white, shimmering sort of light. An Apparition. A mind-manipulator.

"There you are," he said as he drew near to me where I lay trapped, my arms and legs secured in darkness, my soul immobile with fear. "We have been searching for you. Give us your hand."

I did not know him, but he seemed to me like an angel of mercy sent from the Goddess herself. I tried to reach for him.

But my shade shrieked, the darkness billowing over us, cutting him off from my sight. I cried out, my soul wrenching with the pain of hope brought near only to be suddenly stripped away. It was almost more than I could bear, and I nearly let go my hold on my own body and allowed myself to be ousted.

Then the light cut through the darkness again. Just a faint, silver gleaming at first, but it strengthened with time. Although I could not see his face, I heard his voice singing to my soul. "What is your name?" he asked.

I thought he spoke to me, and I opened my mouth to answer.

But out of the darkness came a voice that was no voice, a voice that spoke in no language. Rather, it was an impression of language, of understanding, such as I had never before heard.

I am Irimir, *my shade declared.*

"Irimir," the man replied. And then I realized it was no mere

man who spoke, but a man and shade bound together as one. "We are Stanier and Uzurul. We are here to help you."

I stared in horror as the light once more coalesced into the figure of the man standing before me in that dark hall. I realized then that he was an inborn.

He looked down at me and smiled. "It's all right." He reached out a hand and touched one shining finger to my forehead. "Wake up."

I opened my eyes—

And stared at low ceiling rafters over my head and the flickering glow of firelight playing on a mud-and-wattle wall.

CHAPTER 12

A HORSE AMBLED DOWN THE ROAD, ITS HEAD LOW, its reins trailing.

Gerard stopped, surprised. He shaded his eyes and looked again, uncertain whether or not to believe what he saw. It seemed almost too good to be true that a horse would approach him out of nowhere, saddled and ready to ride. Was this a trick of some kind? Or a dream?

But the horse kept on coming, its ears twitching nervously with every step. Gerard approached the beast carefully. At the sound of his voice speaking gently, it lifted its head, pricked its ears, snorted, and pawed at the ground. But it let him draw near and heaved a great sigh of relief when he took hold of the reins and ran his hand down its dappled neck.

It wore a venator's tack. Gerard recognized it at once, the insignia of Castra Breçar embellishing both the cheek piece and the saddle skirt. This was an Evanderian's horse. There was a spatter of blood on its flank, but no wound. No sign of a rider anywhere either.

Gerard sighed and breathed a swift prayer. It was a long trek from Dunloch to the Witchwood, even cutting straight across the countryside as he intended. If the Goddess saw fit to provide him with a mount, he might as well be grateful.

He unstrapped the sword in its sheath from his back and affixed it in place on the saddle instead. Then he mounted, adjusted the stirrups to fit his length of leg, and turned the horse's head east.

"*Jah!*" he cried, and drove his heels into the horse's ribs. The beast sprang into motion, and they galloped for the horizon.

Hollis crouched in the shadows, her spirit coiled into a tight ball of defense. She sensed the labyrinth of stone around her, the dark twists and turns leading off into even darker places. It was the world of her own mind, a world she barely understood even after years of intense exploration.

She couldn't see anything. The paralysis poison held her too tightly in its grip.

Searching along the soul tether connecting her to her shade, she felt that spirit somewhere in the distance, around many bends and corners, behind many walls of this mind maze. It reacted to the poison even more strongly than she did, hiding its strange face in the many folds of its wings. Hollis wished she dared try to reach out to it, to offer some sort of comfort or to receive comfort in return.

But that was impossible. Her shade was a weapon. Sharpened, oiled, deadly. Nothing more.

So Hollis remained alone, coiled up inside her head. She tried to remember what had brought her here, what events taking place in the waking world had led her to fall prey to an Evanderian poison. But it was all so distant and confused. Fendrel's face flashed before her mind's eye, but that didn't mean anything. He was always there. Close in her mind. In her heart. An object of terror as much as love. Had he done this to her? Had he poisoned her, trapped her in this place?

Would he come soon to finish the job? To kill her? To damn her?

She shuddered, terribly helpless and furious and frightened all at once. She hated Fendrel. She loved him and she hated him, when she wanted to feel nothing for him at all.

Heat.

Hollis's spirit uncoiled slightly, awareness quickening. Heat. Rising heat. She felt it both in her mind and in her unconscious body. Growing, swelling, rushing down upon her. Heat and pain and—

Her eyes flared open. The darkness of her mind vanished, replaced by red, roaring bursts of light. Magic flared through every limb. Her shade screamed in her head and rushed wildly up through her soul, multitudinous wings pounding in her skull, bursting from her head so hard that only the soul tether held it back. All suppression spells were broken, all control momentarily lost.

Hollis sprang upright, reaching out with her mind to catch hold of the tether, to reclaim ascendancy. She felt souls near, and with a scream she directed all the power inside her to attack. Her shade screamed, its voice an echo of hers, and launched itself at the nearest soul.

A pair of wings, shedding drops of light like rain, opened before Hollis's vision. A pair of forearms reached out and caught Hollis's shade as it flew raging in attack. Her shade screeched, tore, clawed, snarled—but the massive light-being caught it close, wrapped its own wings shut, and held it.

Hollis stared, amazed, her shadow sight dancing, unable to comprehend what she saw. For a moment she thought the light-being had devoured her shade. But then a sound filled her ears, filled her heart—a song, soft and soothing. Hollis felt a ripple of relief flow along the soul-tether, emanating from her shade.

What in the Goddess's three holy names was going

on?

Every muscle jumping with energy and tension, she blinked out of shadow sight and gazed into the mortal world. Lantern light filled her vision, illuminating a scarred young face and brilliant blue eyes. She recognized him. She couldn't forget a face like that, though the last time she'd seen him he wasn't quite five years old.

"Terryn du Balafre," she sneered. Then she lunged at him, tearing at his eyes with her hands even as her soul pulled at her shade, seeking to reclaim its power. Her shade shuddered and yanked free of the light-being's arms to dive straight at the young venator. She would plunge into his mind, find some memory, some weakness, and tear it apart, leaving him crumpled on the floor in agony!

But the light-being reacted too quickly. It caught her shade again and held it fast. Her shade fought furiously but couldn't break free. Terryn likewise caught Hollis's wrists and wrenched her hands back from his face.

"I am not your enemy," he growled into her face, his teeth flashing in the lantern's glow.

"Festering Haunts you're not," Hollis spat. "Where's your master, little puppy?"

"If you're referring to Fendrel du Glaive, I don't know. I hoped you would."

"The festering bastard ambushed me," Hollis snarled. She yanked hard, and Terryn let her go, though she knew he could have held on if he'd wished to. "Where's Ayleth? What has your master done with her?"

"Again, I hoped you would know," Terryn replied. Did she imagine it, or was there a flicker of warmth amid those cold words? "Fendrel turned on me as well," he added. "Tried to have me killed. He thinks I'm dead."

Hollis stared at him. She couldn't believe it. Fendrel had turned on Terryn? No. No, no, no. She still remembered when he brought the little boy home from the Battle of Cró Ular, how the almost otherworldly light had glowed in his eyes, in his heart. The hope. The conviction. Terryn was Fendrel's own future embodied. The closest thing to a son he would ever know.

But then . . . Hollis was the closest thing to a lover Fendrel had ever known. Yet he would destroy them both. All for the sake of his Order. All for the sake of his lie.

"*Down,*" she commanded, and her shade stopped

struggling against the light-dragon. It still brimmed with the burst of angry, raw power that had brought it raging up inside her and broken through the paralysis. Such power would have been more than a match for any ordinary Evanderian shade bound by suppression spells. But the light-being had held it off almost too easily.

Hollis, using her shadow vision, looked at Terryn more closely. Her eyes widened. "Your shade," she said. "I sense no suppressions."

"No," he answered. Nothing more.

So he was a heretic. Terryn du Balafre. Fendrel's little protégé. A heretic.

How interesting the world had suddenly become.

Hollis grimaced. Her body quaked suddenly, the aftershock of the various poisons it had just endured. She put a hand to her head and shifted on her feet, struggling to maintain her balance. "What did you give me?"

"Anathema poison," he answered.

Naturally. The best counter to the Apparition paralysis that had been used to bring her down was a dose of Anathema poison. Hollis could probably count on one hand the number of times she'd been paralyzed, and only this once had she been revived with counteractive poison. It was an experience she hoped never to repeat.

The nausea passed, however, and some of the raw magic had already reduced in her soul. Her shade settled back inside her head, still too ascendant for comfort. Realizing she'd need to reassert the suppression spells, she felt for her Vocos pipes on her belt. But it was gone. They'd stripped all her weapons, including her pipes.

Taking a look around, she saw that she'd been left in the same undercroft where she and Ayleth had carried the unconscious Crystalwitch for mental interrogation. The witch's corpse lay to one side, several hours dead by the look of it. How long had she been trapped here? And why had Fendrel not killed her while she was unconscious?

Terryn was already on the move, making for the door. Hollis pushed her unwilling body into motion, following him. "They're gone, aren't they," she said to his broad shoulders.

He nodded without looking back. "Fendrel left two wounded Evanderians behind to deal with the household." He gave her a quick summary of his discoveries since escaping his own near death. As he talked, they passed through the back quarters of Dunloch, leaving behind the humble storage rooms and kitchens, taking the passage leading to the Great Hall. They stepped out into that pillared space, and Hollis stopped dead in her tracks, her whole spirit lurching with a jolt of surprise.

A young untaken woman stood at the bottom of the great staircase. She was delicately built with a pale, pinched sort of face and very little hair on her shorn scalp. She was clothed in rags but carried herself with quiet dignity, her head up and shoulders back, her eyes unflinching.

On her hip she held a shade-taken child. Its ascendant shade gleamed unmistakably to Hollis's shadow sight. And just to one side, seated on the lowest step, was another shade-taken, an old man in velvet robes, with the ascendant spirit gleaming in his eyes. On the young woman's other side sat a nun, her holy robes rumpled and her hood askew. The ascendant spirit in her body was mortal, but a shade presence hovered just beneath, unsuppressed and watchful.

"What . . . what is this?" Hollis gasped.

"Evanderians died in the attack last night," Terryn explained, standing between her and the little assembly on the stair. "These are their shades."

The untaken young woman cleared her throat and looked Hollis straight in the eye. "They are under my protection," she said, adjusting her hold on the little shade-taken girl.

Hollis gaped. Who was this young person to be making such bold and nonsensical declarations? A mortal . . . protecting shades? It was too much, too laughable. But something in that untaken woman's gaze made her swallow her protests.

"Venatrix di Theldry," Terryn said, drawing her attention back to him, "before you were attacked, the prince commanded you to use your powers and glean what information you could from the Crystalwitch's mind. Were you able to discover anything there?"

Hollis nodded. "The Queen's Highway," she said. Trying not to let her gaze drift to the shade-taken more than necessary, she hastily filled Terryn in on what she had learned of the Crimson Devils' intentions. "The Queen's Highway is the swiftest route to Dulìmurian.

With Odile awake, she may be able to control the oblidite in the road and safely navigate through the Witchwood."

"And . . . and it is certainly Odile?"

Hollis looked at Terryn's grim face, his question echoing in her ears. He hadn't been there in the vault. He hadn't seen the Witch Queen sit upright on her crypt slab, her neck still bleeding from the old death wound as it slowly reknit.

She nodded. "She is alive. She is awake."

Terryn bowed his head. But whatever evil thoughts preyed on his mind, he didn't succumb to them. He looked up at Hollis again almost at once, his eyes bright with magic and light. "You must pursue Fendrel," he said. "You must find him and . . . and Ayleth. I don't know what he's done to her. I don't know what he will do. I don't even know if . . . if . . ."

There was real pain in his face. Hollis recognized it and more besides. Oh, Ayleth! What disasters that girl left in her wake, this poor man's heart not the least of them!

"Fendrel won't hurt her," she said firmly. "He won't dare. Not as long as Odile herself breathes."

"Why?" Terryn demanded. "I don't understand. What

is the connection between them exactly?"

Hollis drew a deep breath. "There is no time to explain," she said. "Just know that . . . know that Ayleth is the only one who can kill Odile. Don't ask me why; don't ask me how I know. Believe me. I have no reason to lie to you. Fendrel knows the truth as well, and he will use Ayleth to put an end to the Witch Queen once and for all. Until she has served his purpose, Ayleth is safe. From Fendrel at least."

Terryn nodded. His face was gray, his ugly scar standing out starkly. She could tell he wanted to ask more questions, but something else drove him. "You must follow them," he said. "Fendrel will have gotten the information he needed from Ayleth. They'll have made for the Queen's Highway."

Hollis frowned. "What about you?"

Terryn shook his head. "I have another mission to fulfill. My . . . the prince. The king. Gerard." He firmed his jaw. "He is in danger. I must save him."

"He doesn't matter." Hollis threw up her hands and almost laughed. "Don't you understand, boy? Nothing matters but Odile. Ending Odile. We can't—"

"He matters to me."

His voice held such finality that Hollis stopped short. She could think of nothing more to say, not even when Terryn turned from her and addressed himself to the young woman on the stair. He bowed to her, his fist pressed to his heart.

"My queen," he said. "With your permission, I will now take my leave."

His *queen?* Hollis's brow knotted. Who was this girl anyway?

The young woman merely nodded, her bearing undeniably regal. "Go," she said. "Find him. Bring him home if you can."

Terryn straightened and looked Hollis's way. "Take a horse and ride for Cró Ular and the Queen's Highway. And may the Goddess guide your way."

"You're making a mistake," Hollis said. "They'll need you, Terryn du Balafre. Ayleth will need you."

Another flicker of pain raced across his face. But he schooled his features into an expressionless mask. "When my brother is safe, I will come," he said. With those words, he marched for the door and did not pause. He vanished outside, leaving Hollis to stare after him.

So. It was up to her then. To find and rescue Ayleth. To stop Fendrel before his madness carried him beyond recovery.

Why did she suddenly feel as though her life was one endlessly repeating cycle of the same choices, the same mistakes?

"There were Evanderians left behind," she said, her voice loud in the silence of the Great Hall. "Where are they?"

"We locked them in the buttery," the young woman answered behind her. "Why?"

Hollis turned, glaring at the woman, the child, and the two shade-taken. She clenched her fists. "I need to restock my weapons," she said. "I've got a hunt to pursue."

Cerine stood at the top of the porch steps, watching Venatrix di Theldry's red hood disappear as she rode across the bridge. She felt as though she watched her last ally vanish, though whether or not the venatrix truly was her ally, she couldn't be at all sure.

Little Nilly stirred in her arms. Cerine adjusted her grip on the child and turned to her, offering a smile that was probably not as reassuring as she hoped. She turned that same smile to Yves and Ducette, who trailed after her like two silent shadows, their gazes sometimes mortal and sometimes not.

So, Dread Odile was returned to Perrinion. And Gerard had ridden off alone to fight her and her Crimson Devils, leaving Cerine behind with the shade-taken she had promised to protect.

In one hand she gripped Gerard's note. She couldn't bear to read it. Not yet. If these were the last words she would ever have from him, she would put off the end as long as she could. Instead, she strengthened her smile, facing the shade-taken. Beyond them, she saw the other members of the castle household—the guards, the servants. All of them looked to her now in this moment of fear, of crisis.

She was their queen.

"Come," she said, her voice clear and steady, though her heart thundered in her throat. "Let us do what we can to make Dunloch secure."

The sun reached the noon zenith in the sky and began its descent into afternoon.

WHAT CAN I SAY OF THE MONTHS THAT FOLLOWED? *My legs were broken, and my body was wracked with fever. I drifted in and out of consciousness, and whenever I returned to the realm of my mind, my shade was there waiting for me. But now Stanier was there as well. Stanier and his inborn shade, a being of light who spoke to and calmed my shade in its wrath and spoke to and calmed me in my fear.*

When I woke, Stanier was there also. Everything about him repulsed me. He was an abomination. His very existence spat in the face of the Goddess. I hated him, hated him with such intensity that I once tried to rise up and kill him, though my broken bones betrayed me and I ended up crawling on my belly across the floor of his cottage, weeping with pain and frustration.

He helped me back into the bed, put cooling cloths on my brow, and sang to me in his mortal voice—humble songs about birds and trees and flowers and the pathways of the stars. Songs of love and songs of birth. Songs mothers sing to their children.

And when at last I drifted off to sleep again, he waited for me there as well, a comfort in the darkness.

At last the day dawned that I opened my eyes and the fever was broken. I was as weak as a kitten but no longer delirious, and my hatred seemed to have died back to nothing more than a dull ember in the depths of my soul. I turned my head and found Stanier beside me—his mortal soul gleaming in his eyes, but his shade spirit bright in the center of his being.

"Why haven't you killed me?" I asked. My voice was rough from disuse, and it hurt to speak.

He lifted a wooden cup to my lips, and I drank greedily. "I don't know," he said when at last I had finished. He sat back on the stool he'd drawn up close to my bedside and regarded me, his head tilted to one side. "Something about your face, perhaps." He smiled a crooked sort of smile that made his homely features suddenly bright, not with Apparition light but with a glow altogether unique. My heart seemed to stop in my breast. "It's an uncommonly pretty face," he said.

"I'll kill you as soon as I can stand," I answered before breaking off in a fit of coughing.

"I don't doubt it." He leaned forward with the wooden bowl again. "But in the meantime, drink this."

CHAPTER 13

AYLETH LAY IN THE QUIET OF HER MIND FOREST, curled up, hidden, her arms wrapped over her head, her hair covering her body like a veil.

Laranta was near. The barrier of iron prevented her from coming close, but Ayleth could feel her powerful presence pacing along the edges of her awareness. She wished she could reach out and take hold of her wolf shade, wished she could bury her head in that ruff of black fur. She wished they could be as they had once been—not venatrix and shade, but inborn soul sisters. Wild things running through a pine forest on mountain slopes, far from mankind. The two of them together with their wolf brothers and wolf sisters, owning nothing but their wildness, desiring nothing but their freedom.

That life would never be theirs again. In this huddled hiding place of her own mind, Ayleth wept for her loss, wept for Laranta, wept for her mother and brothers and sisters.

Suddenly, hideously, red light pierced through the quiet shadows, pulsing with pain. She knew what this was—iron poison. Directly impaled through her skin, into her blood, down into her soul where she could not hide from it.

The Evanderians had found her. They'd saved her.

She endured the wave of agony until at last it rolled on overhead. In the mortal world, her eyelids fluttered, then reluctantly opened. Her swimming, pain-wracked gaze focused with an effort, and she saw her hands before her—encased once more in the iron mitts and bound to a saddle.

Ropes secured her on all sides, preventing her from

falling off the horse even in her unconscious state. Not the same horse she'd ridden this morning, she noted dully. The neck bowed before her was a glossy chestnut, and she half wondered if it was Terryn's Fleeta. But no, this beast was darker and stockier than his pretty red mare.

A whole world of aches, pains, cuts, and contusions reached out to embrace her as she came more fully conscious. Along with the broken ribs and the bruises on her neck where dead hands had throttled her, she noted in particular the pain in her thighs. Looking down at her trousers, she saw long cuts in the fabric, revealing bandages spotted with blood. She knew what those must be: Fendrel had purged the Corpsewitch's controlling curses from her limbs. She ought to be grateful.

Instead, she turned her head slightly and glared at the figure riding beside her on a black horse. Her rescuer. Her torturer.

She opened her mouth, tried to speak. Her throat was too sore from the attempted strangulation, and the words wouldn't come without extreme effort. At last, forcing sound through her lips, she rasped, "If you gave my shade ascendancy, I could heal from my wounds much faster."

Fendrel did not turn, though she thought she saw the flash of his eyes casting her a swift sideward glance. Otherwise, he offered no response.

Shuddering, Ayleth pulled herself upright in the saddle, squaring her shoulders and taking care not to move her hands more than absolutely necessary. She could feel those iron spikes ready to bite. Evanderians surrounded her just as they had that morning, but when she did a quick headcount, there were only six, including Fendrel himself. So two others besides her venatrix guardian had lost their lives in the morning battle.

If one of Odile's Crimson Devils could do this much damage, how could they hope to face Odile herself?

But then again, the Evanderians would not face Odile. That was Ayleth's job.

"Take these Haunts-damned things off of me," she growled suddenly, her voice still rough and hideous. She trained a hard glare on the side of Fendrel's face. "I can't fight with them on. You need me. You know you do."

He said nothing. He did not seem to hear her, not even to spare a flicking sideways glance.

Ayleth shuddered again, dizzy with all the myriad pains coursing through her body. "That venatrix," she said, bowing her head but forcing the words out nonetheless. "The one you left to guard me. She died because I was shackled. I could have saved her. If you hadn't left me defenseless, I could have kept her alive."

"Venatrix d'Aril is dead because of you." Fendrel turned his head just enough to fix her with an accusing eye.

Ayleth flashed her teeth. "She's dead because we were overwhelmed by walking corpses."

She felt the sudden bolt of tension shoot through him, felt it as clearly as though he'd struck her. He turned to face her, and the expression on his face was like a blow in itself. "I don't care if it was you who delivered the death stroke or not. *She* died, and you did not. You, who should have been the Corpsewitch's first and only target. He had you at his mercy, and yet you live. And so does he, for you let him escape."

"*Let* him escape?" Ayleth shook her head and then immediately closed her eyes as another wave of dizziness darkened the edges of her vision. Had Fendrel not seen her fight with the Corpsewitch? Had he not seen how she'd tried to kill that man?

Fendrel looked at her with such loathing, she could feel it even with her eyes closed. "You ought to be dead," he said. "You, who are the greatest, the *only* risk to their queen's life—you ought to be dead."

Ayleth cracked her eyes open again, peering through her lashes at the Venator Dominus. He met her eye and shook his head slowly. "She must have some use for you still. Something that makes your continued life worth the risk." His lip curled ever so slightly. "I ought to kill you myself. If I did, we might still bring her down, cut off her head again. She'd be trapped forever this time, without any blood kin to revive her. Maybe . . . maybe . . ."

He was mad. For all his iron-hard will, for all his stone-hard face, he was utterly mad. Ayleth stared into those eyes and saw the whirling vortex of insanity in their centers, and it was all she could do not to spur her horse's ribs, not to make a break right then and there. But if she did, he would surely pursue. He would hunt her down, kill her, damn her . . . and damn the rest of them as well by destroying their last chance to end Odile.

So Ayleth held very still, every muscle tense, afraid to move.

Her horse took a wrong step, jostling the saddle. In reflex, Ayleth tried to reach for a fistful of mane . . . and the spikes of the iron mitts drove through skin, tiny points biting at bone. She moaned, whimpered, and lost herself again in a storm of agony from which there was no escape. Her mind filled with red.

When at last her vision cleared and she was able to think and feel something other than pain, Fendrel was no longer beside her. She saw him up ahead, conferring with one of his men. In his place, when Ayleth turned her weary head to her right, she found Kephan holding her horse's lead. Unlike Fendrel, he looked at her squarely, meeting her gaze as she turned toward him, his face full of concern.

"Don't look at me like that," she snarled.

"Like what?" he asked, blinking twice.

"Like you care. You're one of them. You're helping them. You don't get to care about me."

The venator drew a deep breath and looked away, up the road. His gaze fixed on his dominus. They progressed several minutes before, with a heavy sigh, he spoke again. "I do care, di Ferosa. And I'm going to help you. If I can."

"Help me?" Ayleth nearly choked on the ugly chuckle rising in her throat. She lifted her hands just slightly. "If you want to help me, get these things off."

Kephan shook his head. "You know I can't. Not yet anyway. I have to wait for a chance." He cast her a quick glance. "Venatrix d'Aril . . . we trained together at Castra Breçar back in the day. We were students together. Did you . . . Were you . . . ?"

Ayleth grimaced. "I didn't kill her, if that's what you're asking. She died trying to protect me. Because I couldn't protect myself."

He nodded. She couldn't tell if he believed her or not. What had Fendrel been telling him and the others? Fendrel had a way of speaking outrageous lies so convincingly that one couldn't help believing him, couldn't help *wanting* to believe him. He obviously believed himself. Which only made his lies more dangerous.

Ayleth breathed out slowly through her nose and

gazed around at the countryside through which they passed. They traveled on a circuit trail winding along the upper slopes of hilly countryside, avoiding the valleys. Something about it felt familiar. "Are we . . . are we making for Cró Ular?" she asked.

Kephan nodded. She saw it from the corner of her eye without actually looking at him. "We're not far now," he said. Then he dropped his voice as though afraid of being overheard even by Ayleth herself. "The Dominus hopes the Witchwood will slow down Dread Odile. He hopes we'll catch them before they pass the Great Barrier. But the Corpsewitch effectively slowed us by several hours, so . . ."

So Odile and her escort of Devils could be long gone by now, having plunged into the dark, poisonous depths of the Witchwood. But that haunted air would not poison Odile's lungs, for she alone commanded the power of *oblivis*. And the Witchwood itself . . . would it welcome her like a long-lost sister?

Their horses climbed a steep incline now, and Ayleth recognized where they were. At the top of this rise, they would command a view of the valley in which Cró Ular stood. The ruins of the Queen's Highway would be visible, stretching across the countryside. And beyond the tower would stand the dark mass of the Witchwood, waiting.

Ayleth looked ahead and saw Fendrel just reaching the top of the rise. He pulled his horse up short. She frowned. Something about the way he sat in his saddle, something in the way he held his shoulders . . .

Something wasn't right.

Kephan sensed it too; she could tell by the way he tightened his grasp on her mount's lead rope, causing the horse to toss its head in protest. They continued on up the slope and gained the crest. From there they looked down into the Valley of Blood and Eyes.

Before them lay the tower ruins, just as they had lain these twenty years. And beyond them . . . beyond them . . .

Ayleth stared. Then she blinked and stared again. She could not make herself believe what she saw, could not make herself accept the reality of the vision before her.

The fringe forest was gone. Replaced by a forest of glittering stone.

The air whirled with what she at first took to be ash. But ash did not glint and glimmer with dark magic, catching the light and refracting it into scattered pieces. This wasn't ash—it was *oblivis*.

What did this mean? Was the Great Barrier destroyed? Was the Witchwood breaking through? But this didn't look like the Witchwood's work. There were no vines, no pus-oozing wounds in the trees. In that sickness there had been life.

Now all life was gone.

Only one person could have done this. Only one person could possibly wield such power. In her mind's eye, Ayleth saw again the burned, skeletal form of the Witch Queen crouched on her stone burial slab, her neck still gory with the newly knit wound, *oblivis* pulsing through every limb. She had looked frail then, as though a breath of wind could shatter her. Clearly, she wasn't frail anymore.

Between them and the desolation stood Cró Ular. Something about its ruined walls and fallen tower seemed strangely expectant, eager.

"Venator du Tam," Fendrel barked, breaking the

stillness which had held the whole company captive for too long. Kephan responded at once, passing the lead rope of Ayleth's horse to the nearest Evanderian and hastily riding to Fendrel's side.

"Something doesn't feel right down there," the Dominus said with a wave of his hand. "Use those Feral powers of yours and look for a trap of some kind. Take Harsent and Theutrud with you, and watch yourselves."

Kephan saluted and motioned to the two Evanderians named. The three of them dismounted and, leaving their horses, progressed swiftly and stealthily down the incline. Ayleth couldn't sense their shades, but she knew they must be ascendant, brimming with power only just restrained by spell songs. Despite herself, worry slipped into Ayleth's heart as she watched Kephan creep up to the ruinous walls. She wished it was her down there. She wished—

Her horse shifted its weight suddenly, and she made an instinctive grab for the pommel. The iron spikes bit down hard, like vicious teeth savaging her skin and soul. With a stifled cry, she sank into the pain, cursing and desperate and angry. She'd have been better off with the witches.

When at last the wave passed and she came to herself, it was to the sound of screams. She thought at first they were her own and Laranta's. But no. These were distant, desperate voices echoing outside her head.

She shook her head hard and peered through the haze of pain down to the tower below. The screams she heard . . . they came from down there but were almost drowned out by a terrible roar. One section of the ruinous wall broke in a shower of rubble as something smashed through it—something that flew out from the ruins by several yards and fell to the ground as a bloody pulp that was no longer recognizably human.

A red hood fluttered to the ground as the last gust of a whirling wind returned to the ruins.

Gerard reined in his horse at the top of a rise. The afternoon sun was high above, shedding light but no heat on the winter day. The shadows in the valleys lengthened and deepened, but they were not dark enough to hide what those valleys contained.

They could not hide the field of the dead.

Darkness fell across Gerard's spirit like a cloud passing over the sun. He sat as though frozen, staring down that slope, unable to tear his gaze away from that grim sight.

There were a dozen or more. Men, women. Children too.

These were his people. Murdered. He didn't have to guess by whom. The Crimson Devils of Dread Odile had no regard for mortal lives. Not even the lives of their own host bodies. Certainly not the lives of humble village folk. They used them. Killed them. Like a herd of cattle led to the butcher.

At first, Gerard could see nothing but death below him, could feel nothing but horror. But as the first wave of horror passed, he saw something else—a pattern. Most of the bodies lay in the center, piled up on top of each other, while the others formed circles out from the center. As though all of them were engaged in some sort of strange and terrible dance.

Or controlled by a single mind.

"The Corpsewitch," Gerard whispered.

His horse trembled, snorted, uneasy in the presence of

so much death. But an Evanderian horse didn't spook easily. Gerard adjusted his grip on the reins and turned his gaze east again. To the Witchwood. It was close now; he could see the fringe forest from here.

His heart pounded in his throat. More than anything, he longed to turn from this path, to give up this wild ride. The urge to hunt the Corpsewitch burned in his breast, the desire to avenge these people—*his* people. These innocent souls taken and used as tools, then cruelly discarded.

But there was only one way to end this madness.

"May the Mother receive you, who hath called you." he murmured, raising his right hand in salute to the fallen. *"And may the heavenly spirits conduct you to the Gates of Light. GoddessHead have mercy. GoddessHeart have mercy. GoddessSoul have mercy."*

Then he turned his horse's head east once more and spurred it into a gallop, leaving the valley of the dead behind. He did not see the wind that blew across their still faces, pulling at their hair.

He did not see them open their eyes. Stir. Stretch.

Begin to rise.

I DIDN'T KILL HIM.

My body healed slowly but surely under his ministrations.

One day while he was out of the cottage, fetching herbs to make a poultice, I heaved myself upright and discovered that, although my legs were weak, I could just balance myself on them. With a little searching I found a knife, and by the time he returned, I sat upright on my pallet, the knife in my lap.

"Ah," he said, observing me. "Is today the day then?"

I shrugged and set the knife to one side. "Maybe tomorrow."

But tomorrow he helped me to stand and take my first five agonized steps outside in the yard. The next day he helped me take five more.

Three months later, in the dark of the night, I rose up from my bed and fetched the knife once again. I walked on my own two feet across the cottage to his bed, where he lay fast asleep—both mortal and shade spirit quiet inside him. He was a fool to trust me. He was a fool to think I was less a venatrix now than I had ever been. He was a fool . . .

But so was I.

I drove the knife into the wall over his head. The sound of its impact woke him. He sat upright, his eyes wide, but not with fear. He stared up at me, and it was an entirely mortal soul that I saw gazing at me.

I climbed into his bed that night and committed the great sin. But I never stopped to think of what my actions meant, for my blood was hot, and my body hungry, and my soul ablaze with a feeling I had never before known and did not think to name.

Nine months later, I gave birth to an inborn daughter.

Olena.

CHAPTER 14

AYLETH GAPED, HORRIFIED. SHE COULDN'T BELIEVE what she saw taking place before her eyes. Another figure flew out from the ruins of Cró Ular, soaring high into the air, arms and legs struggling against the wind that bore them. Was it Kephan? Oh, Goddess, let it not be Kephan! He was lifted high—twenty feet, fifty, a hundred feet in the air—and then dropped, cartwheeling through nothing, plummeting to his end. He landed among the ruins of Cró Ular and out of sight.

A second later, a third figure appeared, tumbling through the air, and smashed into the hillside just below where Fendrel and the others stood. Ayleth craned her neck, trying to catch a glimpse of his face, trying to see if she recognized him and if he somehow, miraculously, still lived.

Another roar of wind drew her gaze back to the ruins. Up from the center of the rubble a fourth figure rose, this one not struggling and wheeling about in terror. The Windwitch rode on the air, her arms outstretched to balance on the winds she commanded, her pale hair flying behind her in streaming, tattered pennants. As the winds carried her, they also reached down among the broken stones of Cró Ular, winding invisible bands of power in, around, and under. She lifted her arms, and the stones rose into the air, floating around her.

"Move!" Fendrel cried. His voice seemed to break a spell of paralysis holding the Evanderians frozen. They broke ranks at once, horses squealing, hooves pounding, tails flying, riders' hoods flapping back over their shoulders. Projectiles whistled through the air, embedding into the hillside, some as large as a man.

The Evanderian holding the lead to Ayleth's horse spurred his mount sharply, urging both horses downhill in an effort to escape the assault. The sudden lurch into motion jarred Ayleth's hands, and she lost all sense of her surroundings, all ability to feel fear, all ability to feel anything but the red-hot agony of iron poison lancing through her soul. In the pine forest of her mind she shrieked, begging the Goddess to hear her, to deliver her from this torment. But the poison battered her down until her projected self-image shattered, and she became nothing but her pain.

When she slowly became aware of herself, she was lying on the ground, still tied to her saddle. Her horse lay on her leg, pinning her. The beast didn't thrash or groan, and Ayleth saw a great deal of blood and a huge stone, which had miraculously missed her when it struck. She couldn't move at all, not even to shift her position, for fear of driving the spikes into her hands. She could do nothing but lie there listening to screams, listening to rock thudding into the hillside.

"*Laranta!*" she shouted inside her head. But it was no use. Ayleth shook her head, and her hair, pulled free of its braid, whipped into her face, over her eyes. Through the dark strands, she saw a figure approaching, riding on air currents. The Windwitch.

Her gaze landed on Ayleth, pinned beneath the horse, and her lips stretched into a rictus smile. One arm moved as though throwing wind. Ayleth gasped, struck by a solid wall of air, but the wind broke and moved around her, like so many fingers wrapping under the horse's body, and began to lift both it and Ayleth.

Before Ayleth could even open her mouth to scream, the witch was knocked sideways and lost control of her wind, whirling through the air like the poor men she had tossed and broken so carelessly. But she quickly caught herself, regained her balance, and turned in the direction the blow had come from.

Ayleth also turned, trying to see who had managed to land a blow on the Windwitch, but she moved too abruptly, and the spikes drove home again. She collapsed back into pain.

When she was able to open her eyes, Fendrel stood over her, his legs braced, his arm up, and his right hand bleeding from the cuts he'd dealt himself. Shade power whirled around and through him, so far ascendant that Ayleth didn't need Laranta's powers to feel it. How did he keep his body from bursting into a cloud of dust? Somehow, he held on to control.

Even as Ayleth focused on him, Fendrel drew back his arm and hurled another curse straight at the witch, blasting through her shield of wind. Cuts appeared across her face, across her upraised hands, slicing through her garments. But none of them caused lethal damage, and though she dropped sharply toward the earth, she caught herself and, while still rising, lifted one of her massive stones and flung it straight for Fendrel, straight for Ayleth.

Fendrel brought his bleeding hand down in front of him in a short, sharp gesture. A burst of magic emanated from him, and the stone cleaved in two, falling on either side of them and rolling away. A fine film of dust sprayed in Ayleth's face, but nothing more.

She became aware of footsteps around her. Turning her head, she saw two Evanderians rush in on each side, scorpioni cocked and ready. They took shots. One of them aimed erratically; the other took a good stance and shot true.

But the Windwitch caught both darts in a whirl of air and sent them flying off wildly. Then, extending one arm, she grasped something invisible in her fist and pulled it back hard over her shoulder.

Fendrel staggered, stepping two paces away from Ayleth. He fell to one knee, then down onto his left hand. His other hand grasped at his throat, and he gagged, choking, desperate, trying to catch at the air snatched from his lungs. The other two Evanderians did the same, collapsing, choking, and writhing in their need to draw breath.

The witch, riding high above them, smiled grimly at the sight and looked down at Ayleth. While keeping her one hand in a fist, as though holding tight to the breaths she'd stolen, she stretched out her other hand, pointing at Ayleth.

Ayleth's gaze fixed on the huge block of stone rising slowly beneath the witch, rotating on its axis. It was a missile the size of a horse. It would crush her skull and flatten her to the ground, and she couldn't even lift her hands in a feeble defense.

She wished suddenly that Laranta could be with her. That she needn't face this violent death alone.

But instead of hurtling toward her, the rock wobbled, then thudded straight down on the ground. The witch's eyes widened, still fixed on Ayleth but no longer seeing her. As she stared at something a world away, her fist opened, its fingers splayed, releasing the breaths she had stolen from the Evanderians.

Then she doubled over and blew back several feet in the air, her white hair falling over her face. Her winds caught her before she fell, but her hands moved to her temples, gripping at the hair there, and she shrieked, "No, no, no! Get out, *get out of my head!*"

She dropped to the ground, a fall of some ten feet, and rolled. Her winds rushed wildly and uncontrollably around her, blasting grasses flat, shifting the bodies of the fallen and the broken stones. The witch held her head and screamed, "Zarc! No! No! No! Get out of my head!"

There was a horrible rush, then an instant of hush, as though some great being had drawn a breath, and all the winds temporarily stilled. In that moment, a fletched dart appeared in the witch's throat. Then a second, striking the back of her hand. Then a third, fixing in her cheek.

She screamed. A brutal gale burst from her core, and a tornado of pure magic sent her spinning up into the air. She continued screaming, but her voice was inaudible above the chaotic roar of the wind she had summoned in a last desperate attempt to escape. But the three darts did their work. The tornado stopped as abruptly as it had begun. Zilla d'Utrehd, deprived of her support, plummeted from the sky and struck with a thick, dull, bone-breaking crunch.

Ayleth lifted her head from the ground, turning with care so as not to move her hands too much. Twisting slowly in her position pinned under the horse, she looked up to the top of the rise. There stood a venatrix, her legs in a wide firing stance, her right arm supported by her left, and her scorpiona armed with yet another dart.

It was Hollis.

The shadows of the fringe forest were not yet deep when Gerard slipped in among them. The sun was beginning its descent, but there were still hours of daylight remaining to this interminable day.

Not that the time of day would make much difference when he stepped through the Great Barrier and entered the Witchwood, he reminded himself.

How much farther now? A mile or more, he guessed, though he couldn't say for certain. This was unfamiliar territory to him. The undergrowth was minimal this time of year, so although there were no trails to follow, his horse was able to navigate its own path well enough. He peered up through the branches, keeping an eye on the sun's progress, the best compass available to him as he tried to maintain a steady eastern course.

Something felt strange. Something in the air. His horse sensed it too, judging by the way its ears never stopped twitching and its skin never stopped shivering. He had not traveled more than a few lengths in among the trees before the feeling became almost overwhelming. Almost enough to make him turn back.

But he couldn't turn back. He'd made a vow. And the Goddess had shown him Her will. There was no going back, not anymore.

The horse tossed its head, then stopped and shook its

whole body so hard that it rattled the teeth in Gerard's skull. He held on until the shaking passed, then patted the beast's neck and murmured soothing nothings. Its ears flicked back to his voice. After a heavy sigh it continued, its pace reluctant but steady.

The trees . . . there was something off about the trees. Gerard frowned and pulled on the reins, stopping for a closer inspection of a nearby oak. A strange residue seemed to have grafted to the north side of the trunk. Something black that . . . glittered somehow. Like a fungus, it sprang out between the grooves of the bark, but it was no fungus. More like . . . faceted stone.

"Oblidite?" he whispered. But no. That couldn't be. Could it?

He rode on. The farther he went, the more prevalent the deposits of stone became. Every tree wore a strange coating. But there was something else, something he couldn't at first discern. He realized the truth only after he'd long since left the edge of the forest behind him.

The trees were all dead.

His horse balked and tossed its head, pulling at its bit so hard, it came close to pulling him right out of his saddle and down over its neck. Gerard swiftly took control, mastering both his mount and his own surging heart. He could not surrender to the terror threatening to rise up and choke him. This was only the fringe forest, after all. He hadn't yet reached the Great Barrier. How could he hope to cross over, to pass through the darkness of the Witchwood itself if he couldn't manage this stretch of the journey?

"Come on, then," he urged his horse. It responded to the firmness in his voice and moved forward again. Gerard turned in the saddle, looking up through the branches to check the position of the sun. But the forest's canopy, though bare of all foliage, was thicker than he expected. Very little light filtered through now, and the air was oddly thick. He shook his head and faced forward again, trusting pure instinct to guide him east. Instinct and the leading of the Goddess. He would reach Dulimurian. He had to.

His horse shied suddenly and squealed, springing to one side. Gerard made a grasp for its mane, but lost his seat and fell heavily to the ground, landing flat on his back. For a moment he lay where he'd fallen, stunned.

Then he gasped in a breath.

The stench of rot filled his nostrils and lungs.

He choked, gagged, rolled over, and heaved. He'd eaten nothing that day, so there was nothing to bring up, but his stomach jolted again and again. At last, pulling himself together, he sat up onto his knees. The dirt squelched with each movement he made. More rotten stink rose around him. Gagging again, he reached out and, using his fingers, pulled aside the topmost layer of old leaves and bracken and soil.

His hand hit rot. Foul, putrid rot.

Gerard stood up, his heart thudding against his breastbone. This was wrong. This was unnatural. This was . . .

"The Witchwood," he whispered. The name spat from his tongue, his breath moving the strangely thick air in swirls. Had he somehow passed through the Great Barrier and not realized it? No. No, surely that wasn't possible.

After all these years, had Fendrel's song spell fallen?

"GoddessHead have mercy," he whispered. "GoddessHeart have mercy. GoddessSoul have mercy."

His horse stood shivering not far away, watching him with a white, rolling eye. It was too afraid to run far, however, which was lucky for him, because his sword, his only weapon, was still strapped to the saddle.

Approaching with care, Gerard caught the beast's reins and then, pulling its head to him, rubbed its nose and murmured in its ear. He never would have brought an animal into the Witchwood, not on purpose. But it was a bit late now, and he could make better progress mounted than on foot.

"I'm sorry, fellow," he murmured. But he removed the sword and sheath from the saddle and strapped them to his back. If he was unseated again and his horse should bolt, he didn't want to be stranded without a weapon. He mounted and, using the north-facing deposits of oblidite as a guide, turned the horse's head east.

The air was hard to breathe. Little motes floated in the air before his face. Ash? Was there a fire? The sulfurous stink worsened as well, and Gerard could almost feel his lungs being coated with each breath he took.

A sound reached his ear. A sound he couldn't at first place. Like . . . like breathing. But not quite.

Something watched him.

Gerard turned in his saddle and peered back through the stricken trees. At first he saw nothing. Then, appearing through the thick air, shambling figures came. Two figures, both men.

He drew his horse up short. Better to face pursuers than to flee in this dark place. He waited, and soon enough, the two men stepped into the clear space behind him. They didn't look at Gerard. Not directly. Their gazes went over and around him, their eyes strangely glassy. Nevertheless he felt a strong sense of . . . *studying* emanating from their blank faces.

"Who are you?" he called out, his voice hard. The thick air moved in a whirl before his lips.

Neither man answered.

Were they shade-taken? They must be. Many possessed mortals had fled into the Witchwood over the years in their bid to escape the Evanderian slaughter. Gerard's hand moved for his sword, but he stopped himself. If he fought them, if he dealt them violent deaths, who could say where their souls would end up? Better if he could find a way out of this without resorting to violence.

"I mean you no harm," he said. "We need not be enemies. Be on your way, and I'll be on mine."

They didn't move. They didn't speak.

But their glazed, wandering eyes focused suddenly on him.

Gerard's heart hitched.

Movement and sound drew his attention. He turned to see two more figures step into the path in front of his horse. One man, one woman. They stood much closer than the other two, affording him a clearer view of their faces, their bodies.

He saw their death wounds. He realized what they were.

His horse shuddered, snorted, and tossed its head, reacting to the stench of death. Gerard gripped the reins hard and squeezed his legs around the horse's barrel, desperate to keep his seat. Taking a firm hand, he yanked the bit, pulling the beast's head around to the right. It spooked, sidestepped, and then sprang forward, eager for flight.

Three more figures loomed suddenly in front of them.

Three dead, twisted, pathetic figures. The horse skidded, nearly sitting back on its haunches. Squealing, it heaved upright, then reared, tearing at the air with sharp hooves.

With a wild yell, Gerard fell from the saddle and landed hard in the squelching dirt. For a moment the world went black. He rolled, just managing to avoid frenzied hooves. With another ear-splitting squeal, the horse tore away into the forest, vanishing into the underbrush. Just out of sight, it screamed once more, the sound cutting off abruptly.

Gerard pushed up onto his elbows. The dead closed in around him, moving slowly, as though the commands from their master came from a distance. Breathing hard, Gerard got to his feet. His head spun, his back ached, his limbs jumped with fear and adrenaline. He grabbed for the sword strapped to his back.

He didn't get it free before the first two charged.

I LIVED IN THOSE QUIET MOUNTAINS WITH STANIER *and Olena for two years, watching my inborn daughter grow. It was strange to me, a trained Evanderian, to observe her double soul and to recognize that both beings inside her body were of equal importance to the essence of her. Though the two spirits were distinct, they were only whole when together.*

I was different. I still feared the power inside me. Irimir—*my possessing parasite. I would never be the same as my two loves, my husband and my daughter. But over time, as I observed their interactions with their shades, I sometimes attempted similar interactions with mine. Rarely did I take up the Vocos pipes and spin the suppression songs, for Stanier did not like it and would have preferred to break the pipes if I would let him.*

Maybe someday, *I thought,* I won't fear my shade. Maybe someday I'll be like them.

But in the meantime, I loved them, and I lived with them and learned from them. My infant daughter was a miracle, a thing of such beauty and grace and wonder. She carried an Apparition like her father's, a shimmering star of a spirit that radiated out from her core in a gentle aura wherever she went.

I lived with them for two years. Two beautiful years.

Then the Order came to my rescue.

CHAPTER 15

TERRYN RODE AS IF THE HAUNTS THEMSELVES snapped at his heels. With his gaze fixed on the eastern horizon, he relentlessly spurred his horse onward. Hooves tore up the turf, and dark mane and tail whipped in the wind. The cold air biting at Terryn's face drew tears that streamed from the corners of his eyes.

And all the while, the vision burned in his head—the vision planted by Nilly du Bucheron and her shade: He saw Gerard fleeing through a dark forest, his face wreathed in terror. He saw his brother draw up short suddenly as a mounted figure appeared through the shadows in front of him. A deep hood shrouded the stranger's head, but a skeletal hand reached up and threw back that hood, revealing the face.

It was Terryn's face. But without a scar. Emaciated. A death's mask.

He knew exactly to whom that face belonged. Nilly had given him the vision for a reason. He had to believe it. So he must also believe he would make it in time. He must believe he was on the right track.

Overhead, Nisirdi flew, its mighty wings silently pulsing the air. They passed along a high ridge above a valley. Something drew Terryn's eye, and he looked down to see corpses littering the ground. Only a few . . . but Terryn's trained hunter's eye spotted signs that there had been more. He saw where the grass was flattened, saw where blood stained the ground.

But the dead had risen up and walked. Their footsteps led east. Toward the fringe forest.

Terryn bowed over his horse's neck, urging it faster, faster, as though he could will it into flight. But when at last he drew near to the fringe forest, he pulled his horse up short. As it stood with sides heaving and head bowed, grateful for the chance to catch its breath, Terryn slid from the saddle and proceeded on foot. His steps were quick at first but slowed before he reached the shadows.

He stared. His eyes flickered with shadow-light, but he didn't want to believe what they saw.

"*Nisirdi,*" he said, speaking in spirit, not aloud. "*Nisirdi, what is this?*"

The light-dragon landed beside him, folding its wings along its lithe body. It peered into the forest. A shudder rippled along their soul tether, straight to Terryn's heart.

The Haunts, Nisirdi said. *This is the air of the Haunts.*

Gerard caught the outstretched arm of the corpse closest to him and swung it hard into the second, knocking both off their feet. He staggered at the impact, caught his balance, and saw the other corpses lurch toward him, their glazed eyes fixed with purpose.

He turned and made a break through the trees. Heart pounding in time with his feet, he raced through shadows, ducking branches, pushing through low foliage. His hand reached for his sword, but he couldn't get it free while in motion.

A mounted figure appeared through the thick air as if from nowhere and loomed over Gerard like a hooded specter of death. The prince gasped, recoiling. In some part of his brain not completely dulled by fear, he realized it was his own horse before him, bleeding from a death wound in the neck. Its eyes were blank, filmed over, soulless.

The hooded figure looked down on Gerard from its perch in the saddle. A red hood, Gerard saw. Red as blood. Red as death. An Evanderian?

The figure lifted a hand and flicked the hood back over its shoulders. For a terrible moment, Gerard thought he saw Terryn's face gazing down at him. But then its mouth broke into a smile Gerard had never seen on Terryn's face.

"Well, well." A voice as deep and dark as a tomb rumbled in the air. "If it isn't the prophesied Golden Prince."

This couldn't be Terryn. It couldn't be. It was some

apparition, some manipulation of his mind. Gerard braced himself and drew his sword, holding it high between that spectral form and himself. "Corpsewitch," he growled. "I hoped I might meet you here."

The terrible smile only grew. Corpses moved in from each side, arms outstretched, mouths gaping. With a vicious cry, Gerard pivoted on his feet, swinging his weapon. The blade connected, cutting deeply into an exposed neck. He felt the impact, felt muscle give and bone break. The head tilted, fell, and rolled.

But the corpse didn't stop coming.

Gerard ducked and ran. He heard laughter ripple the air behind him, but he stopped his ears to the sound and ran on. Corpses moved in his peripheral vision, swarming in pursuit. One lurched in front of him, standing directly in his path.

Gerard raised his sword, took a lunging step, and plunged the blade straight into the dead man's heart. A burst of energy coursed along the steel, through the hilt, up his arms, and burst in his chest. He staggered back, eyes wide, and yanked his sword free. The corpse fell to the ground, its curse broken.

There wasn't time to celebrate. The dead closed in around him. Gerard's teeth bared in a grimace that was almost a grin. At least now he knew what he had to do.

Arms reached out to grab him, but he whirled, cut, slashed—and plunged his sword into another chest, breaking through bone to strike the heart. The corpse fell, dragging his sword down with it, but Gerard wrenched free. Hands clutched at his back, weight pushing him down, but he doubled up and flung his attacker off his shoulders. While it lay on its stomach, he skewered it through the back. He felt the burst of energy again as the curse broke.

Yanking his sword free, he went down on his knees and hacked the legs out from under another attacker. It didn't stop trying to reach him, but at least it was off its feet. This cleared a space for him, and Gerard sprang up and ran, putting some distance between himself and the swarm of dead.

Hoof beats reverberated through the ground. The dead horse blocked the path, the Corpsewitch still in its saddle. The horse reared, but this time not in panic. It couldn't feel panic anymore, or anything else beyond the will of its master.

Gerard saw a flash of horseshoes ready to smash his skull. He flung himself to the ground and rolled, just escaping those devastating blows. His brain churned wildly. He knew he could not bring down a living horse, not with a sword. But this beast was already dead. All he had to do was break the curse.

Setting his jaw, Gerard pulled himself upright, still ducking and dodging, the sword gripped firmly in both hands. He saw his moment—a moment that lasted less than a heartbeat.

He surged up, sword flashing, and drove the blade deep into the horse's chest. Another ripple of energy rolled down his arm, striking him in the heart. It was so powerful this time, it sent him flying right off his feet.

He hit a tree and collapsed as if boneless. His ears rang, and darkness closed in around his flashing vision. He blinked. His vision cleared, just a little. Just enough to see his sword lying several yards away, out of reach. He blinked again.

The horse lay unmoving on the ground, its curse broken. The other corpses surrounded him, swaying heavily, waiting. Though he looked, Gerard saw no sign of their master.

"Come on then," Gerard growled, dragging himself to his feet. He clenched his fists, knees bent, prepared for a fight. "Come on!"

The first corpse lunged, reaching for his throat. A second came just behind it, curled fingers groping for his eyes. Gerard went down, both corpses on top of him. He bucked his hips, writhing, trying to slither free. He struck out with both arms, clawing, punching. A third corpse piled on him, a fourth, a fifth. The stink of death filled his nostrils, filled every sense.

Then a wild instant of clarity came over him—

He was no longer on the ground, fighting for his life. He stood high above the world in the palm of a great stone hand. He winced, his eyes dazzled by the blue light blazing from the core of a crown. Through the pulsing, blinding glow, he saw the one wearing the crown, saw her face twisted in pain. Her hair burned away in blue sparks and embers, and her skin blackened where the crown gripped her brow. Her wide, wild eyes sought his, catching and holding his gaze.

He saw it all with perfect clarity, even as dead hands choked the life out of his body—

A flash of light. Many brilliant beams of pure white light.

The corpses stopped abruptly as though frozen. Holes smoked in each of their chests, burned straight through from back to front. They swayed. A stench of burning flesh filled the air. Then they collapsed, one after another, burying Gerard beneath them.

THEY COULDN'T LEAVE ME IN THE CLUTCHES OF THE *inborn, now could they?*

I was special. I was meant for a great destiny.

Only I could wear their crown. Only I could serve their great purpose.

So they came in force, up through the mountains, their shades called to high ascendancy, their scorpioni armed with poisons. And I . . .

I stood on the mountainside, the power of my shade mounting inside me, ready to be unleashed. And I looked down into the face of Domina d'Arcand. My mistress. My savior. The one who had taken me from nothing and remade me into something mighty.

I could have killed her with a single blast.

But I hesitated.

The poisoned dart struck me in the throat, and I fell from the rock on which I stood and rolled down the slope. I was unconscious, succumbed to paralysis long before my body came to a stop.

I woke hours later. Slowly. Painfully. My nostrils were filled with the mingled funk of medicines and poisons, and I looked around at the walls of a tent. A phasmator stood near. He saw that I was waking and bade me be still, to let the poisons work their way out of my system before I tried to move.

With a savage cry, I rolled off the bed on which they had placed me. Knocking aside the phasmator's reaching hands, I belly crawled out of the tent, fighting him for every inch. I pushed back the flap and gazed out to the world beyond, gazed up the mountainside, up those forested slopes.

I saw smoke rising in black coils to the sky.

CHAPTER 16

TERRYN'S ARMS THROBBED WITH THE AFTERSHOCK OF Arcane magic. His head spun, and sparks flashed on the edges of his vision, but he shook himself hard. Now was not the time to succumb to pain.

Unsteady on his feet, he rushed to Gerard's side, grabbed the topmost corpse by its shoulders, and with a grunt and a heave, rolled it away.

Gerard's pale face appeared to his view, scored by the ugly cuts the Warpwitch had given him last night.

"Terryn!" His voice choked through bloodless lips. "You're . . . but you're . . . Fendrel had you killed!"

"He tried to," Terryn growled, hauling the second dead body off his brother. He offered a hand, which Gerard took, and pulled him to his feet. Gerard appeared mostly unharmed, despite his gape-mouthed staring. Terryn took hold of his elbow and pulled. "Were there other corpses besides these?"

"Three. I stopped them. I think I saw the Corpsewitch as well."

"Haunts damn." Terryn wiped a hand down his face. How many corpses could the witch control at one time? He didn't want to stay to find out. "We've got to get you out of this place."

"No." Gerard yanked his arm out of Terryn's grasp, regarding him as though he still didn't believe what he saw, as though he spoke to a ghost. "I'm not going anywhere. If the witch is near, we've got to end him. Now."

"Don't be an idiot." It wasn't the right thing to say to a king, but in that moment, Terryn didn't care. His gaze swept beyond his brother's head and into the trees behind

him, shifting deftly from spirit to mortal vision and back
again. The dense atmosphere of *oblivis* was difficult to
penetrate even with shadow sight. "*Nisirdi, is there another
shade near?*"

The light-dragon streamed out of his head and
manifested in a sweep of sun-glittering wings at his side.
Yes, it said. *I can feel it. But . . . but . . .* The dragon took a
few paces, passing over the fallen corpses, its sinuous
neck outstretched and its eyes wide as it sought to
penetrate the gloom. Its powers were not like those of
Ayleth's Feral shade. Though it could detect spirit traces,
it could not discern how close those spirits were or how
ascendant in power. A rippling sensation of frustration
and unease flowed from the shining being.

Terryn took hold of Gerard's arm. "We've got to go,"
he said, pulling his brother after him as he retreated back
into the shadows through which he had just emerged.

"No, Terryn—" Gerard's voice cut off abruptly, and
his already gray face went white.

The Corpsewitch stood in their path. *Oblivis* swirled in
a thick cloud around him, but he took a step forward, out
of the deeper shadows of the trees and into a place where

a little light fell on his face, illuminating his features. He smiled. And that smile was familiar. Painfully familiar.

Terryn took a lurching step before he could stop himself. His hands rolled into fists, and magic swelled from his core, roiling hot through his arms and swelling in his palms. "Gillotin du Visgarus," he snarled.

"Well, well." The Corpsewitch stretched his stolen smile still further, flashing rotten teeth, which had once been white and strong. "I know you, don't I? You're the offspring of this host body. All grown up now, but somehow these eyes still recognize your face." He shook his head, chuckling softly. "My host cherished many a fond memory of you. But I've purged most of those over the years. They're of little use to me."

Terryn squared off in front of Gerard and raised his right arm. It was a habitual gesture, to take aim with his scorpiona. But it wasn't his scorpiona he now trained on the witch. A sphere of white light surrounded his closed fist, ready for him to open his fingers, to let it loose.

The Corpsewitch's eyes widened. "An Arcane," he said. "And ascendant too. Haunts damn, I wouldn't have expected as much from a castra boy like yourself." His own hands moved, blood streaming from cuts in his fingers as Anathema magic swelled. "You and the little mortal king make for a pretty pair of prizes. I'll carry your heads back to my queen and lay them at her feet in homage."

Everything in Terryn's nature told him to let loose the mounting blast before the witch could complete the spell he wove. The pressure in his hand increased, and power throbbed through his arm, his shoulder, his spirit, power that must be released.

But Nisirdi, standing beside him, swung its narrow head and gazed down at him. *My brother may yet be saved.*

Terryn cast the light-dragon a half glance. *"What? What do you mean?"*

My brother. The shade bound to that mortal's soul. We must set him free.

The strange words entered Terryn's head, and with them, Terryn's shadow vision suddenly flared, brighter, more intense than he'd ever before experienced. He stared at his father's tortured face, twisted into a malicious mask. But his shadow sight forced him deeper, looking behind the face to the spirit of Gillotin, which crouched within his host, a roiling mass of wrath and power and frustration, ugliness without form but more real than physical reality.

Deeper, Nisirdi urged, and Terryn's shadow sight quickened. He saw through the spirit of Gillotin down to the other spirit hidden in that stolen body.

To Terryn's mind, it took the form of a fiendish hound. Paper-thin skin only just contained the protruding bones. Every vein throbbed, every muscle seized, every tendon strained. Its head was long and would have been elegant save for the twisted snarl of its lips, the rabid spatter of foam, the blood staining and dripping from its unnaturally long teeth. It was monstrous.

It was suffering.

We must save him, Nisirdi urged. *This is what I was sent into this world to do.*

Terryn's vision snapped back to the mortal world. He stumbled back a step, staring across at his enemy. Gillotin grimaced at him and lifted the nearly complete curse he wove with his bleeding hands. In another instant, he would send it flying.

Terryn opened his fist.

The blast shot out from his core, a lance of pure, burning light. But he didn't aim it at Gillotin. He shifted his stance at the last instant and let the blast crash into a tree beside the witch. The trunk splintered, the tree groaned, its skeletal branches waving wildly.

Startled, Gillotin flung himself forward as the tree crashed down on him. The trunk was so large and the branches spread so wide that Gerard caught hold of Terryn and dragged him back so they wouldn't be crushed as well. The ground shuddered at the impact, knocking both Terryn and Gerard from their feet. They sprawled in the dirt, clouds of *oblivis* obscuring their vision.

"Terryn?" Gerard coughed on the thick air. His searching hand found Terryn's shoulder and gripped hard. "Terryn, are you all right?"

Terryn didn't try to answer. He pushed onto his feet, his shadow sight flickering wildly as he struggled to see through the poisonous clouds. Nisirdi stepped to his side. "*Did I kill him?*" Terryn asked.

I sense no death, the light-dragon answered, its song voice uncertain.

Terryn slipped a dart from its quiver. He needed to subdue the Corpsewitch quickly while he was still down. Somehow, he doubted Gillotin du Visgarus would be stopped by a fallen tree. He needed to deliver the paralysis, which would give him time to think up a plan, think of a way to separate the conjoined souls.

"What are you doing?" Gerard demanded behind him, but Terryn didn't answer. He pushed through the clouds, stepping carefully over and around the fallen crown of the tree. The broken branches were dark and dense, and the Corpsewitch might lie in that darkness, impaled and bleeding out. Or he might—

Nisirdi's voice rang like a bell: *Ware! Ware!*

Anathema magic flared red in Terryn's eyes. In the glare he saw Gillotin pinned under the heavy trunk, his legs broken, his torso twisted at a dreadful angle, his eyes wild with magic. Drawing power from the blood oozing from dozens of fresh wounds, he flung his still-active curse. Terryn threw up an arm as though to ward it off.

The curse struck, embedding into his flesh like a knife. A shout of pain burst from Terryn's mouth, and he tried to back away. But the Corpsewitch's compulsion took immediate effect. His own hand turned against him, tearing at his face. He was only just in time to catch hold of his wrist with his free hand, to stop the curse from making him rip his own eyes from their sockets.

But the curse went deeper still. Red threads of magic plunged down through his veins, rippling to his core where his and Nisirdi's spirits were anchored. The Anathema shade pulled at the wellspring of Arcane magic there, dragging power straight from Nisirdi's soul, pulling it back through Terryn's cursed arm. Terryn stared in horror as magic he had not summoned and could not control burned in his bones, glowed through his skin.

"Nisirdi! Help!"

His shade responded at once. With a sweep of blinding light, it lunged at the Corpsewitch where he lay pinned. A being of spirit, Nisirdi could not physically touch the witch. It dove instead at the witch's shade, which rose up to meet the dragon head-on. The two beings crashed together in an explosion of spirit storm. Terryn saw the light-dragon tear with razor claws at the rabid dog's flank, saw the slavering hound lunge at the dragon's elegant neck, brutal jaws snapping with bone-breaking force. Though the dragon was the greater spirit by far, it did not wish to hurt the hound, which gave its enemy the advantage.

Gillotin, pinned under the tree, grimaced at Terryn, his hands twisting to manipulate his spell. Terryn's arm responded, lifting his hand toward his face, palm open, fingers spread. He tried to force it down again, but light swirled in the center of his palm, aimed directly between his own eyes.

"*Nisirdi!*" he cried.

His shade, responding to his desperation, turned suddenly vicious. It grabbed the hound in both its front claws and sank long teeth into its spine, shaking it savagely. The hound screamed, spattering foam and blood from its gaping muzzle.

The curse's hold loosened. Just a little. Just enough that Terryn could angle his hand, and the blast of light shot over his shoulder into the forest behind him. Another of the wounded trees groaned, broke, crashed to the ground.

The Corpsewitch spat a vicious expletive and, clenching both bloody hands into fists, yanked on the spell threads he'd woven. The curse responded. Terryn's hand formed a fist and struck him in the jaw, knocking him off balance. Terryn went down on one knee, grimacing. His hand locked around his throat, squeezing, and as he choked for breath he felt the mounting magic pulled from inside him, burning his skin as it responded to the Corpsewitch's summons.

"You can't win, boy." Gillotin's voice was a hideous facsimile of that voice Terryn knew from his childhood. Despite himself, Terryn turned and looked into those dark eyes. Those eyes that once belonged to his father but now gleamed with the Corpsewitch's madness. "You can't win. The Queen has returned. A new age is upon us. This time her reign will have no end, and all the shade-taken of the world will know her for the goddess she is. Odile the incredible, the inevitable, the invincible."

The Corpsewitch wrenched at the curse again, and Terryn's whole body jerked in response. "Go on then. Let that magic of yours loose. It will kill you anyway if you hold on much longer."

Was this the end, then? All that he had fought for, all that he had believed, all that he had struggled and bled and wept and broken his spirit to accomplish—was it all come to nothing?

Gerard . . . Fendrel . . .

Ayleth . . .

"Give up, boy. You've already lost," Gillotin hissed. "Your Order is nothing. Your boy king is nothing. Your Goddess has forsaken you, while mine will ascend to her high throne, and—" His voice broke off in a shocked, sharp intake of breath. Blood poured out over his tongue, down his chin.

A figure stood over him where he lay trapped beneath the trunk of the tree, a figure braced with a sword in its hands, the blade sunk down through the witch's back, through his chest, and into the ground. Gillotin tried to turn his head, tried to look up into the face of his killer. His soul shuddered, and, in a blinding explosion of Anathema magic, burst from his body as it died.

Terryn wrenched his hand away from his throat and, screaming, let loose the accumulated magic in a beam pointed straight up into the sky. It poured out of him in pulsing waves of power that knocked him onto his back. He lay still, trying to catch his breath. His vision blackened. Unconsciousness beckoned.

Through the darkness and pain, he heard something—a rush of souls escaping their broken host body.

Terryn opened his eyes, opened his shadow sight. The tumultuous whorl of the Corpsewitch's spirit, bound to his shade, erupted before him in violence-induced power. "No," Terryn breathed. Then, in his mind, he screamed, *"Nisirdi, stop them!"*

His shade moved quicker than thought. Its wings scattering shards of radiance, the light-dragon whipped its long neck around and caught the writhing Anathema in its jaws. The shade momentarily resumed its hound shape, howling, snarling, terrified. Terryn's shadow sight struggled to make sense of the horror of those souls, but he thought he glimpsed Gillotin himself—not his father's shape, but someone he had never seen before, a hawk-nosed man with a bearded jaw and cruel eyes. Unbreakable spell threads stitched the man to the hound, joining them at their backs. The image of the man kicked, thrashed, and lost its shape entirely, becoming writhing spirit stuff.

The light-dragon held onto the shade, exerting all its

strength against the incredible propulsion. Its jaw slipped, but its claws caught a fresh grip. The shade's and witch's souls fought back for freedom, and Terryn felt Nisirdi's straining efforts as though they were his own.

Then the ripple in reality. The crack. The tearing.

As the Haunts loomed open to receive the unanchored souls, the horror of the void washed over Terryn as though he saw it for the first time. He'd never before faced the Haunts with a fully ascendant shade, with all his shadow senses heightened to such an extreme.

Nisirdi's grip on the shade hound slipped again. The hound roared and snapped at Nisirdi, tearing into the dragon's neck. A shudder shot through the soul tether into Terryn's heart.

"*Let go, Nisirdi!*" he shouted. "*Let the Haunts have him!*"

His shade's answer appeared in his head, soft but firm: *I'll not abandon my brother.*

Terryn pulled upright, grabbing at his throbbing right arm, which felt as though it had been half melted from its socket. But it was still hanging from his shoulder, solid and—physically, at least—whole. He braced himself before the horror of the Haunts, forcing his gaze away from that yawning eternity, closing his ears to the howls that bellowed up from its pit. Gillotin's spirit screamed, and both he and his shade lashed out at Nisirdi again and again, desperate to break free. Each blow radiated down the soul tether.

Somewhere far away, beyond the roar of the Haunts, beyond the reverberations of spiritual blows and the shrieks of the unanchored souls, Terryn thought he heard Gerard's voice crying out his name. But he couldn't think about that, couldn't answer. He snatched his Detrudos pipes from their sheath, uncertain what exactly he'd be able to do with them. Only death by fire could break those binding spell threads and separate Gillotin's soul from his shade, and that death was no longer possible.

But it didn't matter. He had to try. Something. Anything.

He began to play the Song of Separation. Just the melody itself, no variation. His fingers trembled as he picked out the notes, and his lungs struggled to maintain the difficult breath patterns. He'd always been skilled at spell songs, skilled at hearing the variations that would produce the necessary effect. But now his mind drew a blank, so he simply played the song again. And a third time, straight through, one note after the other with no flourishes or trills. He felt the inexorable draw of the Haunts and knew he was powerless against it.

Then his ears—or rather, not his ears, but those unnatural senses awakened by his shade—filled with a new sound. As he played the Song of Separation a fourth time, still without variation, a new line of melody wove in and around the notes as they poured from the pipe heads. No . . . not a melody. A harmony more complex than anything he could have created.

He looked up and saw Nisirdi with the hound clutched close to its shining breast. The shade's luminous eyes gazed down at Terryn, and from its mouth, from its center, the song poured forth. A song of pure spirit—not channeled through mortal instruments such as the one Terryn played. This was shade song performed in shade language, unadulterated. The song of the *Ildrir.*

Terryn watched in awe as the magic wove together— shining Arcane magic, light and song fused, now wrapped around Gillotin's soul and the soul of the Anathema shade. As Terryn played on, the binding soul threads began to snap. One by one, the tethers connecting the two souls came apart and faded away.

The Corpsewitch's soul flailed in despair as it felt itself coming apart. Nisirdi held onto the hound, but the human soul was left to clutch at those fading threads as the Haunts drew it in. Losing all shape of humanity, the mortal spirit streamed away, passed through the gate, and was lost.

Terryn gasped, dropping the Detrudos from his lips. "*You've done it, Nisirdi!*" he cried. "*You've done it, you've—*"

He broke off, letting out a wordless shout of surprise. For just as he spoke the words, his shade looked down at the spirit it held. It seemed to Terryn that the dragon bent its long muzzle and planted a kiss on the snarling hound's head. Then its claws relaxed, and the shade slipped free. With a last bellow and belch of horror, the Haunts swallowed the soul and shut.

The world quaked.

Terryn fell to his knees.

He stared at the ground, at the oozing soil between his fingers. One hand still clutched the polished bone pipes. He thought he heard Gerard's voice calling to him again, but he couldn't answer. It seemed too far away.

"*We lost it,*" he said. He felt Nisirdi's gaze upon him but couldn't lift his face to look at his shade. "*We lost the Anathema.*"

Why do you say that? A flutter of wings in the air, and then light filled his head as Nisirdi poured back inside him. *Why do you despair, mortal?*

"*I saw it.*" Terryn closed his eyes, breathing hard. His fingers tightened around the Detrudos. "*It slipped from your grasp. We were so close, but the Haunts won in the end. We couldn't save your brother.*"

The light in his head warmed, a humming sensation, a comfort. The great opal eyes hovered before Terryn's vision.

My brother has gone to the Haunts. But he is not lost. He is saved from the soul that enslaved him. What will happen next, none of us can say.

Terryn stared into those impossible eyes, his shade's voice echoing inside his head. How could this possibly be? The Haunts were . . . the end. The torment of eternity awaiting all damned souls. So he'd been taught, and so he'd always believed.

But what if the Haunts weren't the end at all? What if they were . . . a beginning?

"Terryn? Terryn, answer me!"

He blinked hard. A pair of hands gripped him by the shoulders. Slowly he looked up into a pale, blood-streaked face. Gerard knelt before him, his sword lying at his side, freshly stained with the witch's blighted blood. His eyes were desperate, confused. Without shade senses, he had seen none of the spiritual battle Terryn had just experienced.

"Can you hear me?" Gerard asked, his fingers tightening.

Terryn nodded. Then he gasped and, with a wordless grunt, caught his brother by the back of the head and pulled him into an embrace.

OLENA.

The Order of Saint Evander is merciful to inborn children. Animals don't matter, and adults . . . well, they deserve their damnation. So they are given the Gentle Death, and their shade-entwined souls are driven to the Haunts.

But not the children. They must be spared. Their spirits must be separated from their shades and sent on to the Goddess's Light.

Olena. Olena.

The Order of Saint Evander is merciful to inborn children. They don't damn them with the Gentle Death.

They save their souls.

CHAPTER 17

HOLLIS FELL TO HER KNEES BESIDE AYLETH, HER hands outstretched to touch her cheeks, to wipe back strands of loose hair. Ayleth had never seen her mistress's face so pale, so gray, her eyes like round pools sunk into shadowed hollows. "Ayleth? Ayleth, are you all right?" she demanded, her voice trembling.

A bitter question flashed through Ayleth's mind: Was Hollis's concern for her real? Or did she worry only for the weapon she had raised to bring down her great enemy?

Rather than try to answer, Ayleth simply lifted her hands in the iron mitts. Hollis caught her breath, horrified. She knew what pain the torturous device inflicted. With a curse, she leapt to her feet again and, springing over the dead horse, sprinted downhill several yards to where Fendrel lay. Was the Venator Dominus dead? Had the Windwitch succeeded in killing him when she stole the air from his lungs? Ayleth couldn't tell as she craned her neck, watching Hollis search the dominus's pouches.

At last, Hollis rose again and ran swiftly back up the hill. Ayleth saw the gleam of the brass key in her fingers, and she nearly wept at the sight. Taking care not to jostle Ayleth's hands unnecessarily, not to send her plunging back into that world of inescapable pain, Hollis inserted the key in the slot and twisted.

The mitts sprang open and fell to the ground. Ayleth stretched and flexed her tortured fingers, little caring for the tiny puncture wounds covering the backs of her hands. Those didn't matter, not now in this moment of sheer relief.

"Come on, my girl," Hollis said, kicking the mitts away. She moved around behind her former apprentice, crouching and slipping her hands under her shoulders.

"How are you alive?" Ayleth demanded, her voice emerging in a breathless whisper. "How did you escape? I thought they'd killed you after we left."

"Terryn du Balafre found me. Got me out."

Terryn.

The world around Ayleth ceased to exist. Just for a moment—a moment of pure, painless, fearless gladness. Terryn was alive. Alive! But of course, he couldn't be dead. Not without her seeing him again. Not without giving her a chance to look him in the eyes, to tell him . . . she didn't even know what. There were no words she wanted to say.

But he was alive. There was still time to think of the right words. There was still time.

Her thoughts broke off as her body exploded in pain. Not spirit pain such as the iron caused, but real, present, earthy mortal pain. "Stop, stop, stop!" she shouted, and Hollis, who had caught her under the arms and tried to pull her out from under the dead horse, let go at once.

Ayleth panted, staring hard up at the sky above. "I've broken a rib. Several ribs, I think. And maybe the leg as well."

Hollis cursed. She knew Ayleth's Feral shade should have protected her from such injuries. "I'll try to shift the horse," she said, moving to reposition herself. "I'll lift, and you slide free. Do you think you can?"

Ayleth lowered her eyebrows and set her jaw. "I'll manage," she said.

Hollis nodded, and on a count of three, heaved at the horse's dead weight. She had no shade strength to empower her, and her skinny arms didn't look as if they could lift much of anything. But there was unexpected might in Hollis's slight frame, and though her face reddened and the tendons of her neck stood out sharply, the pressure crushing Ayleth's leg to the ground eased away.

The horse had fallen on an incline. To pull free, Ayleth had to scoot upward. The iron shackles still ringing her wrists restricted both her range of movement and her strength, but she managed to twist and pull herself just enough to slide the leg free. Painful protests shot through her torso in response, but to her relief, she discovered her leg wasn't broken after all, merely numb from the pressure.

With sweat standing out on her brow, Hollis crouched beside Ayleth, her expert hands testing the leg, then moving to her ribcage and prodding carefully. "What did this to you?" she demanded.

"The Corpsewitch," Ayleth answered shortly and offered nothing more despite Hollis's sharp, questioning look. "Where is Terryn?" she demanded instead.

"He went after Gerard."

"Gerard?" The blood seemed to freeze in her veins.

Hollis's gaze moved to meet hers. "It was the Seer-taken child. She gave him a vision, something that drove him to escape Dunloch and enter the Witchwood on his own. We think he's trying to hunt down Dread Odile. Perhaps still trying to fulfill the *Seion-Ebathe*."

Ayleth stared at her mistress but didn't see her. Through her mind's eye flashed a memory—or not a memory but an image even more vivid, complete with sensations of sound, smell, touch. She saw herself standing in the palm of an upraised stone hand. She felt molten heat ringing her brow, searing her skin to the skull. She smelled her own flesh and hair burning. She saw Gerard approaching her, his face illuminated by strange blue light. Stars gleamed in the sky behind his head.

"I'm so sorry, Ayleth," he said, and swung his sword at her throat.

She blinked and was back in the present, sprawled on that stone-strewn slope, gazing into the face of her mother's murderer. She shook her head and struggled to get to her feet. "We have to find him. We have to stop him!" Blood pounded painfully back into her numbed leg, which nearly gave out under her weight.

"Easy, my girl, easy," Hollis protested. She caught Ayleth's elbows, offering assistance and support. "Terryn will find our young king, never fear. You've got your own hunt to follow."

Head swimming, knees weak, Ayleth leaned into Hollis's strong hands and fought to find her balance. But her mistress's words struck her ears, and she pulled away again. Her own hunt? The hunt for Dread Odile, she meant. Suddenly Hollis's presence no longer seemed a fortuitous blessing. She was, Ayleth remembered, another enemy. Another powerful force that sought to control her, that sought to use her for her own ends. Yet just now, Ayleth had believed that concern in Hollis's voice, had fallen again for the lie that was the mother-daughter bond she felt between them! She took a step back, jerking free of Hollis's grip on her arms.

And she saw Fendrel standing down below, his scorpiona aimed at the back of Hollis's head.

Moving on the impulse of instinct, Ayleth caught Hollis by the front of her jerkin and hauled her viciously to one side. The poisoned dart whirred through the air, just inches past her ear. Hollis staggered, caught her balance, and whirled on her heel.

Fendrel had already loaded again and now lifted his arm, taking aim. The dart's fletching was black. The Gentle Death.

With a savage cry, Ayleth jumped forward, planting herself between the Venator Dominus and her former mistress. Fendrel froze, his thumb poised over the firing mechanism. If he took the shot, if he missed his target, if he struck Ayleth instead . . . it was all over. Odile would win back her crown, and no one could stop her.

Still he hesitated with Ayleth in his sights. She watched his eyes, saw the battle waging just beyond those gray disks, in the world of his mind. The urge to give in to his instincts was strong, the urge to take her down.

"Fendrel, don't be a fool!" Hollis barked, looking out from behind Ayleth's shoulder.

"I was a fool to let you live." He shifted his footing, trying to get a clear shot at Hollis. Ayleth moved in sync with him, keeping herself firmly planted between him and her mistress. "Even now. After all these years, Hollis. You still make me weak. You still compromise everything I work for. I should have ended you before leaving Dunloch!"

"If you'd done that, Zilla d'Utrehd would have killed you by now," Hollis answered, her voice dry and bitter. "She's still alive, by the way. If you're itching to poison someone, I'd recommend you turn your weapon her direction. See her soul out of this world."

Fendrel growled deep in his throat. "One witch at a time."

"You Haunts-damned idiot of a man, you know I'm

no witch!"

"Maybe not. But you're a harborer of witches and a heretic. I have plenty of reason to—"

"Enough of this!" Ayleth cried. Her shackles clanked as she put up both hands, wishing she could throw herself at Fendrel and catch him by the throat. She felt Laranta moving inside her, climbing as far ascendant as she could, despite the iron. Her shade couldn't offer much strength, which was a shame, because Ayleth wanted very much to catch both Hollis and Fendrel by the hair on top of their heads and knock their skulls together.

Instead, she glared down at Fendrel. "You need every ally you can get if you hope to win this battle. Look at this!" She swept her hands, indicating the hillside, cratered with the witch's assault of stone. The other Evanderians were starting to stir and rise, but some of them would never move again. "The Windwitch nearly took us all out on her own. The Crimson Devils are strengthening by the minute, and we don't know how many of them are left. And what of Odile? If she's gaining strength as fast as her devils are, you are going to need every able-bodied fighter you can get."

Fendrel didn't look at her as she spoke. It was as though he couldn't bear to, couldn't bear to acknowledge her presence. But she knew he heard her. She saw the color drain from his face.

"I need people I can trust marching beside me," he said, addressing himself to Hollis.

"You can always trust me, Fendrel," Hollis answered, stepping out from behind Ayleth. When Ayleth tried to shift her position, to place herself between her mistress and that poison once more, Hollis caught her arm and firmly moved her aside. "You can always trust me to do what I know is right, no matter the cost."

They gazed at each other across the body of the dead horse. And Ayleth, shifting her gaze between them, realized both how strangely alike and how fearfully different these two souls were. It seemed they would be better enemies than lovers, and yet one could not deny the cord of connection that ran between them, binding them fast with an unbreakable bond. Ayleth half expected Fendrel to take his shot, to kill Hollis where she stood, just to free himself from her hold.

"Remember," Hollis said, her voice oddly gentle, "we

share a common goal. We *must* destroy Dread Odile. And we both know, Fendrel: this girl is our only hope. Whatever you may decide to do to me afterwards, for today at least, we must hunt together."

How badly he wanted to resist her words! How badly he wanted to squeeze the trigger! Ayleth could feel his longing, as though that stretched cord of connection had been plucked and now vibrated with music too complex for human understanding.

But he dropped his scorpiona and turned away.

Ayleth let out a huge breath. Only then did she let herself become aware of the other figures closing in around them—two Evanderians standing with their weapons raised, ready at a signal from their dominus to let their poisons fly. "Stand down," Fendrel said, and they too lowered their firing arms.

A figure slowly climbed the hill toward them, and Ayleth, her heart pounding in her throat, recognized Kephan. He had somehow survived his encounter with the Windwitch, no doubt protected by his own Feral shade's ascendant power. He made his way to the fallen witch, who lay succumbed to paralysis with Hollis's three darts still protruding from her body. In a few swift movements, Kephan knelt, plucked a Gentle Death from its sheath, and plunged it into the witch's neck.

Ayleth didn't watch him draw his Vocos pipes and play Zilla d'Utrehd's soul on to the Haunts. She didn't have access to her shadow sight anyway. Instead, she staggered down the hill beside Hollis. Looking around at their ranks, she saw that, aside from Kephan, only two other Evanderians had survived this battle. Counting Fendrel, Hollis, and herself, there were now six of them in total. Would they be enough?

"Dominus," Hollis called to Fendrel, who crouched beside the dead body of a venator, taking darts from his quivers and adding them to his own supply. He looked up, and Hollis indicated Ayleth's shackles. "Give me the key to these."

The Venator Dominus did not respond. He merely blinked. Then he finished harvesting the dead man's weapons and closed his eyes before standing. He turned away from Hollis without another word or look.

"Haunts damn," Hollis growled. "He really means to keep you prisoner."

Ayleth shrugged. As long as he didn't try to put the iron mitts back on her hands, she wouldn't complain. Not yet, anyway. But Hollis looked up at her, her expression wracked with guilt. "I'm so sorry, my girl," she said, and extended one arm as though to draw Ayleth into an embrace.

Ayleth stepped back several paces. She shook her head, her loose hair flying. "Don't think anything has changed between us," she said, her voice harsh and low. "I am still your weapon. You are still the murderer of my family. Our goals are temporarily aligned. Nothing more. Nothing less."

With that, she turned her back on Hollis to gaze upon the ruins of Cró Ular, and beyond to the blasted landscape where the fringe forest had once stood and the dark expanse of the Witchwood still lay in wait.

Years ago, the statue stood twelve feet tall, carved of marble rather than oblidite. One of the queen's devoted worshippers had crafted it in her honor and placed it here beside the road to mark the way to Dulimurian. It depicted Odile in the attitude of a loving mother, kneeling with hands outstretched to receive and shelter the shade-taken of the world. A weary traveler on his way to the Queen's City might stop a while at the statue's base and receive balm for the soul by gazing upon the serene countenance of the New Goddess.

The Witchwood had eaten away at the pedestal so that the whole statue listed dangerously to one side. Vines had crawled up the graceful limbs and wrapped so tightly around the statue's neck that its head had broken off and fallen. Now it lay several yards off to one side, half sunk into the muck. Only one eye was still visible, gazing mildly up at its own headless body.

Inren watched Odile approach the statue's pedestal. It was such a strange juxtaposition—that massive sculpture of pure stone depicting the New Goddess in her most idealized form, each limb rounded and muscular, her pose simultaneously gracious and commanding . . . and the goddess herself, this broken and repaired thing, cracked at every seam, only just held together by binding magic that refused to let her suffering body die. Their progress into the *oblivis*-infused atmosphere of the wood had done much to heal Odile, or rather it had augmented the magic by which she sustained herself, strengthening the curse threads and bindings. But would she ever be that beautiful, majestic being again?

Could the Kingdom of the New Goddess be restored?

Inren's gaze pulled almost against its will to the statue's head. That one eye, though half lidded and gentle, seemed somehow mocking. With a shudder, Inren looked instead at Odile. But her queen's living face was even harder to read than the stone. She could not fathom her thoughts or feelings, though she thought perhaps Odile's eyes focused a little too intently on the statue's severed neck and the marks where the vines had wrapped.

The vines were no more. Inren noted this with a shudder. The whole Witchwood was eerily stripped of their thick, draping, tentacle-like curtains. They had retreated from Odile, but somehow Inren knew they weren't gone for good. The Witchwood was biding its time. Waiting for the right moment . . .

She could only hope she'd be swift enough to *evanesce* her goddess to safety before it caught and tore her apart.

Odile turned suddenly and continued down the road

without a word or a look for her trailing lieutenant. With the vines retreated, more of the landscape was visible between the wounded trees. Inren caught glimpses of ruins—towns and temples the Witchwood had swallowed during its swift progress across the land. All were corroded, rotten, covered in layers of *oblivis* like dust. It broke Inren's heart to remember the once beautiful and bountiful land surrounding Dulimurian, cultivated over the two hundred years of Odile's rule. Communities, temples, centers of learning, villages—all made up of shade-taken denizens united in worship of their New Goddess protector.

It was hard to imagine those memories ever becoming reality again. The Witchwood was too great and too terrible.

The road called back to life by Odile's summoning hand pointed straight through the trees. For at least six miles they had progressed without incident. But now, as they left the beheaded statue behind, Inren looked ahead and saw the road disappear. It ran smoothly to a broad, open field covered in a thick layer of *oblivis*, and there it simply sank into the soil and vanished.

Odile and Inren walked to the edge of the visible road and stood gazing across that field. The trees on its edges were tall; their branches still arched over the clear space, blocking out most of the sky overhead. Still, it was strange to see such a broad expanse with no trees growing at all.

"There." Inren pointed to the far side of the field. "There, I see the road again." She took a step, intending to cross the open stretch swiftly.

Before her foot landed, Odile caught her by the upper arm with a grip like stone. When Inren fell back again, glancing sideways at her goddess, Odile knelt and plucked a handful of oblidite from the paving stone at her feet as easily as she might scoop a handful of wet sand. It was soft and malleable in her fingers, and she formed it into a rough stone, which hardened at her command. Drawing back her arm, she hurled that stone with all her might. It arced through the air, disrupting motes of *oblivis* in its flight, then fell into the middle of the field.

It plopped and vanished. The smooth layer of *oblivis* rippled and broke, revealing greasy black water. A waft of stink rose in the air, and the air shimmered, hazy and putrid.

A lake of poison.

Inren felt the blood drain from her face. Uttering a curse, she drew back several paces. But Odile only smiled and stretched out both hands. Instantly, the shadow-being in her core sent long fingers out from her body, down into the water.

The lake began to roil and churn. More of the water became visible as *oblivis* sank beneath its surface. Things moved, black shapes in the darkness. Then, to Inren's gasping horror, heads rose up, one after another. Black, dripping things.

The shades contained within these forms were fully ascendant but fully debased. The air of the Witchwood had warped their host bodies into desiccated husks barely held together by bits of bone and sinew. Only the magic teeming through them kept those bodies alive.

Inren summoned her courage and leaped forward, placing herself between Odile and those fiends. She felt for the stones in her pocket, prepared to plant one, prepared to fight. One after another she would drag each monster to the Haunts, leaving them there where they belonged! She would—

Odile's restraining hand landed on her arm. Inren looked back to behold her queen's stern smile. "Don't be afraid, my dear," Odile said, her voice a rough whisper in her newly repaired throat.

The poison-dripping things swam toward the shore, their jutting spines cutting through the water, their blazing eyes like pinpoints in their skull-like heads. The nearest ones held their heads higher, exposing cages of sharp teeth. But Odile stood at the lake's edge, her hands outstretched. The many fingers of her shade shot out from inside her, plunging into each of those creatures. It found the *oblivis* in their lungs, in their blood, and took control.

The monsters, a dozen of them at least, crawled onto the shore of the lake. Inren's stomach churned at the sight. Most of them were beasts, but some had been human once. They all threw themselves at Odile's feet, groveling, worshipping.

"Go forth, my children," Odile said, speaking the words out loud, though Inren felt the force of her command ripple through the magic threads that connected her to each creature. "Go forth into this forest and summon all my servants. All those who are yet loyal to me."

They raised their heads, jaws dropping open. Hideous ululating cries filled the air, a hymn of praise to their dark goddess. Then they turned and sped away like rats scattering in sudden lantern light, eager to carry out Odile's will.

Once again, Inren and the goddess stood alone on the lake's edge. Inren's fingers gripped the stone in her pocket so hard, it cut into her skin. But Odile, her expression as unreadable as ever, walked to the lake's edge and, lifting her tattered skirts, stepped into the water. It rose to her knees almost at once, lapping and hungry, the poisons eating away at her skin.

The shade in her soul reached again, this time stretching farther than before, and plunged through the water, sinking down to the lake's bed. A rumble of magic shook the ground, and Inren stumbled and nearly fell. She watched wide-eyed as the waters churned and the Witchwood groaned and strained, struggling to resist this surging power.

Odile's jaw clenched. The tendons of her shattered throat stood out beneath her pale skin. A scream broke through her teeth as the shade inside her shuddered and redoubled its magic flow.

Shining stones of oblidite covered in slime and ooze rose from the water in answer to Odile's call until the road formed a perfect arch over the lake. With a final groan, it locked into place. Although the water beneath it continued to roil and the Witchwood itself growled its frustration, Inren knew that span would not be brought down again. Not so long as Odile lived.

The goddess climbed out of the lake. Her skin was scalded from the knees down, but she didn't seem to notice. Without a glance Inren's way, she set out across the bridge, her gaze fixed east to where Dulimurian lay in ruins.

To where Oromor awaited her coming.

Inren bit out a curse. Then she hastened after her goddess, her heart full of desperate prayers she dared not utter out loud.

ARE YOU QUITE CERTAIN, ODILE?" DOMINA D'ARCAND said to me. *"It has been only five years, after all."*

Five years since my re-indoctrination. Five years since I underwent purging and testing and cleansing and renewal. Five years since I reentered the Order and reaffirmed myself as a daughter of Evander, a servant of the Goddess.

"I am ready," I told my domina. My conviction was unwavering. "Take me to the Council of Agla."

D'Arcand acquiesced at last, and we made the journey to Roihm. There, before the Grand Vanderian and all the assembled council, I presented myself—even as I had done thirteen years ago. But then I was a mere child, full of power and passion.

Now I was a venatrix. I had seen. I had done. I had become.

The ardor glowing in my breast belonged to no one but me. I had the will to master any power—even the power of the Eitr Crown.

"Give it to me," I told the Grand Vanderian, "and I will do all that you ever dreamed and more."

No one could doubt my sincerity. And their longing was great. I understood now, as I had not when I was that young girl of twenty. I understood all they had done to protect this world from the powers of the Haunts. I understood the weight of their deeds which crushed their souls. For those deeds were my own, and my soul bore the same cruel weight.

But if I could wear the crown—if I could master its shade— then I could offer salvation where they offered only death.

"Odile, Venatrix di Mauvalis," the Grand Vanderian said, "you have more than proven your devotion to the cause of Evander over the years. Now, prove it one more time. Master the Eitr Crown."

So saying, she motioned with one withered hand, and the crown was brought to me, carried on a litter supported by four strong venators. It pulsed with light and life, the blue metal writhing and liquid and yet somehow contained in that rigid form. I gazed at it unblinking.

And I felt the spirit inside gazing back.

CHAPTER 18

GERARD HELPED TERRYN DRAG THE CORPSEWITCH out from under the fallen tree. The moist soil squelched beneath their feet, and their burden left a long black bloodstain trailing in its wake. Once the body was free of the broken branches, Terryn rolled it over. The head lolled; the empty eyes stared up at the sky.

Terryn grimaced. The death wound was ugly, exposing swiftly rotting flesh. Gerard's sword had pierced the witch straight through the back into the heart and out through the ribcage. No matter how he scraped and polished, the once bright blade would never be fully cleansed of the shadow-blight stain.

Aware of Gerard's intent gaze, Terryn took care not to meet his eye. Instead, he studied the face of the dead witch. His father's features, twisted in pain. The eyes, even in death, retained their startled expression. The mouth sagged, and blood trickled over the curled-back lips and rotten teeth.

"Terryn," Gerard said with what sounded like understanding in his voice. He must have recognized the Corpsewitch's stolen face; he must have guessed to whom this body once belonged.

Terryn refused to look up. His hand trembling, he reached out and tried to close those staring eyes, to smooth those pain-warped features. But no matter what he did, he couldn't make the face belong to his father again.

Sitting back on his heels, he drew a long breath and gazed dully into the shadows of the Witchwood, into the churning atmosphere of *oblivis,* thick with poison. Somehow he'd always believed that if the Goddess granted him the opportunity to kill Gillotin du Visgarus, to avenge his possessed father, it would somehow purge his heart of this pain. But he was wrong. Gillotin was dead, his soul damned.

Yet the devastation of an orphaned boy remained.

For some moments Terryn sat there, kneeling in the muck, insensible to the world around him. Then the pulse in his ears slowly faded and he heard a rich, solemn voice speaking, no, *singing* a prayer:

"May the Mother receive you, who hath called you, and may the heavenly spirits conduct you to the Gates of Light. GoddessHead have mercy. GoddessHeart have mercy. GoddessSoul have mercy."

The words struck him, reverberating through his spirit down to his core—the very core where his soul and his shade's anchored together in his mortal flesh. Terryn became aware suddenly of white light all around him, encompassing him. It was a light that had been there all along, only his eyes had been unable to discern it. His vision flared now, not with shadow sight, but with something more. Something deeper, clearer, keener. And his ears heard, underscoring the prayerful words sung in mortal language, a profound and indescribable song being sung in another language entirely.

He blinked. The vision passed. The light and the song faded away, and he was once again in the murk and muck of the Witchwood. Gerard knelt across from him and, invisible but present, Nisirdi crouched by his side on powerful haunches, its long forelegs elegantly placed and its sweeping wings neatly folded. A hum of comfort rippled along the soul tether he shared with his shade . . . and, to his surprise, along another tether he'd never before noticed. The tether that connected him to his brother. Heart to heart. Soul to soul.

Gerard's prayer ended. He looked up and met Terryn's gaze. Without a word passing between them, they stood and stepped away from the Corpsewitch's final host. Already the Witchwood was creeping in to claim it, the soil itself dragging the body slowly down to be digested. Remembering what had happened to Venator Nane's remains, Terryn watched for signs of the creeping parasitic vines but saw none.

He and Gerard turned their backs to the corpse and moved on. Gerard turned to the east and took several resolute steps before Terryn caught him by the arm.

"Wait," he said.

Gerard gave Terryn a look and shrugged his arm free. "We can't delay," he said. "We've got to keep moving. We don't know how much time we have, and—"

"I've got to take you back," Terryn said. "To Dunloch. Now."

Gerard said nothing at first. His eyelids quivered slightly as he stared back at Terryn. "I'm not going back," he answered at last.

"You are not prepared for all that lies ahead." Terryn waved a hand at the wounded trees, at the horror of tortured branches and struggling half-life fighting against the surrounding decay. "This is nothing. This is a stroll in the park compared to what lies ahead. You are not prepared for the Witchwood, believe me."

"And you are?" With a snort, Gerard turned and started off again, his thin shoes pressing into the soft soil, each footprint behind him filling with ooze. "Admit it, Terryn," he called back over his shoulder. "You would have died just now if not for me."

With a growl in his throat, Terryn hastened after his brother. He tried again to catch him by the arm, but

Gerard dodged him easily. "I'm not helpless, you know. Not here. Out there in . . . in *our* world, I have no weapons to fight the shade-taken. But here? Here I can deal out death, and it doesn't matter. There are no habitable host bodies to be possessed by whatever shades I violently free. And my own body, they tell me, cannot be possessed. So unless that's another lie . . ."

"It's not a lie," Terryn answered, reluctantly honest. "You're an untorn. You cannot be shade-taken."

"Then there you have it." Gerard shrugged and kept on walking. "I may not have your powers, Terryn, but there's nothing to stop me from using whatever deadly force is at my disposal. As I proved just now."

Gerard hadn't seen the battle that took place following his too easy slaying of the Corpsewitch. He hadn't seen how the spirits inside shot free, how the Haunts opened to claim them, how Terryn and Nisirdi had fought to prevent them from escaping. All of that harrowing experience had passed before his blind mortal eyes in a handful of breaths. But attempting to explain to him things he couldn't begin to understand would be useless.

Terryn shook his head and said instead, "You might

not risk your soul, Gerard, but you do risk your life. There are dangers here beyond anything you can imagine. You are king now. Your people need you. Perrinion won't survive whatever comes next without a sovereign to lead."

"I am no king."

Terryn blinked, taken aback by the vehemence in Gerard's voice. He stared after his brother for several paces before redoubling his speed and catching up to him. Matching his stride to Gerard's, he remained silent for the moment, unable to think what he could say.

Gerard lifted his heavy head, peering sideways at Terryn from under his brows. "My father took his throne under false pretenses. He committed blasphemy, claiming the Goddess willed his ascension to power and using Her name to fuel his rise."

"The du Glaive lineage—"

"Doesn't matter. It doesn't matter if my grandfather ruled Perrinion from exile, or if my great, great grandfathers once sat upon the throne. My father's right to rule stems solely from his prophetic claims. Nothing more, nothing less." Gerard drew a long breath through his nostrils, his lip curling as though he inhaled a stench more putrid than the rotten air of the Witchwood. "I will not sit on a charlatan's throne."

They progressed several more paces before Terryn reached out, caught Gerard by the shoulder, and whirled him to face him. Looming over Gerard by several inches, he glared down into his face, eyes flashing with anger. Nisirdi, responding to the flare of Terryn's emotion, stepped up behind him, wings spread as though preparing for an attack. Gerard, unaware of the light-dragon's presence, did not flinch. He met Terryn's gaze without blinking, his expression strangely calm.

"What then?" Terryn demanded, gritting the words between his teeth. "What then, Gerard? Will you let Perrinion fall into chaos and civil war? Even now, with Dread Odile on the verge of reclaiming her crown, her power?"

"Odile will reclaim nothing."

The confidence in Gerard's voice startled Terryn. He stepped back, releasing his grip on his brother's shoulder. There was something unsettling in Gerard's face, something . . . something certain. And terrible. "What do you know?" Terryn asked, half afraid to hear the answer.

Gerard turned his head to the side, looking east into the dense gloom of the wood. The *oblivis* was thicker than ever, obscuring all sight beyond ten paces, but Gerard's gaze seemed to penetrate for miles. "The Seer girl," he said at last, his voice a whisper. "The inborn child."

"Nilly du Bucheron?" Terryn blinked, surprised.

Gerard nodded. "She was there. In Dunloch last night. This morning she found me and gave me a . . . a sight." He glanced at Terryn, not quite able to hold his gaze. "I saw the Witch Queen die. And I was there. I saw how it will happen. Odile will never reclaim the Eitr Crown."

Terryn narrowed his eyes, studying his brother's face. There was no triumph in his expression, nor any hope. "What are you not saying, Gerard?"

The muscles in Gerard's face tightened, the lines around his mouth deepening. He didn't speak.

Terryn cursed softly. Whatever it was that Nilly had shown him, it wasn't good. Dread Odile's defeat would come at a cost. Perhaps Gerard had seen his own death. Or . . . or possibly Terryn's. That would explain his unwillingness to answer. A thrill of trepidation rippled through Terryn's soul at this thought. But it passed, leaving behind a strange calm. He had trained all his life, preparing himself for death and for the damnation likely to follow. Only now, connected to Nisirdi as he was, he no longer feared damnation. Even if his soul was taken to the Haunts, the Haunts were not an ending. His eternity was not a foregone conclusion. There was still hope beyond death, and with that hope, he could face the prospect of death without flinching.

"Gerard," he began, "I need you to—"

"No, Terryn." Gerard met his gaze at last, his eyes sharp and bright with resolve. "You need to listen. I *must* do this. I have no choice. What the girl showed me . . . that is my path, my destiny. I knew it the moment I saw it. I am meant to be there. I am meant to see Dread Odile's power broken once and for all. I am meant to prevent the Eitr Crown from enslaving our people. It doesn't matter what happens to me, to you, to any of us. I have to see this through. *I* must do it, Terryn."

For an instant, Terryn saw Guardin's face before him, the desperate face of the hero king who was no hero at all. It was Guardin's despair speaking through his son's mouth, Guardin's unatoned sin shining through Gerard's eyes.

Terryn's stomach twisted in a sickening knot. He had not seen the Witch Queen either beheaded or restored. He still struggled to believe that she really could be alive, that she really could be returned to this world, threatening all that had been built in her absence over these last twenty years. But as Gerard spoke now, bizarre though his words might be, his very tone convinced Terryn of the grim truth.

Still, he had one weapon remaining. One weapon he was loath to use, and yet . . .

"What about your wife?"

The silence that followed was like the void after the blade falls, the scream is cut short, and the ring of the axe's edge on stone fades away. Gerard's face lost all color as he stared at Terryn.

"You say nothing matters," Terryn persisted. "What about Cerine?"

Sweeping a hand down his face, Gerard wrenched away until Terryn saw only his profile. He drew several long, careful breaths, and when he spoke again, his voice was perfectly controlled. "Cerine knew. All along, she knew I was no Golden Prince, no divine promise. She knew the prophecy was false and its supposed fulfillment was false as well. And now, after everything . . . she won't bear looking at me."

"Gerard, that couldn't be further from the—"

"No, Terryn. No. Don't say anything more. It's like I just said: It doesn't matter. Nothing matters. Only ending Odile. No one will be safe, Cerine included, if the crown is reclaimed. Fendrel can't do it. He couldn't before; he can't now. And Ayleth . . ."

Terryn's heart went stone-cold and dropped in his chest. "What about Ayleth?" he said, his voice sharp and quick.

Gerard pressed his lips together and shook his head slowly. "I know what I saw. What the Seer showed me. It will come to pass. I must be there."

And Ayleth too. Gerard didn't have to say it; Terryn felt the truth in the silence of that unfinished sentence. Ayleth would be there at the end. As Fendrel's weapon or as her own dangerous self, he couldn't guess. But she would be there.

Which meant he had to be as well.

Terryn stood there in that thick, poisonous air, gazing at his brother. His lord. His king. Sighing heavily, he took three steps closer to his brother and clapped a hand on Gerard's shoulder. "Come on, then."

Gerard raised an eyebrow at him. "Where?"

"If you're going to make it to Dulimurian in time to fulfill any visions, we'd better get moving."

I KNELT FOR THE GRAND VANDERIAN TO PLACE THE *crown upon my head. As though I were a queen claiming my kingdom, not a warrior about to go into battle. The whole of the assembly seemed to be holding its breath as the cold metal came in contact with my brow.*

Then my world exploded in black fire.

I had long ago learned to manipulate and control oblivis *using the power of my possessing shade. But this . . . this was something else entirely. This was* oblivis, *not as an element, but as a living entity in its own right, full of creative and destructive forces always at war with one another. Pure, living chaos, like the whole of the Haunts itself made manifest in my head.*

And in the center of that chaos—the Presence.

It looked upon me and laughed. Its voice was nothing like a mortal voice, but I understood it better than I understood mortal language. I understood its mockery, its mirth. Its hatred. It had been bound in this eitr *prison for centuries now, and though time means little enough to beings such as it, it began to grow impatient.*

I felt its desire. It wanted a host it could use, could turn to its own dire purpose. Eitr *is inert, immobile. The Presence longed for a chance to work its will through a mortal host again.*

You, *it said in its language that was no language.* **You are of the blood. You can survive me.**

It was surprised and delighted and hungry all at once.

My mind reeled under that voice, and I felt the firm footing of sanity slip away beneath my feet, the yawning gulf of madness open wide to receive me. If I fell, I would be lost. This Presence would rip my soul from its anchor and cast it out from my body, taking full possession. I felt the threads that bound me to my mortal frame straining, thinning, breaking.

But I wasn't about to give up so easily.

"Irimir!" I screamed.

As a venatrix of Evander, I ought not to know the name of my possessing shade. But I was no venatrix. Not anymore. So I grabbed hold of that name, and I grabbed hold of my shade, and I dragged it up and flung it before me as a shield against the profound assault of darkness. Irimir manifested in the form of a thundercloud, black and flashing with magic.

The Presence drew back, startled. In that moment, I saw how like the two of them were—like mirror images, opposite and equal.

I braced myself and, channeling Irimir's power, I lashed out at the Presence. "Tell me your name, Dark One!" I cried.

It resisted. It fought. Oblivis *clashed with* oblivis *in a storm of pure rage. But whatever rage the Presence felt, mine was more than match for it. My eyes saw only red flames. My ears heard only a child's screams. My skin felt only burning, burning.*

My soul cried out for vengeance.

The Presence roared in terror and pain as the power I channeled at it dug deep into its essence, clutching down to its core. The two shades became inseparable, and the wildness of the oblivis *storm whirled into a maelstrom inside my head that should have killed me in an instant. But I withstood it. I, the last of Mauval's kin, survived the onslaught according to my destiny.*

"Tell me your name!" I cried.

And this time, the Presence responded: **Oromor.**

With that, it bowed to me, relinquishing control. The magic and the might of the Eitr Crown was mine.

CHAPTER 19

FENDREL'S COMPANY OF SIX RODE THROUGH A FOREST OF petrified oblidite. Each tree was perfect—every twig and curl of bark, every lingering autumnal leaf, all intact. All frozen. All black and multifaceted and glittering in the sunlight.

Hollis recognized the signs at once. This was the work of Dread Odile. The Witch Queen had entered the wood and breathed in the atmosphere of *oblivis,* feeding her shade, feeding her magic. She would soon be glutted on power.

Twenty years, she had lain headless upon the stone slab. Twenty years, she had suffered, broken and defeated. If mere hours later she was already strong enough to blast this entire forest, what would she be by the time they caught up with her?

If she regained her crown, she would be unstoppable.

Hollis turned her gaze from the trees and focused instead on Ayleth, who rode just ahead of her in the procession. The girl sat very straight in the saddle, her shoulders back, and her head high. Pretending not to feel the pain of the iron shackles binding her wrists.

Never had Hollis encountered a soul more courageous, a heart more ready and willing. And she did not doubt the girl's battle training, which she herself had honed over the years to blade-like sharpness.

But Ayleth carried nothing more than a Feral shade. Even with all her powers called up to full ascendancy, how could she hope to fight an Elemental such as Odile wielded? She may be the only means to kill Odile and break the curse, but that didn't mean she actually had the strength to do the deed.

Well . . . Goddess help them, they would just have to find out.

Hollis realized suddenly that Fendrel rode beside her. She glanced sideways at the Dominus but wouldn't let herself look at him straight on, despite her curiosity. In the past twenty years, she had caught only fleeting glimpses of him during her yearly visits to the castra. He never spoke to her during those times, and she never sought him out. They were like strangers. Less than strangers. How much had he changed? Her brief stolen glances saw few alterations on the surface. Some gray strands twining through his tight golden braids. A few lines around his steel-hard eyes. His mouth was a little grimmer, his jaw a little firmer.

The greatest change lay in his soul. Her shadow senses didn't need to reach far to feel the encroaching blight of his shade inside him. Those three iron spikes he wore on his left bracer were testimony to his struggles. He would not be able to hold his shade at bay much longer. Not with song spells. Not even with iron.

Hollis focused between her horse's ears. It was strange to ride beside Fendrel now, even as she had ridden beside him all those years ago. Those years of campaigning, of struggle and triumph. But then he was a hero in her mind, a legend sprung to life before her very eyes.

She had loved him—with romantic love, yes, but also with a love much stronger. He had inspired loyalty in her heart. Passion.

She glanced his way again, noticing how his gaze rested on Ayleth. There was torment in his eye, such a conglomerate of emotions. She would be afraid to use her shade to pry into his mind. The fire in his soul might slay her the moment she crossed the threshold.

"Would you have killed her, Fendrel?" she asked suddenly. He didn't start at the sound of her voice. Perhaps he had been aware of her scrutiny all the while. "Would you truly have killed our last hope to end Odile's life in this world?" she continued when he did not answer right away. "All for the sake of your lie?"

He drew in his lips, pressing them into a hard line. Then he said only, "Yes."

Hollis wanted to curse him. To hurt him. But what was the point? She couldn't actually cause him more suffering. Only hours ago he'd seen the last of his jealously guarded honor crushed to dust, leaving him with nothing but an empty shell.

She swallowed back her curses and instead, in a quiet, curious voice, asked, "Why didn't you, the moment you recognized her, take the girl down to the vault, put a knife in her hand, and have her end all of this? It could have been done in a moment."

Fendrel's jaw hardened. "The risk was too great," he said. "She may just as easily have awakened the witch as killed her."

Hollis looked at him, his excuse ringing false in her ears. She knew the truth well enough: He simply did not want *his* solution—the solution he had given *everything* to bring about—to be insufficient. After all these years, he had convinced himself that his lie was the right truth for this world. The only truth. Better that Dread Odile go on being suppressed under his curse than that she actually die. Because he was Fendrel du Glaive. He could not be wrong.

They continued in silence through the petrified forest, surrounded by red hoods as they rode for Dulìmurian. Just as they had marched to face Odile twenty years ago.

Only then, they'd had two hundred venators at their backs, armed with the *atacara.*

At length, Hollis asked, "Why didn't you simply kill her? She was at your mercy. You could have ended her life many times over. Why keep her alive? Why go through the bother of summoning the castra, of the tear test, of everything?"

Here, at last, Fendrel turned his head and looked at her. His iron gaze met and held hers fast. "For you," he said. As though it were the most obvious answer in the world.

Hollis gaped at him.

"She was yours. Your apprentice, your protégée. I thought you must have cared for her. I thought . . ." He shook his head and faced forward again. "I thought you would prefer that I save her soul."

What could she say? What could she think? How could she possibly answer?

She glimpsed in his face, for just a flash, the hard, horrible truth: Fendrel still loved her.

He loved her enough to burn Ayleth alive for her sake.

Bitterness rising in her soul, Hollis turned her gaze

back to Ayleth. They kept the girl in the center of their small company, where she could be best protected. But Hollis's gaze slipped away, drifting far back to times long gone. She saw Guardin instead—the king as she had known him, young and golden-haired and strong and fearful and entirely devoted to his older brother. Just as they all had been. But their devotion hadn't sprung from nothing. No . . . it stemmed from Fendrel's own love for them. His deep love, which fountained up from the depths of his heart and rushed in a torrent to overwhelm them, to drown them.

She thought of Terryn and Gerard—Fendrel's apprentice and his nephew, young men now. The older one, dark and stern and full of power. The younger, beautiful and golden and full of goodness. Fendrel's fingerprints were all over them. Did they know? Did they recognize his influence in their lives? Did they, like she and Guardin and the whole of the Chosen King's army before them, know the truth and yet eagerly give themselves up to his will?

Did they realize what a terrible thing it was to be loved by Fendrel du Glaive?

Hollis drew a deep breath . . . and suddenly noticed how thick the air was. The atmosphere was darker than it should be at this hour, with blue skies overhead and the sun still high. Fendrel pulled his horse up, and his voice echoed against the stone trees: "Halt!"

The riders obeyed, turning in their saddles to look back at him. Bitter lines scored the Dominus's face. He breathed in, breathed out, and then cursed through his teeth. With a shake of his head, he looked round at the company. "The Great Barrier has fallen," he said.

A murmur of dismay rippled through the Evanderians. Hollis's heart sank like a stone. If Fendrel was right—and she knew him better than to doubt him—then nothing held the Witchwood at bay. This darkness in the air was *oblivis* pouring unchecked into the mortal world.

"It's unsafe to breathe the air," Fendrel continued. "Inhaled *oblivis* will make you susceptible to control."

To Odile's control. For she commanded her element like none other.

The Evanderians, as though of one mind, reached into their saddlebags and removed masks that had been prepared in advance for the journey. Fendrel, without a word to Hollis, handed her a spare he'd taken from the bags of one of the fallen hunters. Hollis slid it over her face. It felt familiar. She'd worn something like it twenty years ago when battling Odile. Crushed calendula petals were pressed into the end of the long pointed beak, serving to filter out the stink of *oblivis*.

With her mask in place, she helped Ayleth with hers, since the girl couldn't manage it with shackled hands. Ayleth wouldn't look her in the eye. Hollis's heart twisted painfully, but she shoved the feeling aside. There was no time for whatever pain lay between them. Not now. Not until the job was done.

"We'll leave the horses," Fendrel said, his voice strange and hollow through the beak of his mask. "They will only make us vulnerable."

The company dismounted. Again Venator Kephan took the lead, his Feral senses alert as they continued onward through the petrified forest. And then . . . Hollis sucked in a deep breath of calendula-scented air. It wasn't the petrified forest anymore. The trees they now walked among were living—living, wounded, and suffering. Gashes oozed infection up and down their twisted trunks, and their branches twined together tightly, as though they sought to hold each other up. The interlacing canopy blocked out all sight of the sky.

I OPENED MY EYES.

Once more I stood in the council room of Agla, surrounded by the domini on their high seats. The Grand Vanderian stood but a few paces from me, her wizened face a mask of utter horror, her mouth gaping, her eyes wide.

Looking down, I saw a ring of black-fletched darts around me on the floor. So, the venators hidden in the galleries above had taken their shots, had tried to bring me down in the midst of my battle with the crown. They had believed I was losing my fight, had thought I would not maintain control.

But I, without even knowing I did so, had caught each of those deadly darts, broken them in half, and let them drop to the ground around me in a perfect circle.

"*Odile di Mauvalis?*" *the Grand Vanderian whispered my name, uncertain who it was looking out at her through my eyes. "Is that you?*"

"*Yes,*" *I answered.* Oblivis *slid from my tongue and billowed out into the air as I spoke. "It's me." Then I smiled and lifted my right hand, aiming my palm straight at her heart.*

I slaughtered them all. One after another. Violently. I caught their liberated souls—shade and mortal alike—and when the Haunts opened, I hurled them through to their damnation. When they were dead, I turned on the hall itself, sending great bolts of hardened oblidite crashing into the walls until the entire structure rained down upon me, until I stood in the center of destruction with power pulsing through my veins.

I left the following day and returned to the castra. There, I commenced another cleansing slaughter. Domina d'Arcand first. Yes, she looked me in the eye as I killed her, and she knew what it meant for a great destiny to at last be fulfilled. When she was dead and damned, I turned on the rest—the venators and phasmators, the indoctrinates and initiates and apprentices. All of them.

And when my work there was finished, I marched upon the Citadel of the Goddess and razed it to the ground.

CHAPTER 20

WHILE CARVING ITS WAY THROUGH THE ROLLING HILLS surrounding Dulimurian, the Queen's Highway steadily climbed. Odile led the way up the steep incline, her pace never flagging. Inren struggled to keep up. Although her goddess was renewed with every breath of *oblivis* she drew into her lungs, Inren felt her strength flagging the more she inhaled the poisonous element. It would stain her very bones black and leave them weak as butter if she had to continue at this rate.

As they approached the top of the rise, reluctance as well as exhaustion slowed Inren's pace. She knew what view would meet her eye when she crested this hill. During her four years of captivity in the Witchwood, she had never dared venture this deep but always stayed on the outer edges, close to the Barrier or the rivers. She disliked looking on the ruined City of the New Goddess, preferring to remember its former glory.

Odile, however, marched onward undaunted, increasing the space between herself and her remaining lieutenant. Inren saw her reach the top of the rise, saw her pause . . . and saw her go so still, she might have been turned into a pillar of oblidite.

Summoning up her courage, Inren redoubled her pace, hastening to join her queen. This host body she now wore wasn't as tall as Odile's emaciated frame, so she peered around her shoulder. Her eyes widened as she took in the panorama below.

The mighty idol of Odile was still there—fallen to its knees but still upright, its hand raised to the sky and visible above the tree line for twenty miles around. It had once stood on a broad, circular platform of oblidite, which rested on the top of a many-tiered mound high above the rest of the city. The mound was now cracked, its stairways broken.

The city radiated out from the statue in concentric circles, and the five roads of Odile had once converged at the statue mound like the points of a star joining at a nexus. But four of the roads were lost, broken, swallowed by the wood. Only the one Odile had called back to life was still visible.

The Witchwood had done its work on Dulimurian. It had dragged down the tall spires of oblidite, crushing them to dust. It had opened the ground beneath the foundations and half sunk the west end of the city in muck and mire. Vines had torn at the once graceful lines of the amphitheater in the south quarter until it lay collapsed like a broken animal. The Library of Odessa was no more, its precious contents lost forever. The temples, the squares, the graceful dwellings of impervious oblidite—all smashed like so much fragile crockery.

And surrounding the city was a massive wall of black vines.

Inren stared, certain she could never tear her gaze

away. All the vines of the Witchwood must have gathered here, slithering across the miles of forest. Woven together in a wall, they were as impassable as granite. The magic, the pure power emanating from them was palpable. It made Inren's shade scream and dive deep within her host body, where it hid, quaking with dread.

The upraised hand of the statue glowed, pulsing with blue light.

There the crown lay.

There Oromor waited.

The hope that had tentatively blossomed in Inren's heart over the miles of her journey now choked and died. Odile was great. Odile was mighty. Odile had taken the song spell of Fendrel du Glaive and torn it apart like spider-web threads. But no one, not even Odile, could penetrate that living wall. This was more than song spells, threads of magic spun together. These vines were pure, dark, living magic. Living *oblivis*.

Inren glanced at her mistress's face. The queen's expression was implacable. Whatever her thoughts might be, Inren couldn't fathom them.

Suddenly Odile turned her back to her city and stared

into the forest they had just traversed. "Come out," she said, her voice dangerously soft.

Inren recoiled as the desiccated beings from the lake emerged suddenly from the pervasive shadows. They crawled out onto the road, and others followed—shade-taken figures she'd not realized were there. Her shadow senses must be dulled by the *oblivis,* otherwise surely she would have detected the approach of so many souls. So many monsters. Some retained traces of their original mortal hosts. But, like the Crimson Devils themselves, none of them had escaped the warping influence of the air they breathed. They were tumorous and grotesque, skeletal and oozing. Nightmares made flesh, and flesh made nightmarish.

But Odile extended her hands as though to embrace them. "My children," she said.

As one, they fell to their knees, threw themselves on their faces, and groveled before her. More and more of them appeared, silent as wraiths while their very spirits screamed with the agony of hope suddenly and unexpectedly resurrected. Odile simply stood there, arms wide, and accepted their obeisance with stern grace.

At last, she commanded them: "Rise."

They obeyed at once. The queen's right hand moved, one finger crooking, and the foremost of the lake beasts crawled on its belly to her feet. It touched what might almost pass for a nose against the ragged, burned hem of her garment. "What of the Evanderians?" Odile asked.

A hiss rippled through the company, followed by deep, loathing growls. The creature at Odile's feet snarled and writhed, somehow communicating to her, though Inren couldn't understand it. Odile nodded grimly. Then she lifted her head, addressing the assembly.

"Fendrel du Glaive is in our land," she said.

At the mention of that name, the shade-taken sufferers threw back their heads and howled and screamed and chattered, wild with hatred and bloodlust.

"He who hunted us," the goddess continued. "He who hounded our brothers and sisters, who ousted our shades and damned our souls—he even now marches on Dulimurian."

Another uproar. Inren's own spirit surged within her, and she nearly opened her mouth to bellow seething hatred along with the horde. The shade inside her churned and, down deep, the parasitic mortal soul shivered with dread.

"I charge you, my children, my darlings," Odile said, "to hunt him down. Him and all those Red Hoods who march with him. Kill them and let their souls go to the Haunts where they belong. But . . ." She held up a warning hand, stopping the shade-taken in their tracks before they could turn and bound off through the trees. "There is a girl among them," she said. "My own kin, my granddaughter. See that she is not harmed. Bring her to me, alive and whole."

Many frenzied eyes turned the queen's way, blinking with slowly dawning understanding. Inren clenched her fists, clenched her jaw. None of these monsters knew about the *Cravan Druch*. None of these monsters knew what a danger the granddaughter posed to their goddess. But *she* knew. She knew all too well how everything she and her brethren had worked and died for could be undone in a moment . . .

"Go," Odile said. "Go now, my children. Find Fendrel du Glaive and his followers. Find my granddaughter."

With pounding hooves and slithering scales and

groans of unrelenting pain, the monsters turned and vanished into the shadows of the trees, eager, no, *desperate* to fulfill their goddess's decree. Inren followed them, moving with quiet stealth. Odile had scarcely deigned to acknowledge her presence for hours. Surely she wouldn't notice if her one remaining lieutenant slipped away now. If she was lucky, she might find the granddaughter first. She would drag her off to the Haunts and leave her there, where she could never again pose a threat to the goddess. She might—

"Inren."

The witch stopped short, hissing a breath through her teeth. But she quickly pulled herself together and turned to salute her queen. "My Goddess."

"Stay close to me." Odile put out her hand and gently gripped Inren's fingers. "We are near the end now. You must help me finish what we have come here to do. You must help me get my crown."

FOLLOWING THESE EVENTS, I WORE THE CROWN ONLY *periodically. Its power was so great, and the strain on my body and mind so severe, that I knew better than to toy with it. But it did not matter. After what I had done, the mere mention of my name made entire castras tremble and run. I scarcely needed the crown's gifts.*

Shade-taken flocked to me. I spread my wings and took them in, be they inborn or newly possessed or witches. It did not matter to me. I accepted them all, made them my people, made them my kin.

We carved out a place for ourselves. On the ruins of Roihm I built my own city and established my throne. I paved roads of oblidite and sent them out like the radiant arms of a star, carving into Perrinion. Along these roads I established towers, and so my kingdom grew, and the Order of Evander trembled and fled before me.

And when members of the Order came to me, when they fled their castras and prostrated themselves before me, did I turn them away? Did I raise my hand against them? No. For they, like me, were victims of Evander's lies. They, like me, needed only the chance to have their eyes open, to have their hearts purified and their souls made strong. I took them to my bosom. I blessed them. I transformed them.

They became my Crimson Devils. And with them, I went to war against Evander's followers. I became the Poison. I became the New Goddess, the Witch Queen.

Odile, Venatrix di Mauvalis, ceased to exist.

There was only Dread Odile.

CHAPTER 21

THOUGH SHE'D KNOWN IT WAS FOOLISH, AYLETH HAD almost dared to hope her previous experiences in the Witchwood would prepare her for this new venture. But no. All those smells, all those tastes, and that pervading, inescapable oppression of dread crashed down on her senses in a reality far worse than memory.

Somehow, knowing that the Great Barrier was gone made it worse. The last time she'd passed through that web of spell song, she'd known it was still there at her back somewhere. That no matter how deep she went, that no matter how lost she became, there was always the chance of returning to the barrier and crossing back over into clear air and open skies. Now it was broken. There was no separation between this unnatural realm and her own world. She had seen the Witchwood send out shoots and roots, encroaching on Wodechran Borough. If she survived this journey to Dulimurian, would there be any coming back again?

Even to ask that question seemed stupid.

Glittering *oblivis* floated before her face, drifting in whorls and eddies, never settling. She raised her shackled hands to fiddle with the strap of the mask wrapped around the lower half of her face. Every breath pulled the soft mesh fabric up into her nostrils and mouth, and the pointed beak end was an odd weight swinging out a foot from her nose. The masks made them look like a cluster of ugly flightless birds waddling through the shadows of the Witchwood, their cloaks hanging like broken wings from their shoulders. But the crushed dried calendula petals at the end of the beak served their purpose well. The scent was unpleasant but strong enough to mask the far more disgusting funks of the wounded trees, and the mesh spared her from breathing *oblivis* into her lungs.

The Queen's Highway cut straight through the forest beneath the canopy of interlacing branches overhead. It was strange to see those paving stones gleam as though newly polished. The road itself was broad enough that six horses could ride abreast down its center. The little cluster of Evanderians hastened on foot along the middle, keeping Ayleth surrounded at all times.

The road offered firmer footing than Ayleth had enjoyed during her last visit to the Witchwood. She didn't have to squelch through putrid, sucking soil with every step. But this was no comfort, for the repaired oblidite road could mean only one thing—Odile was strengthening. She was using her shade's powers to solidify the *oblivis* in the air and build back the broken patches of her highway, everything the Witchwood had eaten away over the last twenty years. For the first stretch of the journey, the patchwork was rough, the oblidite not quite solid, and the broken spaces still large, with roots of the wounded trees twining through like grasping fingers. The deeper they went, however, the more polished and refined the road became. After the first mile or so, Ayleth could no longer discern the seams between stones.

Her heart sank. If Odile was already this powerful, what was to stop her from retrieving the crown? Even if by some miracle they did manage to overtake the witch and her devils, how could Ayleth hope to combat such might? Laranta at her highest ascendancy was no match for magic like this.

She ducked her head and focused on placing one foot after another. All she could do was keep going. According to Fendrel, it was twenty miles to Dulimurian, and, barring accidents, they would reach the edge of the city sometime in the next six hours if they kept up a brisk pace. It would be dark well before then. Ayleth shuddered. The atmosphere was already so heavy in the half-lit pall of the Witchwood. How much worse would it be after nightfall?

A wave of hopelessness rising inside her threatened to choke her spirit. Desperate, she reached out for Laranta. But her shade had retreated, hiding from the iron influence. Ayleth could catch only the barest trace of her presence.

At least . . . She licked her dry lips, then pressed them together in a tight smile. At least Terryn was alive. Or had been a few hours ago when he helped Hollis escape Dunloch. Where was he now? Did he also stride through the Witchwood's shadows, hunting after Gerard, the Haunts-fool prince? Or had Terryn managed to track down his brother and drag him back to safety?

This last thought had scarcely formed when an image flashed through Ayleth's mind again—an image of a starlit sky and a gleaming sword's edge. An image of Gerard's face illuminated in pulsing blue light, his eyes staring up at her, white-ringed with dread.

"I'm so sorry, Ayleth."

She shook her head, pulling away from that thought, that vision. She dared not think on it too closely, dared not consider what all it might mean or imply.

Hollis walked beside her. She'd quietly approached just behind Ayleth's right shoulder, hovering on the edge of her peripheral vision. How long she'd been there, Ayleth couldn't guess. She cast a quick sideways glance her mistress's way before focusing her gaze on her feet.

They progressed in silence, scuttling along in the wake

of their prey with their pointed beaks cutting the thick air before their faces. Kephan led the way, his shadow senses alert, his scorpiona ready to fire. All the Evanderians had loaded their weapons with black-fletched darts. Here in the Witchwood, there was no need to worry about paralysis and careful killings, no need to fear loosed souls. Unlike the battle in Dunloch, there were no untaken host bodies here to be possessed by violently liberated shades. Each hunter could go directly for the kill.

But the Gentle Death was useless against the Witchwood itself.

Why did it not attack? It was all so quiet, so tame, so . . . docile. It must be a pretense. Ayleth knew how dangerous the Witchwood was, how viciously it could kill when it wished. But though she searched the branches overhead, she caught no glimpse of the parasitic vines, which had been so prevalent during her last visit.

She cursed softly. Without Laranta's power, she was as helpless as a newborn kitten—worse even, for a kitten doesn't know what abilities it lacks. Still, was she simply going to roll over, expose her soft underbelly, and let monsters devour her while she mewled pathetically? No.

She'd fight to the bitter end.

With an effort of will, she concentrated her mortal senses through the soles of her feet. Her boots clunked on the oblidite paving stones, but deeper still she felt . . . something. A distant but consistent pulsing, perhaps. Like a heartbeat.

Boom . . .

. . . boom . . .

. . . boom . . .

The Witchwood was still alert, alive. Its attention was diverted elsewhere, but the pulse of life remained.

Ayleth stopped just long enough for Hollis, taken by surprise, to almost run into her from behind. Hollis flung up a hand to catch Ayleth's shoulder and keep herself from stepping on the backs of her heels. Ayleth wrenched away from that touch and resumed walking, but she didn't put distance between herself and Hollis. Instead, she said in a low voice, "It's not a curse. This wood, I mean."

Hollis understood what she was saying. Ayleth counted ten steps before her mistress's voice finally breathed an answer in her ear. "No."

Another ten steps. With each touch of her foot to the ground, Ayleth felt the pulse of that heartbeat below.

Boom . . .

. . . boom . . .

. . . boom . . .

"What is it exactly?" she demanded. She spoke so softly into the beak mask that she half wondered if Hollis would be able to hear her. Then again, her mistress's shade powers were currently called to high ascendancy. She could probably read the question in Ayleth's mind without need of spoken words.

Hollis hesitated before answering. Then, quickening her pace, she drew up closer to Ayleth and spoke her answer in a hushed rush of words. "When we played the *atacara*—when we empowered the spirit in the crown so that it could overcome Odile's control—we did not consider the lasting effects. The crown retained the magic channeled into it. With Odile's fall, it lost a host body through which to move and act in this world, but . . . but that magic found an outlet. The crown pulled *oblivis* from the Haunts, like water seeping through cloth, and this forest grew as a result. The crown . . . it created a host for itself. A living, thriving host."

Ayleth's heart shivered as though shot through with ice.

"It all happened so fast," Hollis whispered. "We couldn't hope to fight it. We could only contain it. And pray."

Boom . . .

. . . boom . . .

. . . boom . . .

A shade that created a host for itself. A host comprised of elements both of this world and the Haunts. A *being*, sentient and complex and utterly vast.

And Dread Odile thought she could tame it? Thought she could take it back, control it? What kind of force did she house in her body to give her such confidence, such arrogance?

And what arrogance made Ayleth think she could stop her?

"You did this." Her voice was dull in her own ears. She hadn't realized she intended to speak until the words were suddenly there, hanging in the air between her and Hollis. "You gave it the *atacara* and all the strength of those brave venators and venatrices. You handed their magic over like a gift."

Hollis made no answer. Her silence was more dreadful, more damning than words.

Ayleth shook her head, snarling behind her mask. Then she swung around, her gaze stabbing into Hollis's face. "Every good deed you've ever done . . . have they all come out so ugly in the end?"

Hollis drew back from her as though stung. Though her face was half hidden behind that pointed beak, her eyes flashed with sorrow so profound, it hurt like a physical blow to see it. For an instant Ayleth remembered the mistress she had loved with such devotion, the woman who had raised her, cared for her, trained her, sheltered her. The memories cut through her anger like a knife, and she wished suddenly to be that child version of herself again, wished she dared to love so innocently, wished she dared return to the ignorance that had made such love possible.

The instant passed. Ayleth turned away, concentrating her gaze on the red hoods in front of her, leaving Hollis to follow in the wake of her silence.

They marched on, the only sound their heavy footfalls on the oblidite paving stones and their labored wheezing through the beak masks. Ayleth lost all sense of time. They may have journeyed for hours, but it might as easily have been no more than a few minutes. The weird light was unchanging, the floating motes of *oblivis* unrelenting, and the filtering stink of calendula turned her stomach. Her cracked ribs made it difficult to draw full breaths, and all the aches and bruises across her body protested against this endless march.

With every step she took, her certainty grew: Odile was already too far ahead. They would never catch her in time. But there was nothing else to be done. She couldn't pause, she couldn't rest. None of them could. They had to keep going until the end.

Until Odile reclaimed the crown and blasted them all into damnation.

Up ahead, Kephan suddenly stopped, stiffened. Ayleth narrowed her eyes, watching him closely. The way he tilted his head told her that his Feral senses were alert, warning him of something. He lifted a hand, silently signaling the others to halt. Then he made a quick, circling motion with one finger.

Immediately, as though moving in response to a barked command, the Evanderians acted. Ayleth found herself crushed in the center of a tight circle as they gathered round her, backs to her, scorpioni upraised in a wall of defense. Hollis was directly in front of her, so short that Ayleth could easily peer over her head. Fendrel stood just to Hollis's right, his broad frame taking a wide stance, his whole body a shield. Even without Laranta's awareness, Ayleth could sense the power of ascendant shades around her, could almost hear the hum of the spell songs straining to contain them.

What had Kephan sensed? Ayleth peered into the dense gloom of the Witchwood, cursing her lack of shadow sight. Her mortal vision was too willing to play tricks on her. Did she see movement in the darkness? Did the *oblivis* move and whirl unnaturally in the wake of some creeping figure? Did the ground shift as something crawled between trunks, its belly close to the dirt?

Ayleth leaned into Fendrel's back, her beak mask resting on his shoulder. "Take off my shackles," she hissed. How many times that day had she already made this plea? "Let me fight."

He tossed a short glance over his shoulder but answered only with a growl.

"She's right, you know," Hollis said, not taking her eyes off the forest. "She's no use to us restrained like this. Let her go and——" She broke off abruptly, choking on her words. Her body doubled up, and a thin cry squeezed through her clenched teeth.

"Hollis?" Ayleth whispered, trying to catch her mistress's shoulders from behind. Her Apparition powers must be reacting to something, some thought she'd just discerned approaching through the trees. "Hollis, what's wrong?"

"There." Kephan, standing to Fendrel's right, turned sharply, swinging his scorpiona and pointing it into the forest. Every pair of eyes looked where he indicated. The next moment, the rest of them saw what he and Hollis had already discerned.

A horrible figure emerged from the shadows. It was taller than a man and approximately man-shaped, as though whoever formed this thing possessed a vague notion of what a man looked like and had pulled this monstrosity together with bits and pieces of sinew, muscle, and bone. It slumped heavily forward, its huge, sloping shoulders and massive head too heavy for its crooked spine to support. Were it to stand upright, it would be twelve feet tall at least. A multitude of wounds ravaged its body, white bone showing through gaping red flesh in places. Its face was hidden behind a deer-skull mask, and the bent and broken antlers branching up from its crown might have been part of the mask or might have grown from its own head. White, frill-edged growths climbed its torso and neck, extended down its back.

But worst of all were the hands. They had been broken so many times, the bones had splintered into spur-like protrusions, dripping with blood. Its own blood, perhaps.

It was shade-taken. It had to be. But what kind of shade could be housed in a horror like that?

Pure, palpable terror surged through the souls around Ayleth. Even Fendrel took an involuntary step back. He braced himself the next moment, however, and fired straight at the monster's head. The black-fletched dart flew true and stuck between the thing's hollow eyes, quivering. But it could not penetrate that skull mask.

The creature dropped to all fours, shaking its head. Its hideous broken hands tore into the dirt, and it charged their ranks.

Another five darts flew through the air, three of them hitting their marks. One prick of the Gentle Death was enough to kill a grown man in a matter of moments, but that thing kept coming. It leapt out of the forest onto the oblidite paving stones, and with a sweep of one long arm sent Hollis flying through the air, her cloak flapping behind her.

The other arm swung, this time for Fendrel. The Dominus ducked, avoiding the blow. He caught Ayleth's elbow and yanked her down to the ground beside him so that the horrible, broken fingers passed through the air overhead. She rolled, and the splayed, broken fingers of the monster crushed the stones where her face had been an instant before.

She stopped rolling, caught in Fendrel's embrace, both his arms wrapped protectively around her. He let go with one hand, lifting his scorpiona, and took another shot. The dart passed through the monster's antlers. It turned its massive head, and black, shadow-blighted blood dripped through the mask's long teeth and out through the corners of the empty eye sockets.

Two boots stepped in the way, blocking Ayleth's vision. She craned her neck, looking up at the back of Kephan's square head. The monster loomed over him, but as its arm swept down, he caught it and, channeling the strength of his Feral shade, twisted hard. The creature fell heavily onto one shoulder. Kephan took the advantage while it lasted, leaping onto the thing's chest and pummeling it with his bare fists. The skull mask cracked, and more blood flowed, and still Kephan pounded, harder and harder, using all the force of his ascendant shade.

The monster pushed itself upright and, with a wave of its arm, knocked Kephan away. He landed hard and didn't move. The shade-taken surged to its feet, masked face swinging heavily as it searched. Though she could not see its eyes through those sockets, she felt the moment its gaze landed on her. It took a step. Then it staggered. Swayed. The poison of the Gentle Death from those several pricks had at last worked into its system. It took another step, tried to lift its arm . . . and fell so hard, it cracked the oblidite beneath it. Its body shattered at the impact, turning to black, shadow-blighted dust even as the spirit inside shrieked free of its mortal husk and sped away into the thick, dark air.

"Ayleth! Ayleth, are you all right?"

It was Hollis's voice in her ear. And Hollis's hands grasping her upper arms, pulling her out of Fendrel's grasp. Ayleth shook her head, trying to clarify her swimming vision, trying to focus on her mistress's pale face. Blood poured from a cut in Hollis's temple and matted in her hair, but she looked otherwise unhurt.

Another hand closed down hard on her arm, and Fendrel yanked her to her feet so fast that she fell into him. He caught her roughly, forcing her to stand. Ayleth glared at him, ready to lash out. But he wasn't looking at her. His gaze was fixed on the forest.

"There are more," he said.

The words had scarcely left his lips when the air shattered with a ululating chorus of voices. Unnatural shapes swarmed through the branches, crawled among the roots, and lumbered between the trunks of the wounded trees. The shade-taken of the Witchwood descended upon them, closing in on all sides.

I NEVER FORGOT MY OLENA. I NEVER FORGOT STANIER.

I have, however, forgotten the face of the man I took as my lover. He was some mortal, unpossessed, unremarkable for anything save his beauty. I don't know if I bothered to learn his name. I simply took him and made use of him. For years he was my pet, my plaything. In due time he gave me what I longed for—a child.

I don't know what became of him after that. Perhaps I killed him. Perhaps I gave him to one of my Devils. Perhaps he escaped. It did not matter to me. Once I held Olecia in my arms, nothing else mattered anymore.

I gazed into her face. I gazed into her soul and saw the inborn shade entwined with her spirit. And I thought: This is why. This is why everything happened as it did. This is why I have done what I have done.

For Olena. For Olecia.

My children. My darlings. My own.

CHAPTER 22

HUNDREDS OF TORTURED MINDS EXPLODED IN HOLLIS'S head. She felt their rage, their hatred, their bloodlust. Worse still, she felt their hope. It was like looking on a body pulled taut on the rack, joints breaking, ligaments tearing, muscles screaming, mind despairing . . . and suddenly, a promise of freedom. An offer, a taste of freedom that will never come to pass no matter how the soul grasps for it with desperate need.

That sensation a hundred times over fell upon Hollis's

mind like an avalanche, and it was all she could do to grab hold of her shade's soul tether and pull its powers around her in defense. If she let her mind be overwhelmed by that suffering, she wouldn't be able to see, think, or fight.

"Protect the asset!" Fendrel called out to his followers.

Shade power rippled in the air above the Evanderians—all of those ascendant shades straining at the few remaining suppressions binding them to the wills of their hosts. Hollis's own shade struggled for freedom. She'd given it so much leeway, and she wasn't sure she'd be able to control it much longer. But she had to. It was her only chance.

There were too many of them appearing through the trees. She concentrated her attention on the three directly in front of her, just off the edge of the road. Three low-crawling things, their elbows jutting up over their backs and shoulders, their knees angled out weirdly on each side. They may at one point have been human. Their noseless faces were close to the ground, their tongues protruding, trailing purple and swollen across their chins. Their eyes fixed on her.

Hollis raised her scorpiona. In her mind, she gripped

tighter hold of the soul tether connecting her to her shade and swung its power out from her in an arc of defense. In a flurry of multitudinous wings, her shade streaked into the space between her and those creatures. Their mortal eyes could not perceive it, and even if their shadow senses did, it didn't slow them. Galloping on all fours, one came straight at her, while the other two closed in at angles on either side. They struck the wall of Apparition power, and their tortured minds flared in reaction to the shade's assault as it turned all their hatred, all their horror, back on themselves, like a mirror reflecting the truth of their souls directly into their eyes. It was one of the most vicious defenses Hollis knew.

But the shade-taken kept coming. They'd suffered so much mental anguish already, they scarcely noticed the assault.

Hollis aimed her scorpiona. She could take only one shot at a time and wouldn't have a chance to reload before the other two were upon her. She had less than half a second to decide. Her instincts, honed over the years, sensed the angle of each attack and distinguished which of her assailants not only posed the greatest threat to herself but was also most likely to harm Ayleth, standing behind her.

Her arm moved. Her thumb pressed the triggering mechanism. Her scorpiona jolted on her arm as the dart sped through the air and struck the monster angling in on her left.

She didn't have time to see if her poison took effect. The middle shade-taken was already on her, diving for her face. She flung up her left arm, and the monster drove its own open mouth onto the spike on her bracer. Its skull cracked as the iron plunged deep and protruded through the back of its head. The impact sent her rolling with the dead thing on top of her. A rush of screaming, liberated soul brushed her skin as it flew into the ether.

The third monster lunged. Her shadow senses, seeing through the eyes of her shade, perceived a dozen more closing in behind it. She had no time to arm her scorpiona, so she grabbed a Gentle Death from her quivers. Dully, in the back of her mind, she realized that she had only nine darts left. Most venatrices carried no more than ten on a hunt. Most venatrices didn't expect to battle swarms of shade-taken all at once.

Using the Gentle Death like a knife, she rolled, her arm arcing over her head, and plunged it into the shoulder of the third monster. Its tongue lashed out as a gargled cry shot from its throat. It fell.

The next four monsters leaped.

She kicked one in the head, slashed at another with her spike. In her mind, she yanked at the soul-tether, pulling her shade back into the attack. Her shade might hate her, loathe her, long to overtake and oust her—but it also wanted to protect this body, which had been its host and safe haven for many years. So, despite its loosened suppressions, it obeyed her command. Sweeping down across the monsters that hurtled toward her, it filled their minds with pain—raw, searing, soul-burning pain. The attack was so intense, Hollis felt the heat of it radiate against her own soul, potent enough to make her gasp.

But this attack was most effective when focused on a single mind. Spread out like this, it could not kill. Five of the monsters screeched and flung up their hands, claws, and jointed arms, falling on their faces, writhing on their bellies. Another three merely shook their heads and drove onward. And it wasn't just the monstrous forms themselves. The shades inside them reared up, powers bursting. Hollis's shadow sight beheld an oncoming rush of magic. So much ascendant magic, surging from all directions.

A blast of raw, red curse landed at her feet, and she was only just quick enough to dodge to one side. An explosion of Elemental fire singed her hair and skin as she managed to plunge another Gentle Death into a shade-taken heart. The screams of loosed souls filled her ears, and she could not tell if they were friends or foes.

Hollis turned, searching for Ayleth in the sea of horrors. She saw her grappling with a cat-like thing that dripped poison from pores across its face and neck. Her shackled hands were up, and she'd forced the iron chain between them into the cat's mouth like a bit so that its jaws could not clamp down on her throat. Although she had only her own mortal strength to hold it back, with no access to her shade, the monster reacted to the iron, and she was able to toss it to one side. Another shade-taken caught her by her long braid from behind.

"*Ayleth!*" Hollis screamed and took a lunging step toward the girl.

Something struck her, and she flew through the air. Her body hit the ground hard and rolled, falling off the oblidite road into the sick, rotten soil of the Witchwood. The stink of death and decay filled her nostrils, and she cursed. Her bones were jarred, her body quaked, but she got her hands under her, pushed herself up.

She felt the heartbeat of the Witchwood through her palms.

Boom . . .

. . . boom . . .

. . . boom . . .

And she realized.

How much time did she have? The shade-taken must not have seen where she fell— their attention remained fixed on the figures on the road, particularly the tall young woman in the center. Any second now, they would see her. They would turn on her. They would tear her apart.

But for the moment . . . for the moment . . .

Hollis dug her hands deep into the rotten soil, fingers curling tight. *"Come to me!"* she cried to her shade, mentally yanking on the soul tether.

It obeyed at her slightest touch and, sensing her will, sensing her command, plunged down into the ground. Hollis's shadow sight saw the flurry of feathered wings disappearing into the fetid dirt, and she reached out with her own mind, catching hold and plunging with it.

Together, they penetrated the mind of the Witchwood.

It didn't try to block them. There was no barrier, no wall to fight through as Hollis would have expected. It took them willingly, and she found herself in a world of twisting, manic insanity. Her own mind, trying to make sense of madness, presented her with images of tentacles as huge as mountains, twisting and twining with each other, the vast and complex network of a mind so far from human, so far from nature.

She could not stay here long and survive. She had to get out. But first . . .

"*Help us!*" she cried into that mind.

Could a consciousness like this hear her small, mortal voice? Could it understand her? Was it too far beyond mortality for them to share any form of communication?

"*Odile is coming for you! She'll take you again; she'll make you her slave. But we can stop her. We have the means.*"

The twisting vastness seemed suddenly to be aware of her. She felt it closing in, ready to crush her mind like a pebble of clay. "*Read my thoughts!*" she screamed, desperate as the pressure closed in. "*See that I speak the truth!*"

A hundred black tentacle feelers shot out toward her, plunging into her mind. She felt them like a physical sensation of roots and vines tearing into her eyes, her nostrils, her mouth, her ears, winding through her inner workings, sucking on her life. Her very essence pulsed out through those feelers into the greater consciousness controlling them. Her shade screeched and tried to fight back. But Hollis, in a last, desperate maneuver, caught the soul tether and restrained it, giving herself over to the Witchwood.

It knew what she knew. She felt its understanding. She felt its belief. She felt something like . . . like words. Or meaning without words, but which her mortal mind twisted into language she could grasp.

I've been waiting for her.

Suddenly, Hollis was back on her belly in the muck of the Witchwood. She was alive. Her face and head were on fire, and her hands moved to her eyes, her ears, her nose, feeling for plunging vines that were not there. The Witchwood had let her go.

Screams filled her ears, and her shadow senses exploded with spirits and magic. She looked up, looked to the road. A flash of red hood appeared through the tangle of limbs and miasma of magic, but she could not see to whom it belonged.

The ground beneath her moved. Slithered. Vines like undulating snakes crawled down from the trees. Hollis leapt to her feet and staggered back, her eyes wide. But the vines had no interest in her. They plunged into the thick of the battle.

The first of the shade-taken screamed. Then another. Then another.

More vines poured out from the forest, darting into the throng, grasping, pulling, and tearing. The monsters squealed and roared, and Hollis's shadow sight saw the surge of terror rolling through their spirits. They turned and fled, scattering every which way, their terror like a hurricane carrying them away on its winds. But they couldn't escape. Their mangled, skeletal limbs were caught in loops of vine, lifted, broken, and ripped apart as they were dragged away into the trees. Death cries rattled the air; violently expelled spirits shot through the ether.

It was over in a matter of moments. The wild cacophony ended so suddenly, it was like the slamming of a door.

Careful to avoid stepping on the last few trailing vines as they retreated, Hollis staggered out of the wood. The relief of returning to the solid oblidite paving stones was so great, tears sprang to her eyes. She stared in disbelief at the little cluster of red hoods and masked faces, all untouched by the Witchwood.

Fendrel stood protectively over Ayleth, who lay panting but alive at his feet. Kephan, his Feral shade bristling, stood at Fendrel's right, and the others, one venator and one venatrix, flanked them.

"Hollis!" Fendrel cried. His gaze locked with hers, and for a moment she saw, not Dominus du Glaive, the hero of the Witch Wars. She saw Fendrel. She saw the youth he once was. She saw him with his face lit in a glow more brilliant than lantern light, gazing at her as though she were an angel come suddenly to deliver him from certain death. Her heart spasmed with something that felt like pain but wasn't quite.

But this expression vanished the next moment, replaced with hard lines. "Hollis, what did you—" He didn't get to finish.

Thick vines shot out from the trees, twenty of them at least, black and twisting. They knocked aside the venators, including Fendrel.

Hollis lunged forward. "Ayleth! *No!*"

There was nothing she could do. The Witchwood wrapped its hideous fingers around the girl and pulled her away into the shadows so fast, Ayleth didn't even have a chance to scream.

TIME PASSED, BUT IT MEANT LITTLE ENOUGH TO ME. *Years melted into decades, which in turn became centuries. Dulimurian grew and prospered, and when I stretched out my arm, my power extended for a thousand miles in any direction. The Evanderians had long since abandoned Perrinion; my people walked and lived and loved in safety.*

My own heart was full, for my daughter Olecia grew in grace and loveliness and power. In due time, she took a lover for herself— an inborn shade-taken, a man of rare magic. And one night, in the very deepest, darkest hour before dawn, she gave birth to my granddaughter.

"I named her Olena, Mother," she said when she placed the child in my arms. "So that you will remember all you have done and

realize all you may still do."

I looked down into the infant's eyes—those black-as-night eyes, owl-large and innocent, gleaming with shadow-light. But I did not see her.

It was another babe I saw. Another pair of dark eyes. Another Olena.

Around her burned the deadly flames of Evander.

"I swear to you," I whispered, gazing into those eyes, gazing into that long-ago memory. "I swear to you, I will never let Dulimurian fall."

CHAPTER 23

THE GATE OF THE SETTING SUN HAD ONCE STOOD IN this very spot. Inren remembered it well, its huge arch, its ornate design of a black sunburst etched in oblidite—one of the most beautiful of the entrances to Dulimurian. The gate was gone now. And the huge wall that had once encircled the city like loving, protective arms was no more.

Another wall stood in its place, a wall of vines rising at least six meters high. Its depth, Inren couldn't guess. The vines twined themselves together so tightly, they seemed to strangle each other, pulsing like constrictors in a slow, steady rhythm. Odile looked so small, standing before that monstrosity.

Inren waited, standing back from both wall and queen. She hoped to see her goddess gather the *oblivis* from the air as she had done at the Great Barrier. She hoped to see her form it into a solid mass and send it shooting like spears through this living wall, tearing those vines to shreds, clearing a path for herself.

But Odile simply stood there. Her eyes were closed, and Inren, watching with shadow sight, saw how the dark spirit inside her stretched out, reaching along the wall and plunging into the soil. Feeling for weaknesses, no doubt.

Suddenly, Odile opened her eyes and turned to Inren. "You have an anchor?" she asked.

Inren felt in her pocket for the three stones she still carried. Smooth and comforting, they rolled between her fingers. She nodded.

"Plant one," Odile said. "This wall cannot be more than a mile thick. You can carry us to the other side."

Inren's breath caught in the throat. She wanted to

protest. Yes, she'd used anchors to travel back and forth across the Great Barrier. But that was merely a spell song woven by a mortal man. This was . . . something else entirely.

Reluctantly, Inren pulled out an anchor and, kneeling, planted it in the rotten soil. With a twist of magic, she activated it, and the stone flared, its heart glowing as the curse threads came alive, binding her soul and body to the stone. She stood upright and nodded, extending one hand. Odile stepped forward and wrapped her arms around Inren's waist.

Inren clutched her goddess close. Then she stepped— and the Haunts opened to her.

Chaos. Void. Crushing.

An instant of damnation. A taste of hell.

She stepped again, and the mortal world opened. She felt it, but she didn't pass through in the usual way. She took a third step. A fourth. Something resisted. The air was too thick, too solid. The *oblivis* barred her entrance. Inren's soul jumped with panic as she felt the curse threads anchoring her to the world strain. One of them snapped.

With a cry, she stumbled back and fell out of the Haunts into the gloomy atmosphere of the Witchwood. With Odile still held tight in her arms, she landed flat on her back and lay panting, her eyes spinning in her skull, her head whirling, her soul screaming.

Odile sat upright, pulling free of Inren's grasp. Her face was like stone as she looked up at the wall. Then she directed that same hard gaze down at Inren. "What happened?"

"Forgive me, my Queen," Inren panted, suppressing the squeal of terror still trying to push its way up through her throat. "It would not let me through."

"It?"

"Oromor." Inren got her elbows under her and propped her head and shoulders up. Her vision still swimming, she closed her eyes. "It knew I was coming. It blocked me."

"Try again."

Inren's eyes flew open to stare at her goddess. "It took all my strength to get us back out!" she gasped. "The curse threads were already breaking. I . . . If I try again, we will be lost to the Haunts. Forever."

The muscles in Odile's face tightened. For a moment Inren feared she would repeat her command—and how could Inren deny her? But before her goddess could speak, a sudden yelping drew her attention away. Odile stood, gazing back along her road, and Inren breathed a sigh of relief that was almost a prayer. Then she twisted her head around, trying to see what had caught Odile's eye. One of the shade-taken loped down the road, its right arm dangling limp from its shoulder, held in place only by a bit of sinew and skin. It left a trail of black, blighted blood behind it, and its eyes smoldered with shadow-light.

It prostrated itself on the ground at Odile's feet. Others came as well, creeping through the Witchwood from all directions. Limping, frightened, whimpering, weeping. Odile stood tall before them, her expression not that of a loving mother, but of a vengeful goddess.

"Where is my granddaughter?" she demanded of the first creature at her feet. "Where is the head of Fendrel du Glaive?"

The shade-taken whimpered, hissed, and screeched, communicating without language. Its meaning was clear enough. Inren felt the dread of the Witchwood in its soul, a terror equal to or greater than the terror Odile herself inspired.

Odile's mouth was a grim line. Before the shade-taken finished speaking, she thrust out her hand and, with a sudden jolt of magic from her core, sent a shot of pure *oblivis* straight to the creature's heart. Poison flooded its body, and it rolled over, writhing in death agonies that would last for some while.

With a shudder, Inren pulled her gaze from the suffering thing back to her queen. Odile faced the wall of vines and studied it for a long, silent moment. Then she approached it, put out both hands, and before Inren could utter a cry of warning, gripped the vines tight.

Inren expected them to lash out, to sweep her goddess into their snarled midst and pull her to pieces. She scrambled to her feet, half intending to fling herself after Odile, to bodily drag her away.

But the vines were still, aside from their ongoing, rhythmic pulse.

Odile held them tight, her eyes closed, her head bowed. Looking with shadow sight, Inren saw the darkness of Odile's shade plunge into the ground and wind deep like a root system. More tendrils of shadow branched out through the air, flowing along eddies of floating *oblivis*.

Then, drawing a deep breath through her nose, Odile let go, took three steps back, and looked up and down the length of the wall.

"Tear it apart," she snarled.

The shade-taken, moving on the impulse of her command, threw themselves at the wall. Ripping, shredding, biting, clawing. It was no use. For every vine they destroyed, another wound in its place. Several of the unfortunate creatures were caught by coils and dragged inside, screaming. But more shade-taken threw themselves forward, and soon the whole wall was covered in their bodies, the air bursting with the assaults of their magic.

Inren backed away, casting uneasy glances at her queen. Odile watched the fruitless attack, her face implacable. For some moments they stood side by side, silent.

"I have sensed something in the air," Odile said

suddenly, turning to Inren. Her eyes were a mystery of darkness, deeper than the night sky. "There is a presence in the forest that gives me some unease." She blinked, momentarily relieving Inren of her gaze. But the relief lasted only a moment before her delicate lashes lifted, unveiling two wells of roiling hatred.

"The blood of the Chosen King walks beneath these trees. He searches for me." Odile's hand crept to her neck, to that ugly, ragged scar, the only remaining evidence of her beheading. For an instant almost too brief to be believed, fear flashed across her face.

"Find him," she said. "Find him, my loyal Inren. Put an end to the line of the Chosen King. Forever."

Inren's heart stopped. She pulled herself together for another salute and opened her mouth to answer in the affirmative. But no words came, for deep down inside her, the parasite soul jolted suddenly and painfully against her suppressions. A voice in Inren's head screamed, *Gerard! Gerard! Gerard!*

At last she managed to speak: "What will you do, my Queen?"

Odile smiled grimly. "I am going to find my granddaughter," she said.

Before Inren could think of a word to say, her goddess turned and marched away. Not along her newly risen road, but into the Witchwood itself.

There was a strange emptiness to the air.

The *oblivis* was as thick as ever, slowly coating their throats and lungs. But the emptiness nagged at Terryn's senses nonetheless. Something was missing: the ever-present *awareness* that had followed him through the Witchwood the last time he was here. It felt as though the sentient mind at the heart of the forest was distracted elsewhere.

Terryn looked back at Gerard, who walked close behind him, his sword sheathed. If he were meeting the prince in the halls of Dunloch, Terryn doubted he would recognize his brother. *Oblivis* dust crusted over the cuts on his face, his skin was sallow, and purple smudges rimmed his eyes. A silent curse hissed through Terryn's teeth. He could only hope to get Gerard out of this place before the poison set in too deep. They had no masks, no means to protect themselves. And Gerard possessed no shade power to support him.

Nisirdi moved at Terryn's side, its bright scales undimmed by the gloom of the Witchwood. If anything, the light-dragon seemed clearer, purer in this setting. Terryn leaned into its presence, feeling the Arcane magic ready for him to use at need. So different from the last time he walked in this dark place.

"Can you sense shades nearby?" Terryn asked. Many shade-taken haunted the Witchwood, and he didn't understand why they had met none so far other than the Corpsewitch.

Nisirdi's brilliant wings fluttered in response, equivalent to shaking its head.

"Keep careful watch," Terryn urged, his jaw hardening. Not for the first time, he wished Ayleth walked beside him, her Feral shade ascendant, its many senses keen to detect the first trace of shade presence. Was she somewhere in this forest, trudging through this slime-thickened dirt, breathing this foul air? Did Fendrel have her in chains, or had she somehow managed to escape him? Terryn's mouth pulled in a half grin at this thought.

He wouldn't put it past her.

Would he ever see her again?

But that wasn't a thought he dared dwell upon. So he shook his head, focusing his energies on the journey ahead. They made good progress, though it was hard to discern distances in this place. They must have covered at least five miles, uphill and down, trudging through this strange stillness.

Gerard stumbled. Terryn heard him grunt and turned to see his brother down on one knee. Quickly he leapt to his side, catching hold of his elbow. "No, I'm all right," Gerard gasped, his voice hoarse. The poison he breathed was getting to him, weakening him. How much longer could he last at such a pace?

"You need to rest," Terryn said.

"There's no time." Gerard shook his head, grabbed hold of Terryn, and pulled himself up. But he staggered again almost at once, nearly falling flat on his face.

"We'll make time," Terryn said firmly, and led Gerard to a fallen tree lying close by. Its rotted trunk was hollow, offering uncertain support, but better than sitting on the ground. "Your destiny can't very well take place without you."

Gerard chuckled grimly at this but didn't protest further as he sank down. *Oblivis* dust rose in a cloud around him, and he coughed.

"Here," Terryn said and held one hand in the air before Gerard's face. "*Nisirdi*," he called, and his shade sensed his purpose. A trace amount of magic flowed through his fingers, more controlled than anything else he had managed that day. His hand glowed and heated, the bones shining white through his dark skin. He concentrated.

The *oblivis* around his hand vaporized in tiny bursts of light. The air cleared.

Gerard stared at Terryn's hand, then turned his gaze up to his face. "That . . . that's impressive," he said. "I've never seen you control your magic like that."

"No," Terryn answered. He wanted to explain further, but how could he begin to describe to an untaken what he was now experiencing? He held his tongue.

Gerard eyed him closely, reading his face. "There's *more* of you somehow," he said. "I don't know how to explain it. But I feel it. It's like you've . . . grown."

Terryn nodded and, with a sigh, sat down on the log beside his brother, breathing the temporarily clearer air. "I've turned heretic," he said simply.

"Ah." Gerard nodded. He was silent for a bit. "Well, I think I may have also. It's probably for the best."

"Probably," Terryn agreed.

They were quiet again, gazing ahead at the miles and miles of endless forest. Not far off, a statue lay half devoured by the earth with only its eyes still visible, gazing thoughtfully up at the world, one broken arm outstretched as though hoping some help might yet come to it. Beyond it were the ruined walls of what could have been a shrine house or even a mighty lord's stronghold. So little of it remained that it was impossible to say for certain.

Gerard breathed a heavy sigh. "Do you think there's any chance that we—"

"Wait." Terryn raised a hand. His eyes widened, switching to shadow sight. The soul tether between him and Nisirdi tensed as his light-dragon spread its wings wide. *"What do you sense?"*

Magic, Nisirdi answered. It opened up its awareness,

allowing Terryn to perceive what it did.

Terryn leapt to his feet, his left hand moving to spring his scorpiona into firing mode. He knew that sense—he'd felt it before. It was the magic of an active anchor. Somewhere near.

"What is it?" Gerard whispered, rising and drawing his sword. His exhaustion seemed to vanish in the face of danger, and he braced himself in a fighting stance. "Shade?"

Terryn nodded. "The Phantomwitch," he whispered.

A crack broke the air behind him. Terryn whirled, scorpiona upraised, and stared into the pale, wild face of Liselle di Matin.

"There you are," Inren snarled through her stolen host mouth.

IT SEEMED TO ME IN THOSE WILD, GLORIOUS DAYS, THAT MY *reign would have no end.*

Then the rumors began. Mere whispers at first, and I took no more notice than I would of a gnat buzzing in my ear. But the whispers grew to murmurs, to growls, to roars.

The Chosen King, they called him. They whispered of him with dread in the city streets. Apparently he was some prophecy come to life—a prophecy I'd never heard of and cared little about. But that didn't matter. Evanderians flocked to his banner. And when he marched on the first of my strongholds, they took it almost without trying, killing all they found within.

Only then did I begin to take notice. We'd had mortal uprisings in the past, but they'd never amounted to much. When faced with the Crimson Devils, they always backed down again. But this was different. This time, the mortals had shade-taken on their side. They had the Order.

Fendrel du Glaive. That was the name that finally reached my ear. Fendrel, Venator du Glaive of Castra Iarcand. A young hunter, but full of Evander's own zeal, they said. And his brother, an untaken yearling of a lad—he was to be king.

Time and again, I sought to bring them down. They were nothing! They were rats scuttling in the basement. And yet none of the traps I set worked; none of the poisons I laid down succeeded. They took another stronghold, slaughtered another town of inborn. And more mortals rallied, and more Evanderians joined the cause.

I wore the crown. Again and again I put it on my head, accessing the power of Oromor until I thought my body would shatter. But it was not enough. The very night I held my granddaughter in my arms for the first time, the night I made my promise to her, the Chosen King set his sights on Dulimurian.

The final battle was upon us.

CHAPTER 24

AYLETH OPENED HER EYES.

She stood in a cloud of *oblivis* so thick she could scarcely discern her hand in front of her face. Her breath caught, and she held it as long as she could, unwilling to breathe in that poison. The beak mask was gone. Somehow she'd lost it, though she didn't remember when. Flimsy protection though it may have been, she felt bereft without it.

But eventually she had to breathe again or risk

fainting. She let the air rush out of her lungs in a gust that sent the *oblivis* whirling before her face. Dark motes coated her tongue, her throat, sinking down inside her as she sucked in small sips of breath. Only . . .

Only she realized that it wasn't *this* body that breathed. It wasn't *this* body that drew in those poisonous gasps. This body, standing tall and straight, felt nothing, breathed nothing. It was merely a projection of her imagination. Her real body lay somewhere else. Somewhere far away. Unconscious, unguarded, helpless. Her consciousness walked in a dream.

Ayleth blinked once, twice, three times. With each movement of her eyelashes, the *oblivis* seemed to recede a little more. Her feet stood on a road of paved oblidite very like the road she'd been walking in the waking world. Only this one was broader and more firmly established, and it led between tall buildings, not trees. The buildings themselves clarified before her vision—great structures of faceted black stone. So many of them and so tall.

Ayleth shuddered. Somehow she knew where she was, knew where her dreams had brought her. Her lips formed a name: "*Dulimurian.*"

At the sound of her voice, the clouds of *oblivis* lifted like curtains drawn back from a scene. They gathered overhead, thick and dark enough to blot out all trace of sun or sky, casting the city in a weird half-lit dusk, full of malicious shadows. Ayleth stood at the top of a rise, gazing down the sweep of the road into a labyrinth of towers, domes, and byways. She glimpsed gardens, or what might once have been gardens, with dry pools and empty flowerbeds and bordered paths crisscrossing beneath cage-like arches. Mighty pillared edifices, possibly temples or centers of learning, stood with doors wide open like hungry mouths eager to swallow those willing to enter in. Bridges arched over dry riverbeds, and barges and ferries and little dinghies lay in perfect condition in the dirt. Carts and carriages without horses dotted the broad highway as far as her eye could see. It was as though all life had been abruptly stripped away from the thriving streets, leaving behind only the empty shell of the city. Like a host body deprived of its soul.

This dream did not belong to her.

She couldn't dream of Dulimurian with such profound clarity of vision. It was nothing more than a name to her, a figment of an idea. This view spread before her under the canopy of *oblivis* was intricate to the last detail, from the carvings on the temple doors to the spokes of the wagon wheels to the cracks in the paving stones at her feet. This dream was born of a mind that *knew*.

"*It created a host for itself.*" Hollis's words came back to her, bringing with them a chill of understanding. "*A living, thriving host.*"

This dream belonged to the Witchwood. Born of its mind and memory.

She must have been knocked out. Confused images of violence returned, images of vines snaking around her limbs and waist, yanking her off the road and in among the wounded trees. She must have been knocked out almost at once, the mask torn from her face. In her unconscious state, she couldn't fight as her mind was dragged into this realm where she stood naked and unmasked and helpless.

"*Laranta?*" she whispered, the word a silent puff of air before her face. Her soul tether twanged, but nothing more. Laranta was far away in another mind, still bound to her mistress's host body. She could not hope for help from her shade.

Fine then. She'd face this dream alone.

Although she knew it wouldn't make any real difference, Ayleth took a moment to conjure up clothing for herself, her familiar venatrix uniform and riding boots. But she didn't bother with the mask. Not here. It would make no difference here. Somewhere in the mortal world her body lay unconscious, dragging more poisonous fumes into her lungs as the Witchwood strengthened its hold over her mind. She had to find a way out of this dream if she was to have any hope of saving herself from pollution and ultimate death.

With escape in mind, she looked back over her shoulder, away from the city. But that way lay . . . nothing. Only dense clouds of darkness in which motes of *oblivis* gleamed threateningly. No, the only way out lay through the dream. Though she hated it, she turned her feet down that road and began her descent into Dulimurian. As she walked, she peered into the churning sky above the city towers. She couldn't discern even the faintest outline of Odile's great idol through the thickness of *oblivis*; nevertheless, she knew it must stand there, high above all. She could feel it . . . or rather, she felt the Presence within it.

She shouldn't let it control her, couldn't let it make her afraid. She would face her fate, be it dream or reality. She would track it down, run it to ground, and if it killed her, at least she would die the hunter and not the hunted.

Ayleth quickened her pace, her boot heels clunking on the oblidite pavers, the sound echoing hollowly off the looming walls around her. As she went deeper, those echoes seemed to transform strangely, becoming new sounds, distant and yet alive. Passing one pillared structure, she believed she heard chanting coming from within, in a language not quite human. When she turned, she half thought she glimpsed figures in long robes standing among those pillars, like a choir of holy sisters gathered in prayer. But the song they sang was nothing like the prayers to the Goddess, and the music itself was profane in its strangeness, its carefully wrought discord.

The instant she looked, the figures flitted away, and with them the echoes of their voices. Only the structure remained. The dark facets of oblidite stone gleamed dully with their own weird light. Ayleth hurried on.

The deeper into the city she progressed, the more of these echo voices and echo images assaulted her senses. She passed through a market center and heard merchants and sellers calling out to one another. She hastened across an intersection and glimpsed oncoming horses and wagons and carriages, street dancers whirling on bare feet at the corners. She heard groans and caught an almost-glimpse of ornate litters carried on the shoulders of slaves. She heard hammers ringing and snatched a sight of scaffolds and strong men hauling great blocks of oblidite. And everywhere, everywhere, she felt phantom traces of shades like icy breaths on the back of her neck, there and gone again in a flash.

Suddenly, a roar of sound exploded to her left, a great crowd erupting in cheers. She turned, and the roar vanished at once, leaving only the memory still echoing in her ear. The great amphitheater stood before her vision, its ringing columns tall and graceful, oblidite tiers descending to a deep pit below. It was utterly empty save for the fog of *oblivis,* but a wave of fear—fear not her own—fear belonging to hundreds, thousands of others—seemed to roll up and strike her so that she almost lost her footing.

Ducking her head, she hurried on in an effort to avoid the phantom sights flitting on the edges of her vision. She didn't want to see the mortals in chains being hastened along by powerful shade-taken. She didn't want to see the men, women, and children gathered as fodder for the theater games. She didn't want to see these dreamed-up memories of what Dulimurian had been in its glory days, back when witches ran rampant over the ruins of the Holy City, back when the temple of the Goddess was cast down in favor of a new, dark goddess of *oblivis*.

Phantoms appeared suddenly before her, blocking her way, but when she darted to one side to avoid them, they vanished. Distant voices echoed through the air, chanting, *"Odile, Odile! Our Queen! Odile!"*

Then, hauntingly, those voices seemed to change. The crowd continued to chant *"Odile!"*

But when the name struck her ear, it warped somehow and sounded instead like, *"Olena! Olena!"*

She didn't know that name, but hearing it . . . hearing it was like being shot through the heart with an arrow so sharp, she didn't feel the pain of its entry. And the phantom faces she glimpsed no longer looked through her, but at her.

Ayleth turned to stare back down the road, the way she had come, desperate to see someone else, anyone who might be the object of this ghostly throng's adoration. But the road was utterly abandoned and silent. No phantom voices or faces. No dancers or banners or music or chariots. Just tall structures of oblidite and the heavy miasma of *oblivis*.

A shudder coursed down her spine. Ayleth broke into a run, her feet pounding down the center of that road. She no longer tried to dodge the phantom figures that appeared suddenly in her path but simply ran through them. She poured all her will into making her limbs—dream limbs though they were—move faster. She had to get out of this dream, and somehow she knew that her way of escape lay in that place where the five Queen's Highways intersected in the heart of Dulimurian.

But when she dared to lift her eyes to the sky, she still could not see the idol through the clouds.

But it *was* there. She knew it. She felt it loom above her, vast and horrible. And the Presence inside was unmistakable in its potency. So she ran on, determined to reach the heart of the city, determined to—

Sudden sunlight exploded in her vision. Ayleth screamed and fell to her knees, her hands hitting the paving stones so hard, the skin of her palms tore. At first she could do nothing but kneel where she'd fallen, her body quaking with the shock of that light. Then, slowly, she gathered her wits and pulled back upright. Wincing against the glare, she peered through her eyelashes at the world around her.

A city of faceted white stone rose all around her. The pavers at her feet were white with a translucent quality containing all the colors of the rainbow—and colors of the shade spectrum, which her mortal vision should not have been able to see. She was standing in the city center, in that place where the highways intersected, and directly before her stood the feet of the statue. Only, these too were carved of white stone.

She looked up. The idol looming above her was as tall as the original and carved of oblidite . . . but the oblidite itself had been fashioned in such a way as to reflect and clarify light, not absorb it. The arms of the idol stretched out above the city, extended in a gesture of benevolence. The head was gently tilted to one side, slightly inclined, and wearing an expression not of power and pride, but of gentleness, of adoration. That face didn't belong to Dread Odile, though the features were terribly similar, almost indistinguishable.

It was her own face, not Odile's, Ayleth saw.

A peal of laughter shattered the stillness. Ayleth's soul lurched, and a thrill ran up her spine. A thrill of surprise, not fear. Wait, no . . . *surprise* wasn't the right word. A thrill of . . . she couldn't quite define it. She'd never felt this sensation before.

She turned on her heel and saw a little figure running toward her across the sun-bright stones. No clouds of *oblivis* marred this vision, and pure light shone on the face of a small child. Or rather . . . no. Ayleth blinked. Light shone *from* the child's face, from her core. A fully ascendant Arcane shade glowed in the center of her soul, interlaced with the little one's own mortal spirit, and the two sang in perfect harmony, a music uniquely their own.

The child ran toward Ayleth with an awkward, gamboling sort of gait, little arms pumping. Her nose wrinkled with the hugeness of her smile, and her hair, too short to tie back properly, flew wildly about her little face. *"Mum-Mum-Mummy!"* she cried and, before Ayleth could recover from her own shock, flung herself into Ayleth's arms.

Ayleth caught that small body. And it felt real. More real than anything she'd ever felt in her life. She lifted the girl up, swinging her onto her hip, and it was all so natural, as though she'd performed this same act a thousand times. She looked over the girl's head, some instinct telling her eyes where to go.

There they were. Just as she'd known they would be. A man, dark-skinned, light-eyed, with an ugly scar on his cheek. His shade was also ascendant, brimming in every vein of his body yet perfectly harmonized with his soul. It lit him up but did not burn.

"Terryn," she breathed. Then, more loudly, *"Terryn!"*

At the sound of her voice, he looked at her. It was a look unlike anything she'd ever seen or even imagined on his face. A look of pure confidence mingled with pure contentment. His smile flashed her way and held no trace of bite or sarcasm, only warmth. In his arms he carried another child, smaller than the first. It clung to his shirt and clenched chubby fingers in his hair, pulling hard enough that his smile twisted with amused pain. A Feral shade twined in the soul of that child. An inborn spirit.

Ayleth stared at that vision, at that child, even as her arms tightened around the little one she held. A surge of emotion welled up inside, a feeling for which she had no name. *Belonging*, perhaps. A sensation of rightness, of joy. A sensation of—

—of a hot iron band ringing her brow.

"It is all a lie, you know. Nothing more than a beautiful lie."

Ayleth gasped, and her arms automatically tightened in protection. But she gripped too hard, and the child she held in her arms melted away, becoming a cloud of drifting *oblivis*.

"*No!*" Ayleth cried out, trying to catch hold of vapors and dust. She turned again, desperate, just in time to see Terryn and the other child vanish as well. The clouds of what they had been rose, thickened, and obscured the blue sky overhead, casting the intersection of roads into shadow. The stones under her feet blackened.

"Don't think you're the only one who has dreamed this dream, the only one who has felt this longing. None of it is real. Not in this life. Not anymore."

Her arms empty, her heart aching, Ayleth lifted her head toward the sound of that voice.

A spectral shape moved toward her down the center of the oblidite road. It was nothing more than a shadow without clear form or definition beyond the faintest outline of a woman. A gust of wind blasted Ayleth from behind, whipping her hair before her face. *Oblivis* stung her skin as it rushed past her, gathering together into a bolt of solid darkness as it shot straight for that shadow.

The shadow lifted a hand. The bolt of *oblivis* broke and crashed around it, billowing like waves. The specter continued along the road unhindered, solidifying as it came.

"I was like you once. Long ago. Eager to devour all the lies they could feed me. Eager to ingest them and make them my own. But you will learn, as I did. You will learn, or you will break."

The space between them shrank to nothing. Ayleth, hating to run, hating to show weakness, stood her ground. When no more than a foot of distance separated them, the specter stopped. Its formlessness seemed to tense as though with concentration. The darkness coalesced, features appeared, faded, reappeared, and hardened.

She stood before Ayleth, not the burned, corpselike thing she had been in the vaults of Dunloch. This was a young, powerful, beautiful woman with eyes like chips of oblidite and hair like a raven's wing. Her soft mouth fixed in a hard, grim line.

"*Olena,*" Dread Odile said. "*My love. My pretty child. The time has come for us to be acquainted with one another. The time has come for you to know who I am.*"

ABOUT THE AUTHOR

Sylvia Mercedes makes her home in the idyllic North Carolina countryside with her handsome husband, sweet baby-lady, and Gummy Bear, the Toothless Wonder Cat. When she's not writing she's . . . okay, let's be honest. When she's not writing, she's running around after her little girl, cleaning up glitter, trying to plan healthy-ish meals, and wondering where she left her phone. In between, she reads a steady diet of fantasy novels. But mostly she's writing.

After a short career in Traditional Publishing (under a different name), Sylvia decided to take the plunge into the Indie Publishing World and is enjoying every minute of it. The Venatrix Chronicles is her first series as an independent author, but she's got many more planned!

Don't miss the climactic finale of Ayleth's adventures in
Book 7 of The Venatrix Chronicles!

Who lives?
Who dies?
Who will be changed . . . forever?

CROWN OF NIGHTMARES

Meanwhile be sure to read Song of Shadows:

Visit www.SylviaMercedesBooks.com
to get your free copy.